CONVERSATIONS OVER COLD SOUP

PHILIP MAZZA

OMNI PUBLISHERS

Also by Philip Mazza

From Under a Tree Book One; The Harrow Saga

Shadow in the Flame Book Two; The Harrow Saga

Children at the Gate Book Three; The Harrow Saga

The Child of Fire Book Four; The Harrow Saga
(Coming 2026)

The Neon Hive

The Quantum Gardener

At the End of it All

Beneath the Ashen Sky

I Know God is a Cat

The Road to Stillwater

The Never-Ending Road

The Cosmic Vending Machine

The Wicked Man Cometh

Gideon Rex

Mother

The Quantum Messiah

The White Buck of Ash Hollow

The Iron Rose

Voidfall

The Soft Cage

CONVERSATIONS OVER COLD SOUP

PHILIP MAZZA

OMNI PUBLISHERS

Cover and book design by publisher

www.philipmazza.com

Omni Publishers of New York
ISBN 979-8-9940486-1-0
Printed in the United States of America

First Printing: March 2026

To all the grumblers, the skeptics, and the ones who refuse to call life a "journey" unless there's a map and a very good reason to leave the house.

For the nurses who keep smiling even when we're at our worst, and for the mothers who bridge the gaps we're too stubborn to cross ourselves.

And finally, to the "Star-Eyes" of the world—the ones who listen to our terrestrial nonsense with patience, serving up something warm while we wait for the long walk into the Great Beyond.

This one is for the empty chairs that still hold the loudest echoes.

A NOTE FROM THE AUTHOR

I've always been fascinated by the friction between the dignity we imagine for our later years and the reality of fluorescent lights and cold soup. Nursing homes, waiting rooms, grocery aisles at 10 p.m.—these are not places we usually grant existential weight, yet they're where most of us actually live out our days. I wanted to sit with that, to build a story that took those small indignities and tiny mercies seriously enough to laugh at them, and to let the laughter sting a little on the way down.

This book is about noticing—the small, stubborn decision to pay attention to your own hands, your own pulse, your own boredom and grief—and to let those moments count, even if they aren't useful or shareable. It's a story about aging, mortality, and the peculiar humor and insight that emerge when we refuse to be reduced to schedules, metrics, or "productivity units."

Ultimately, it's a reminder that even the coldest soup can matter, and that paying attention—really noticing—is its own kind of warmth.

Chapter 1

David Miller sat in his car and stared at Sunny Meadows, as if staring might make it less inevitable. He took a breath that smelled faintly of regret and exhaust fumes, then looked down at a Tupperware of cut fruit—the fruit being an ironic gesture of virtue he would almost certainly forget to deliver to his mother, because memory is a cruel prankster and negligence is its jester.

There are smells worse than a nursing home, sure, but none so efficiently engineered to make a man question the entire purpose of existence while simultaneously whispering that entropy is winning, and winning badly. The automatic doors to Sunny Meadows sighed open with a sound like a sigh from God himself, weary of creation and particularly unimpressed with midlife crises. Inside, the air was a delightful stew of disinfectant, wilted peas, and the faint electric tingle of despair, the kind that hums like a broken neon sign just beneath the incessant chatter of daytime television.

David didn't want to be there. Then again, he was the sort of man who never wanted to be anywhere, not even in the good job he'd somehow landed through a clerical oversight, or on the vacations he never took because they required optimism and sunscreen. At forty-two, he existed like a construction project abandoned by its workers—scaffolding up, no blueprint, the foreman missing, presumed drunk. His hair had retreated into patchy outposts, as if scouting safer territories, and whatever optimism he'd been issued at birth had defected to a different universe with better benefits. He had no wife, no prospects, and no real desire for either, because he had spent his entire adult life tethered to his mother like a balloon tied to a wrist: floating, but never free, occasionally bumped against doorframes.

He stepped into the facility, the automatic doors performing their magic trick — whooshing open, then close. At the front desk sat Nurse Kelly, who smiled like the sun being forced to clock in for a double shift. "You're here to see Margaret, right?" she asked.

"Yeah," David said, adjusting his coat. "And . . . her friend. The one with the opinions."

Kelly giggled in that way nurses do when they've seen enough to know laughter is the only antiseptic left. "That'd be Arthur. They're down the hall. Oh, and it's soup day."

Every day was soup day.

The common room looked like eternity's waiting room, if eternity had a sense of irony and a shoestring budget: plastic flowers that smelled like postponed ambitions, laminated posters shouting about the importance of drinking water, and a television endlessly playing reruns of a fifty-year-old game show where contestants guessed the prices of products long dead.

"A can of pork and beans from 1972?" David muttered. "Really? Even the universe wouldn't bother with that."

Old men popped their knees like cheap popcorn. Old women's eyes darted like startled birds. "What's the price of a vacuum cleaner?" croaked a man with a hearing aid. "I can't remember." The laugh track didn't care. Neither did the universe. Certainly not David.

"This is cruel," he whispered. "Polite cruelty. Fluorescent-light cruelty. Bureaucracy cruelty." Everyone was trapped. Trapped, watching, remembering nothing that mattered, chasing prizes that nobody ever needed. A can opener. A toaster. Oh, and a car that was later found out to be so defective, if it was ever rear-ended could explode in a spectacular way and probably take the universe with it.

"Life," he said, "in microcosm: entropy, canned applause, and the faint hope of ascending to heaven in a moderately impressive fireball."

David imagined the producers in glass offices, sipping martinis. "Yes," they'd say, "this is joy. This is meaningful. Let us watch the last vitality fumble for nonsense." He laughed softly and immediately felt guilty for laughing.

A man groaned like a freight train climbing a hill that didn't exist. He had a cane, a hearing aid, and the look of a man abandoned by the universe. Yet he smiled at the television. "Alive," David thought. "Or as alive as reruns will let you be."

The absurdity of it was exquisite. To ask anyone, much less someone whose memory was now a collection of loose screws and faded photographs, to recall the price of a product long since annihilated by progress and inflation—it was like forcing Shakespeare to write Yelp reviews for fast-food restaurants. David considered the moral calculus and concluded that it was the sort of cruelty that was probably worth doing, just for the sheer comedy of it all, if only someone had the guts to laugh properly.

He blinked a few times and tried to shake the canned applause out of his head. It lingered there anyway, like a cheap jingle you can't stop humming.

He was looking for her.

Mom. Margaret. Maggie.

She was his whole universe in orthopedic shoes.

He was an only child—no siblings to absorb the blast radius of her affection—and his father had checked out early, leaving the two of them to improvise a family out of mismatched leftovers.

She raised him with equal parts devotion and critique, a one-woman civilization held together by casseroles and impossible expectations. And now she was somewhere in that fluorescent purgatory of a room, maybe pretending she hadn't forgotten things. Maybe pretending everything was fine.

His stomach twisted. That could have been guilt. It could have been hunger. It might've been that special nausea you get when you discover the ground you built your life on has started cracking like old plaster.

He shuffled farther into the room.

"Where the hell are you, Mom?" he whispered.

The universe didn't answer.

The universe rarely does. It has other hobbies.

And then he saw her. Right there. Not behind the fake ferns, but there, sitting in the corner—Margaret Miller—a small woman with hair the color of cloud margins. She had puzzle books stacked beside her like they were important work. A knitted blanket was across her knees like she planned to stay warm forever. And there was lavender in the air.

Lavender is what people use when they want a room to smell like peace instead of endings.

"David!" she said, waving. "You're early. The world must be ending."

He kissed her cheek, which felt like folded tissue paper. "Traffic was light."

Margaret smiled. "How's the job?"

"It's still there."

"Well," she said, "so are we. Miracles all around."

David nodded. And for a moment, just a moment, the absurdity of everything—canned laughter, pork and beans, entropy, fluorescent lighting—felt slightly, gloriously alive.

Arthur Trent sat in a chair opposite her, scowling into a bowl of something gray-green that pretended to be soup, sitting atop a small table in front of him. He was eighty-four, a retired machinist, and the kind of man who looked like he'd been built from gravel and spite. His eyebrows alone could have served as small woodland creatures' shelters.

"Who's this clown?" Arthur said without looking up.

"Arthur, this is my son David," Margaret said patiently. "He's visiting."

"Visiting," Arthur said. "People always visiting. Never staying."

David offered his hand. Arthur didn't take it. Instead, he squinted at David's shirt. "That polyester?"

"Cotton blend," David said.

"Looks like polyester to me," Art muttered. "You look like the kind of guy who Googles his feelings."

Margaret clucked. "Arthur."

"What? I'm old, not wrong."

Nurse Kelly appeared with more soup. It steamed faintly, then gave up. "Beef barley!" she chirped.

Arthur sniffed. "Barley's just rice that gave up on itself."

Kelly smiled and left before he could elaborate. She was good at that.

Arthur and David's mom ate in the kind of silence that's only quiet on the surface. David looked at the cold soup, unsure if eating hospital-grade food qualified as an act of filial piety.

After a couple of spoonfuls, Arthur pushed his table away. "Cold again," he said. "They must refrigerate it just to watch us suffer."

Margaret rolled her eyes. "You're such a drama queen."

"Queen, my ass," Arthur said. "If I were a queen, I'd have hot soup."

"Arthur," she said, "maybe try gratitude."

"I did. Didn't take."

David smiled despite himself. "You're like Statler and Waldorf in therapy."

"Who?" Arthur asked.

"The old guys from the Muppets."

Arthur stared. "You calling me a puppet?"

"No," David said. "A Muppet. There's a difference."

Arthur grunted. "Don't care. They're all unemployed. Aren't they now?"

Margaret laughed, that thin, reedy laugh of the very tired. For a moment, David saw her the way she must have been before arthritis, before hospital bracelets—a woman who loved absurd people. He felt bad that her social life had come down to bingo and barbed banter.

Arthur noticed him noticing. "You staring at her or thinking of something sentimental? Either way, knock it off. It's contagious."

David wasn't sure if he should apologize, so he settled for a shrug that conveyed the general message of a man trapped between emotions and upholstery. Arthur kept glaring, the way a guard dog might glare if it had long ago given up on biting but still believed in the principle of intimidation. David shifted, sensing the air thicken with the prelude to one of Arthur's trademark pronouncements—the kind that sounded like prophecy but smelled like sarcasm.

"So," Arthur said, looking David square in the eye with the kind of menace only eighty-four years of disappointment can give a man, "your mother ever tell you I do reality jumps when I doze off?"

Arthur had a way of saying things that sounded both completely insane and eerily bureaucratic, like someone confessing to tax evasion on a spiritual level. His eyes were two tiny interrogation lamps powered by caffeine, regret, and stubborn cellular survival.

David, who had already been regretting the visit since the automatic doors had whooshed shut behind him, managed a polite smile. "Honestly, I didn't know she had found a friend here."

"Don't change the subject," Arthur said, stabbing a bony finger through the air, which trembled slightly, either from righteous fury or low blood sugar. "Did she ever tell you I do reality jumps?"

David blinked. He wasn't used to this kind of thing—old men in nursing homes declaring themselves reality jumpers, whatever the hell that was. But Arthur had the unnerving composure of someone who might actually be telling the truth. "Ah, no. Reality jumps?"

Arthur leaned in just a bit, smelling faintly of antiseptic and determination. "You fall asleep here," he said, "and you wake up somewhere that makes more sense. You don't ask why. You just punch your ticket and hope the bartender remembers your name."

David looked down at the table, where a cup of cold soup sat like an accusation. "Right," he said carefully, "so . . . like dreams?"

Arthur snorted. "Dreams are reruns. Reality jumps are premieres. I fall asleep, and I wake up somewhere else. Not just the other side of the bed. Somewhere else entirely. Vacationing, mostly."

He sat back, satisfied that he had either enlightened or unsettled his guest—both perfectly acceptable outcomes for an afternoon at Sunny Meadows.

"Vacationing?" David said, unsure if this was a euphemism for drinking too much.

Arthur leaned back and gestured vaguely with a finger. "On a star cruiseship, called The Great Beyond, for God's sake. You know. Stars. Space. Cosmic martinis."

David frowned. "You . . . travel when you sleep?"

"Travel?" Arthur barked, a laugh like gravel in a wind tunnel. "I live, you nitwit. I live on that ship. Mostly at the bar. Talking about life. Talking about the universe. Talking about why anyone pretends soup should be warm. The bartender—she's spectacular, got seven fingers, beautiful boobs, and eyes, several of them, that look like little dying galaxies. I call her Star-Eyes. You'd like her."

David tilted his head. "Does she have seven boobs?"

Arthur squinted. "What? No. Don't be an idiot. Two is plenty."

Margaret giggled, a little musical chime of disbelief. "Oh, Arthur."

David frowned. "And nobody notices that you're gone? I mean . . . the reality jump?"

Arthur grinned, tapping his knee. "Notice me? Son, you've got to understand: the universe doesn't take roll call. Everyone here is too busy. Trying to stay alive. I leave. I come back. No one cares. That's the beauty of it. Absurdity is on my side."

"So," David said, "you just fall asleep . . . and wake up on a spaceship?"

Arthur tapped the side of his head like David should have known better. "Exactly. Not metaphorically. Literally. Drinks, conversation, cosmic revelations . . . sometimes karaoke. Interstellar karaoke. Terrible. Everyone sings in the key of existential dread. And sometimes I take excursions. Visit other planets."

David chuckled nervously. "That . . . sounds impossible."

Arthur smiled faintly, a curl of gravel and spite. "Impossible? Son, life itself is impossible. Reality jumps just make the absurdity more interesting. I've met philosophers out there. Psychics. One guy claimed he was an accountant for a company that owned several dying stars. Can you imagine? Dying stars! And me, listening over a glowing martini, telling him soup at Sunny Meadows is cold again."

David laughed. "You mean . . . you actually enjoy it?"

Arthur shrugged. "Enjoy? Sure. Enjoy the only thing that makes me forget the smell of this place and the cold soup. And the humans, here. Oh, the humans. They think this is life. I tell them otherwise. Sometimes they believe me. Sometimes they just hand me another tray. Your mother, though, she gets it."

Margaret's voice piped up from across the table. "Arthur, are you teaching him how to dodge soup or just frightening him with your silliness?"

Arthur squinted. "Both. You've got to frighten them to make them listen. Soup, son, soup is life. Cold soup, colder truths. Star-Eyes tells me everything matters, and nothing matters. I tell her she's full of cosmic bullshit, even though she doesn't know what a bull is."

"Does she know what shit is?" David asked.

Arthur threw back his head and laughed like a gravel truck with a loose muffler. "What the hell's wrong with you, son? Everybody in the galaxy knows what shit is. It's what keeps the universe from falling apart.

David shook his head and smiled the way people do when something sounds ridiculous but might also be true.

"So let me get this straight," he said. "Your headquarters for jumping between realities is a bar. On a stellar cruiseship."

Arthur leaned forward like he was about to share a state secret. Or maybe the punchline to a joke he'd been saving.

"Exactly," he said. "Headquarters."

He ticked things off on his fingers.

"Lounge chairs. Fluorescent lights. That's here. The regular universe. Nothing fancy."

Then he gestured vaguely upward, as if the ceiling might open and let the stars pour in.

"But up there. Bar. Stars. Cosmic revelations. That's the other one."

He sat back, satisfied with the explanation.

"And right between the two," Arthur said, "you've got me. Arthur Trent. Crossing the universe in first-class comfort."

He shrugged.

"One nap at a time."

David raised an eyebrow. "And this . . . never gets boring?"

Arthur laughed. "Boring? Son, the joke's on us. Life's always boring if you let it be. But throw in reality jumps, a bartender with great boobs and galaxy eyes, and cold soup as a running gag, and suddenly the universe looks like a cosmic vaudeville. You'll thank me when you're eighty-four, and someone asks if you want another bowl of soup again."

David shook his head, trying not to snort. "I'll . . . uh . . . remember that, I guess."

"Remember what?" Arthur smiled. "That life is absurd, the soup is cold, shit keeps the galaxy together, and reality is just a polite suggestion? Excellent. You're learning, or at least faking it convincingly."

David slumped into the chair, gazing at the ceiling, which may or may not have been made of the same material as the universe. "Not too sure what I'm learning, exactly."

Arthur grinned, eyebrows twitching like overachieving hedgehogs with a caffeine addiction. "Of course you're not sure. No one ever is. That's the whole point. Enjoy the confusion. It's cheaper than therapy."

David took a deep breath, looked down at his watch, and stood to leave. "I'll come by in a couple of days," he told his mother.

"Bring something sweet," Margaret said. "These desserts taste like . . . "

". . . shit," Arthur finished the sentence for her.

"Oh, Arthur," Margaret giggled playfully. "Such language."

David smiled. "Sure Mom. Something sweet."

As he left, Arthur called out, "Hey, polyester!"

David turned. "Yeah?"

"Life's just soup, kid. Always colder than you expect."

David didn't know whether to laugh or pity him. So he did both, which is the most efficient emotional multitasking a man can manage without getting a nosebleed. Arthur had that effect on people—he made you want to cry for him and strangle him in the same breath. It was practically a superpower.

Outside, the rain began its half-assed descent, each drop taking its sweet time, as if the clouds were on union break. The kind of rain that couldn't quite commit—too lazy to pour, too proud to drizzle. The parking lot shone like an oil painting left out overnight.

David sat in his car with both hands on the steering wheel, performing that sacred suburban ritual known as "thinking." He tried to decide whether the visit had been good. It hadn't been bad, which, in the arithmetic of human connection, was roughly equivalent to love. He counted that as progress.

Then he noticed the Tupperware of cut fruit sitting on the passenger seat, sweating like a guilty conscience. Grapes, melon cubes, a slice of pineapple pretending to be tropical. He had meant it for his mother, who, despite the advanced age and the failing infrastructure of her body, still maintained a childlike, glorious, and totally reliable sweet tooth. It was a small, doomed gesture of love against the vast, cold emptiness of the nursing home. But now he stared at it as though it were radioactive.

"Fuck!" he said, with the conviction of a man betrayed by his own good intentions.

For a moment, he considered walking back into that sterile building again, where everyone smelled faintly of sanitizer and surrender. Then he told himself he wouldn't. No chance. He was exhausted. He wasn't ready for another philosophical debate about soup with his mom's cranky friend.

Yet, there was something about Arthur that intrigued him—maybe it was the stubborn glint of someone who refused to go quietly, or the way his words carried both absurdity and truth, like a man who'd seen too much and decided to make jokes until the end credits rolled. Arthur was a reminder that getting old didn't mean surrendering; it just meant developing new hobbies, like irritating nurses and confusing your son.

David sighed, turned on the wipers, and watched them sweep away the indecision one streak at a time. Somewhere inside, a thought lodged itself like a splinter: maybe he wasn't visiting out of duty at all. Maybe he was visiting because he wanted to understand how a man could face the slow collapse of everything—and still find something funny to say about the soup.

Meanwhile, Arthur Trent, eighty-four years unbowed, was losing his battle with consciousness. It wasn't that he wanted to sleep; sleep just happened to him like a recurring tax audit.

He heard Margaret say, "Goodbye, Arthur. Have a nice trip. I'll be here waiting for you." She said it with the patient cheer of someone who'd been waiting her whole life for people to come back from places they never returned from.

This made him smile—half amusement, half surrender—as he closed his eyes and woke somewhere else entirely.

Arthur was traveling again, though he hadn't packed a thing.

He found himself at a bar that was made of glass and light. Stars drifted past the portholes like lazy plankton. The drinks glowed faintly, neon ghosts of things once alive.

Arthur sat on a stool that rotated very slowly, because in eternity, nobody's in a hurry.

The bartender, Iris, wasn't human, but if you'd been drinking enough, you might wish she were. Her skin shimmered like oil on water, a plum hue that shifted with the movement of the stars. And yes, her boobs were impressive—round, generous, and utterly pointless, like everything else in the universe. Her eyes—there were several—held galaxies, literal galaxies, the way a goldfish holds guilt.

"Rough day planetside?" she asked. Her voice was chime and velvet.

Arthur blinked. "Just visiting hell."

"Population?" she asked.

"Mostly the living," he said. "A few ghosts in attendance. Some bored demons. And the occasional soup."

She poured a steaming drink, which floated upward like it had somewhere else to be. "To your continued suffering," she said.

He sipped. "Burnt nostalgia. Again. Not as warm as yesterday."

"You know everything cools eventually," she said. Seven fingers tapping the counter like a lazy drum solo. "I could heat it up."

"Why?"

"Because some souls need scalding," she said. "Yours isn't one of them, yet."

He peered through the viewport. Below, a small blue planet spun lazily, white scars marking the skin of it.

"That one's mine?" he asked.

"Used to be," she said softly. "You visit often?"

"I come for the cold soup," he said. "And the insults. Those are hot. Though I could use your help. Add a few new ones to my collection."

She laughed. It sounded like wind chimes somebody forgot inside a snow globe.

"You're already one of the galaxy's great insult artists," she said. "You don't need help."

"I always need help," he said. "And you're good at it."

"Flattery will get you nowhere," she said, tilting her head.

"That's where I live now," he said. "Nowhere."

She slid another drink toward him.

"I hear the views there are spectacular."

Arthur took a long sip. "I should go back. Everyone will think I'm lost in fluorescent hell forever."

"Or maybe they won't care," Iris said. "You like the soup there, eh?"

"Always cold," he said.

"Good," she said. "Consistency is important in the universe."

Arthur nodded slowly, letting the glow of the stars seep into his bones. "I'll drink to that," he muttered.

"And to you," Iris said, her many eyes twinkling like guilty galaxies. "Because the universe, my dear Arthur, may be consistent, but has never been known for kindness—or taste."

He woke to Nurse Kelly tapping his shoulder. "Arthur? Wake up. You were talking in your sleep."

"I always talk in my sleep," he grumbled. "It's the only time people listen."

"You said something about a woman with stars for eyes."

"Probably a hallucination," he said. "Or a nurse I liked back in '72."

She smiled. "Sweet dream, huh?"

"Not sweet," he said, staring out the window. "Just familiar."

Margaret watched him quietly. "You always drift off like that."

Arthur shrugged. "World's boring. I visit better ones."

"Yes, I know. You tell me. And who's that special person there?"

He met her eyes for a long moment. "A bartender who knows when to shut up."

Margaret chuckled. "Maybe she can teach me."

"No one can teach you," he said, but his voice softened. "That's why I like you."

Chapter 2

You could measure the optimism of any nursing home by the number of paper crafts taped to its walls. It was a kind of barometer for denial. The more crooked hearts, lopsided pumpkins, and cotton-ball snowmen you saw, the more the staff insisted that death was just another seasonal theme—something you could cut out with safety scissors and tape to a bulletin board.

Sunny Meadows scored high on that scale. If optimism were gold, the place would've been Fort Knox. The hallways glowed with construction-paper suns, macaroni rainbows, and inspirational quotes written in fonts so cheerful they were practically manic. Glitter clung to everything, including the residents, as though the staff had decided immortality could be achieved through static electricity.

David took a deep, shuddering breath, a sound that registered somewhere between a sigh and a desperate, internal gear stripping. He wasn't sure he wanted to come back. But he felt he was failing at his life, failing at his job, and failing spectacularly at the simple task of being with his mother during these, her final days. Yet, here he was, returned out of a dutiful obligation, but drawn back by the crusty, cynical, fascinating gravity of Arthur Trent and his insults. The world outside was confusing, but inside this place, Arthur was the one man telling him the naked, depressing truth—that it was all just a lot of glue and paper hearts, and that the soup would almost certainly be cold.

He arrived just after breakfast, which meant the hall still smelled faintly of oatmeal and Lysol. His mother, Margaret, was in her room, sitting by the window with a magazine upside down on her lap. "I wasn't reading it," she said when he entered. "I just like pretending."

He kissed her cheek, feeling both affection and guilt, which was the standard cocktail of emotions in a nursing home. "You ready for Craft Hour?" he asked.

"Oh yes," she said, brightening. "Arthur will be there. He's saving me a seat."

"Arthur," David repeated, as if it were a new diagnosis. "Do you like him?"

"I do," Margaret said, standing slowly and patting his arm for balance. "He makes me laugh."

As they shuffled down the corridor together—past bulletin boards announcing chair yoga and funeral dates—David said, "So… what's the deal with you and Arthur?"

Margaret smiled the way people do when they're about to tell you something simple and true. "He's funny," she said. "And kind, in his own cranky way. We talk about everything—music, the moon landing, soup. He says soup is proof that hope dies last."

David raised an eyebrow. "That sounds like him."

"He makes me laugh," she said again, more softly. "And when you're our age, laughter's not just good—it's medicine. The real kind. The kind that doesn't get cut off when your insurance runs out."

David nodded, unsure what to say, which was his usual conversational stance with his mother.

They reached the craft room, where the smell of glue and determination hung in the air. Nurse Kelly stood at the front like an over-caffeinated camp counselor, armed with glitter and slogans.

Arthur Trent sat near the window, surrounded by a defensive perimeter of colored paper. When he saw them, he smiled—not a big smile, just enough to prove he wasn't entirely extinct—and lifted a glue stick in greeting.

"Ah, the cavalry's arrived," he said. "Margaret, your chair's safe. And David," he added, nodding toward the pile of supplies, "you can have the glue with teeth marks. Builds character."

Margaret chuckled, taking her seat beside him. David sat down too, trying not to look as though he was joining a cult of cheerful decay.

Outside, the trees swayed in the wind. Inside, the glitter fell like radioactive snow.

"Arthur," Nurse Kelly said, planting herself next to him with the kind of relentless cheer reserved for kindergarten teachers and hospice workers, "do you want to make a friendship collage?"

"I already made one," Arthur said. "It's called my obituary."

The other residents tittered. This was entertainment. Arthur was the show.

Kelly wasn't deterred. "C'mon, I know you're creative! Look, I've got glitter glue!"

Arthur squinted at it. "If you're trying to impress me with shiny snot, it's working."

Margaret giggled behind a paper snowman she was making. David smiled in spite of himself. Kelly sighed the sigh of the eternally patient.

"You know, Arthur," she said, "a little color might brighten your mood."

He tapped his glue stick against the table. "At my age, I don't need color. I need temperature. Warm soup. Warm room. Warm body would be nice, but I'll settle for the soup."

Kelly gave him the smile nurses reserve for men they wish would shut up and live another week.

Margaret leaned over, whispering conspiratorially, "You could at least glue something. It'll make her happy."

"She's young," Arthur said. "She'll recover."

If you've never seen a room full of octogenarians crafting, you've missed one of humanity's more noble farces. Imagine twenty people who have outlived their joints, coordination, and most of their original organs, sitting at tables like soldiers briefing for battle—with glue sticks instead of rifles. Their hands tremble as if negotiating peace treaties with gravity. Their glasses fog. Someone is always muttering, "This glue smells funny." But it's not the glue. Not in the least. That would be too logical. No, it's the person next to you, passing gas—a little silent, internal combustion engine of decay. It's the smell of human industry, just the body's little way of admitting that somewhere along the line, something went in, and something absolutely had to come out—in some form.

But Margaret, God bless her, was enjoying herself. After the paper snowman, she was onto something new. "I'm making a butterfly," she said, pasting pink wings onto blue paper with the grim concentration of a bomb technician.

Arthur squinted at a pair of scissors like they were some kind of alien technology designed to test his will to live. He held them backward for a while, just to make sure everyone knew he didn't care about the rules. Then he grabbed a magazine photo of a smiling couple—young, glowing, disgustingly hopeful—and sliced it neatly in half.

"I'm making a mess," he announced, voice flat as hospital wallpaper. "They look happier this way."

Nurse Kelly, whose job was to interpret despair as progress, clapped her hands. She had that relentless optimism found only in people who still believed in personal growth. "That's the spirit, Arthur! Expression over perfection!"

Arthur blinked at her like a man being congratulated for falling down the stairs. "Good," he said. "Because I've perfected the art of not giving a damn."

It was glorious, in a doomed sort of way. All around, the old folks wrestled with paper, glue, and the sheer absurdity of continuing to make things when everything they'd made for eighty years had already been taken apart, thrown out, or forgotten.

It was human civilization in microcosm. You take two useless things, attach them with hope, call it meaning, and pray it doesn't fall apart before lunch.

And of course, it will fall apart. The butterfly wings will droop, the glue will dry into scabs, and the mess will be swept into a plastic bin marked Memories. That's the punchline of being alive: everything eventually ends up in the trash, and somehow, that's still worth doing.

Arthur stared at his creation: a crooked paper bird, one wing larger than the other, its beak pointing at nothing in particular. "Well," he said, "look at that. I've made a self-portrait."

Ten minutes later, Arthur was gluing googly eyes to the legs of his walker.

Margaret noticed. "Arthur, what are you doing!"

"I'm improving it," he said. "Now when I fall, at least something's watching."

Kelly clapped her hands. "That's the spirit!"

"I'm not dead yet," Arthur said. "Just rehearsing."

Kelly moved on to another table, where Mrs. Franklin was trying to attach macaroni to a tissue box. David just sat there watching his mother and the old man interact with the faint suspicion that they were having more fun without him.

"You ever think about getting out of here?" David asked Arthur.

"Every day," Arthur said. "But then they wheel in dessert."

David chuckled. "Jell-O."

"Sometimes with chunks of stuff in it."

"What kind of stuff?"

Arthur squinted, as if considering whether the answer was worth the oxygen. "Could be fruit. Could be medical waste. At this point, it's a texture adventure."

David laughed. "You eat it anyway?"

Arthur shrugged. "At my age, everything's either poison or salvation. Might as well let the Jell-O decide."

He jabbed his glue stick at the legs of his walker, gluing yet more googly eyes to it. "Besides, it jiggles. That's more movement than I get most days."

Margaret put down her scissors. "Arthur, behave."

"I am behaving," he said. "Badly, but consistently."

Arthur pressed one more set of googly eyes into place, then leaned back to admire his walker like a primitive idol. "Behold," he said, "the God of Ambulation."

David couldn't help but laugh. "You're crazy."

"Took you this long to figure that out?"

Margaret smiled warmly at both of them. "You two get along better than you think."

Arthur turned to her. "I don't get along with anyone. It's my charm."

Now, I should admit something right here, before it's too late: Arthur didn't much care for crafts or art. He believed in torque, balance, leverage—the kind of things you could measure, tighten, fix. That was the machinist in him. A wrench could not lie. A gear didn't gossip. A nut didn't need encouragement.

Glue, on the other hand, was for children and bureaucrats. Both used it to hold together things that had no business being held together. Paper, pride, promises—stick it, smear it, pray it lasts until lunch.

Margaret laughed. Not the brittle, polite kind of laugh people use when they're afraid of dying in public, but the real kind—the kind that drizzles down softly, like rain on a kid's window during summer vacation. It said: yes, the world is stupid, but it's still here, and so are you.

Arthur liked that laugh. Hell, he liked her. She didn't talk to him like he was a malfunctioning appliance or a crossword clue that couldn't be solved without sympathy. She talked to him like he was still alive—which, technically, he was, though the evidence was mixed.

So, he played along. Said the funny things. Rolled his eyes in all the right places. Because he didn't want her to stop laughing. That laugh made the room warmer. And when it stopped—when it was just him and the hum of the building's systems—everything felt colder than the soup they kept insisting was food.

That's the thing about people who pretend they don't care: they care more than anyone. They just don't want a receipt. No signatures. No paperwork. Just the quiet, stubborn knowledge that they notice—and sometimes, that's enough.

David Miller, like many middle-aged men, was stuck between guilt and practicality. He had bills, deadlines, and a boss who measured worth in calendar invites. He had a mother who needed him and a father who'd left before David learned how to shave.

And now he had Arthur Trent—a human barnacle attached to the hull of his conscience.

He watched his mother glue paper daisies to construction paper while Arthur grumbled about the tensile strength of glue sticks.

"She seems happy," David said.

"She is happy," Arthur replied without looking up. "You should try it sometime."

"I'm serious."

"So am I."

David sighed. "It's just strange. She never used to laugh like that. Not since Dad."

Arthur looked at him—the kind of look that could sand paint off a Buick. "Let me tell you something, son. People don't stop laughing because they're sad. They stop because nobody's funny anymore."

Margaret waved her scissors like a white flag. "Gentlemen, please. This is arts and crafts, not a philosophy class."

Arthur smirked. "Same thing, if you think about it."

David watched his mother laugh again, her eyes creasing in that way that made him feel six years old and forgiven for something he hadn't done yet. He felt a sting of jealousy—absurd, but real. Arthur had found a way to reach her through sarcasm and complaint, the universal languages of the elderly.

He wondered if that was what he'd become one day: a man who could only communicate through irritation. Maybe it was genetic.

At the other end of the room, someone sneezed glitter. Time passed like molasses on morphine.

Margaret's collage looked like joy distilled into paper form. Arthur's walker now resembled an alien crab, or perhaps Iris, the multi-eyed bartender from his starship reality jumps. David's own contribution was pitiful: a pile of uncut magazines, a glue stick cap glued to his thumb, and a feeling that he was always a beat behind, forever trying to catch up with the absurd choreography of old age.

He wasn't sure if this was therapy or punishment.

Lunch time.

The great, rolling metallic trays arrived, pushed by an orderly who looked like he'd just discovered the ultimate meaninglessness of existence—which, of course, is part of the job description here. Each tray bore a bowl of that famous, institutional mystery liquid: the cold soup. It was a kind of beige that suggested defeat, a flavorless sludge that was less a meal and more a culinary white flag.

Arthur Trent, a man entirely allergic to surrender, poked at his bowl with a spoon, holding the utensil like it was a tiny, inadequate weapon.

"I ask you, young woman," he called out to Nurse Kelly, who was dispensing trays with practiced, synthetic cheerfulness. "Is the stove here merely a decorative piece? A monument to lost warmth?"

Nurse Kelly paused, deploying a smile that was too tight, too bright, and probably mandated by state regulations. "We follow dietary protocols, Arthur. Hot soup, especially for those with . . . reduced reflexes, can be dangerous."

"Dangerous?" Arthur took a sip of the soup. He scowled. "So is boredom. But you serve that every day. A vast, unending, lukewarm ocean of boredom, and we are all forced to paddle in it."

Margaret, a woman whose life had trained her in the fine art of diplomacy over despair, tried to intercede. "I think it's fine, Arthur. Maybe it's gazpacho. A Spanish delicacy."

"It's not gazpacho," Arthur informed her, with the certainty of a man who had seen cosmic horrors while half-asleep. "Gazpacho is honest about being cold. This," he jabbed the spoon at the beige liquid, "is revenge, served cold and without flavor. It's the universe reminding us we asked for too much."

David felt compelled to defend the indefensible, a peculiar instinct common in men who felt guilty about not visiting enough. He tentatively tried a spoonful. It tasted, remarkably, like beige.

"Maybe it's supposed to be cold," he offered weakly, instantly regretting the words.

Arthur looked at him as though he'd just confessed to eating glue stick. "You're defending the soup? You're defending the culinary apathy of the twenty-first century?"

"I'm just saying," David quickly amended, wiping his mouth with a napkin that felt suspiciously like paper, "maybe it's intentional."

"Oh, it's intentional," Arthur said, sinking back into his chair with a heavy finality. "Everything's intentional. That's the part that makes it truly tragic. Someone, somewhere, designed this cold soup and signed off on it. We live in a world where someone chooses the beige."

Nurse Kelly, sensing the rapidly descending philosophical atmosphere, moved on before she could be drafted into another philosophical war she couldn't win against an octogenarian machinist who traveled through time when he napped.

Margaret leaned in toward Arthur, whispering a gentle reprimand. "Arthur, stop driving Nurse Kelly crazy. She's only trying to help."

"Too late," he said, taking another sip of soup, then another and another after that before flipping his spoon onto the tray with a decisive clink. "And that, my friends, is how civilization ends—one beige spoon at a time."

Arthur never finished his soup, which is to say he never finished complaining about his soup, and then, like a tax accountant at the end of a fiscal year, his eyelids decided to resign without notice.

The mind is a curious little tyrant. Some people dream in color; others remember in sepia. Arthur didn't bother with either. He simply shifted, like a train whose engineer had gone on vacation and left the schedule to a committee of bureaucratic ghosts. Somewhere in the background, time yawned.

Suddenly, he was at the bar again—aboard the star cruiseship The Great Beyond. The counter shimmered like liquid mercury, infinite, reflecting stars as though someone had dumped a cosmic bag of marbles and left the vacuum uncleaned. The barstools had no legs, the floor had no gravity, and the air smelled faintly of ozone and regret.

Iris was there, of course. She always was. Like fate, like bad news in the morning paper, like a hangnail you can't stop thinking about. Her plum-colored skin rippled faintly, her multiple galaxy eyes orbiting in slow constellations. She wiped the bar with a cloth made of light, because ordinary rags could not clean the cosmic grime.

"How's your day going?" she asked, voice a melodic collision of chimes, warning bells, and distant traffic reports from worlds that didn't exist.

Arthur rubbed his temples. "Craft Hour. Glue. Glitter. Death with better lighting."

Her laugh—or maybe it was the death rattle of a tiny star—shimmered around him. "Humans make things that fall apart. Then glue them back. Again and again. Call it progress."

Arthur smirked. "Yup."

"It seems strange," she said.

"What's that?"

"You humans specialize in temporary repairs. You try to patch meaning into everything, then act shocked when the universe doesn't applaud."

Arthur lifted his steaming drink—a deep, impossible blue that smelled like engine oil, and slightly scorched toast. "We can't help it. Everything falls apart. We just like pretending it doesn't."

Iris tilted her head, seven delicate fingers polishing a glass that wasn't really there, or maybe it was, depending on how honest you were feeling about quantum physics. "And does pretending make it better?"

"No," Arthur said. "But it makes it last longer."

She smiled, a supernova sighing quietly. "You're learning."

"Learning what?"

"That it's all arts and crafts, sweetheart. Everywhere. Everything. Even planets. Even soup."

Outside the viewport, a planet drifted lazily past, its surface a floating patchwork of paper cities tethered by string. They collapsed, reassembled, swayed like drunk ballet dancers at a cosmic prom. Children—or something pretending to be children—floated between them, gluing towers back together, like janitors in a school play no one attended.

"They never stop, do they?" Arthur muttered.

"They can't," said Iris. "They create what cannot last, and in doing so, they last a little longer."

Arthur sipped his drink. "That's not purpose. That's stubbornness."

"Same thing," she said softly, like the universe delivering a telegram via butterfly.

He leaned back, watching. Perhaps his life had been nothing but temporary fixes: machines patched, marriage patched, friendships patched, the glue of life applied liberally, hoping gravity wouldn't notice.

"Maybe that's all we are," he said. "Just stuff held together by whatever sticks. Bits of cardboard, old tape, regrets, cold soup."

Iris poured another drink. "Even stars burn out. They're brighter when they're breaking."

Arthur didn't answer. He stared into his glass and saw glitter floating inside, tiny, mocking, cosmic flecks, like the universe was sneering and winking at him at the same time.

"Dammit," he muttered. "Follows me everywhere."

Back at Sunny Meadows, his eyes fluttered open. Margaret was chatting with Nurse Kelly, whose smile could probably be patented as a weapon. David scrolled his phone, pretending not to, and the soup was still cold. Arthur sighed, long and low, as though dragging the weight of infinity behind him.

"Well," he said, "at least the universe is consistent."

Somewhere, somewhere out there, stars twinkled like they were laughing at him—or maybe just enjoying their own terrible soup.

Chapter 3

Lunchtime was over, which meant the residents had survived another round of mashed nostalgia disguised as nutrition. Arthur adjusted his bib, which was neither ironic nor optional, and muttered, "If they served dignity here, it'd come in single servings."

Arthur looked at his walker strewn with googly eyes—a bold aesthetic choice that made the contraption look like a paranoid insect—when Nurse Kelly declared Craft Hour officially over. The residents applauded weakly, the way people do when they're just happy something ended without casualties.

Margaret, proud of her butterfly, lifted it up for inspection. "What do you think?"

Arthur squinted at it. "Looks like it's been through a divorce."

Margaret smirked. "Everything beautiful has."

"Christ," Arthur said, "you've been listening to me too long."

David watched the exchange with the peculiar admiration one reserves for master craftsmen—except instead of woodworking or painting, Arthur specialized in weaponizing pessimism until it circled back around to something that looked an awful lot like enlightenment.

When the room began to empty, Margaret went off with Nurse Kelly to return the glue sticks, leaving David and Arthur momentarily alone.

"You really think you're funny, don't you?" David said.

Arthur leaned back in his chair, hands on his belly like a retired philosopher who'd given up on students. "No. I think I'm correct. Funny is just a side effect."

David crossed his arms. "You know, most people would call that cynicism."

Arthur shrugged. "Most people call soup hot. Then they come here and learn otherwise."

David grinned despite himself. "That's the thing about you, Arthur. You say the most depressing shit in the most comforting way."

"That's wisdom, kid," Arthur said. "Cynicism with rhythm."

He turned his walker slightly, the googly eyes wiggling like an audience. "You see, the trick to surviving this dump—or any dump—is realizing you're in one. The minute you start pretending it's paradise, you're doomed. You'll glue macaroni to a Kleenex box and call it self-expression. Me? I just call it Tuesday."

David laughed. "So you'd rather be miserable and right?"

Arthur looked him dead in the eye. "Wouldn't you?"

David hesitated. He wanted to say no, to defend optimism like a man defending a childhood pet from euthanasia. But optimism had long since run off, probably to join the circus. "Maybe," he said. "But doesn't it get tiring?"

Arthur grunted. "Sure. So does breathing. Don't mean I'll stop."

They sat there in companionable silence for a while, watching as Nurse Kelly fluttered about, sweeping stray glitter into a dustpan like a fairy janitor.

Arthur leaned closer. "You know what I like about you, David?"

"I didn't know you liked anything about me."

Arthur ignored that. "You listen, polyester. Most people come in here, they talk at you. Tell you to think positive, stay active, eat your goddamn fruit cup. You just sit there and take the beating. That's rare."

David chuckled. "So, I'm your ideal audience?"

Arthur snorted. "Nobody's ideal. But you're tolerable, which is the nursing-home equivalent of charming."

Margaret returned just then, barely holding onto three cups of pudding like offerings to some ancient, lactose-tolerant god. "Chocolate," she said, "and still cold."

Arthur grimaced. "If this turns out to be vanilla in disguise, I'm revolting."

"You already are," she said.

David nearly spat up his pudding laughing.

Arthur looked at him, mock offended. "Don't laugh at that. You're supposed to defend my honor."

"I would," David said, "but I'm not sure you have any."

Arthur pointed a trembling spoon at him. "See? The kid's learning. Sarcasm: humanity's last reliable form of affection."

Margaret shook her head. "You two are ridiculous."

"Ridiculous keeps us alive," Arthur said. "Ask any clown. Or president."

For a moment, they just sat there, spooning pudding and pretending the world made sense.

Then Arthur broke the silence. "You know, kid, your mother tells me you work with computers."

"Yeah," David said cautiously. "IT project manager. Mostly spreadsheets and misery."

Arthur nodded as if this confirmed a long-held suspicion. "Figures. You look like a man who spends his life explaining to machines why they shouldn't kill him."

"Not far off."

Arthur stirred his pudding like a philosopher at a mud puddle. "Machines don't hate us, you know. They just imitate. We hate ourselves first, then they learn from example."

David blinked. "That's actually . . . pretty deep."

Arthur raised an eyebrow. "Don't sound so surprised. I've had decades to practice despair."

Margaret sighed. "Arthur thinks he's Kierkegaard with constipation."

Arthur grinned. "Damn right. Existentialism and fiber—keeps a man regular."

David laughed so hard he dropped his spoon. "You should write a book."

"Too late," Arthur said. "The title's Life, or Why Bother? Every chapter ends with a nap."

David shook his head, still smiling. "You know, I think I'm starting to get you."

Arthur leaned in. "Don't. The moment you think you understand someone, you've stopped listening."

"Fair," David said. "Then maybe I just . . . appreciate you."

Arthur squinted suspiciously. "Appreciation? That sounds dangerously close to affection. Keep that up, and people'll think you're joining the cult of kindness."

"Maybe I am," David said. "You'd make a hell of a prophet."

Arthur chuckled. "All prophets are just pessimists with better PR."

He gestured around the room. "Look at this place. The elderly gluing paper to paper, pretending that if they just make enough butterflies, maybe death'll get distracted. It's beautiful, sure. Pathetic, too. That's the secret, kid—beauty and futility always travel in pairs."

David looked at his mother, still fussing over her butterfly. Her fingers trembled, but her eyes were bright. "Yeah," he said quietly. "Maybe that's what makes it worth it."

Arthur studied him for a long moment, his expression softening by millimeters. "You're not a total idiot, you know that?"

"High praise."

"Don't get used to it."

Nurse Kelly returned, chirping like an overfed parakeet. "All done here? That was wonderful, everyone! So much creativity today!"

Arthur waved a dismissive hand. "Yeah, yeah. We'll be signing autographs later."

Kelly smiled sweetly. "I'll bring more glitter next time!"

Arthur groaned. "Of course you will. God forbid we face mortality without sequins."

When she left, David said, "You really hate her optimism, don't you?"

Arthur shook his head. "Hate? Nah. I envy it. But envy's just admiration that's been mugged by experience."

They sat there until Margaret yawned, signaling the end of visiting hours in the quiet, polite way old people announce bedtime.

David helped her to her room, placing the butterfly carefully on her dresser. "You should hang it up," he said.

"I will," she said. "But I like knowing it's safe first."

When she'd settled in, he turned to leave. Arthur was waiting by the door with his many-eyed walker.

"Hey, polyester," Arthur said.

David turned. "Yeah?"

Arthur's voice dropped, suddenly serious. "Don't wait till you're eighty-four to figure out it's all a joke. Laugh now. It's cheaper."

David nodded slowly. "You ever think maybe laughter's the only thing that makes it bearable?"

Arthur smiled. "Kid, it's the only thing that makes it human."

David walked away feeling oddly lighter. The hallway still smelled like antiseptic and surrender, but now it also smelled—just faintly—of glue and paper and something like grace.

Outside, the afternoon sun fought through the clouds with all the enthusiasm of a hungover god. David sat in his car, watching the light dance on the hood.

Arthur was right, he thought. Everything was absurd. Everything was falling apart. And somehow, that made it funny.

He laughed to himself—a small, startled sound—and started the engine.

Back at Sunny Meadows, Arthur leaned back in his chair, eyes half-closed, smiling faintly as if he'd just remembered the punchline to a cosmic joke.

Then, softly, he muttered to himself, "Soup's probably cold again."

And for once, he sounded almost happy about it.

David was back. He knew he should have been at the office, filling out spreadsheets or performing whatever nonsense ritual his job required, but instead, he was here, pulled back by the crusty orbit of Arthur Trent. Why? Because Arthur was a glorious, certified lunatic who managed to make his mother, Margaret (a perfectly sane woman), laugh more than David had in the last two decades. It was an appalling truth, a little slip of paper proving the universe didn't need him. David was essentially a tourist on his own planet, and Arthur, the retired machinist, was the only local attraction that wasn't selling postcards.

He found his mother, Margaret, and Arthur in the sunroom, which was neither sunny nor particularly room-like. It smelled faintly of old library books, lemon polish, and that weird mix of resignation and Lysol that comes free with aging.

Margaret sat at a little table surrounded by clippings and photographs that had clearly survived more years than anyone expected them to.

She was carefully pressing a poem clipped from an old Reader's Digest onto a square of cardboard. The way she did it, you'd think she was signing a treaty with death itself. And hoping death would read the fine print.

"It's for my memory album project," she said.

She didn't look up. Looking up is something beginners do.

"Always liked this poem."

Arthur sat next to her, hiding behind a copy of Popular Mechanics that had likely been printed during the Nixon administration. "The prodigal son returns," he announced without enthusiasm. "Did you remember to shower this time, or are we basking in the musk of middle-aged gloom?"

"Good morning to you too, Arthur," David said. He kissed his mother's temple—it was warm, soft, and smelled faintly of hand sanitizer. "Making an album of dust, Mom?"

Margaret smiled that lovely, crinkled smile that made David forgive everything—the years, the distance, the pudding. "No, dear. It's an Album of Memories. See?" She lifted a scrapbook that had "ALBUM OF MEMORYS" written across the front in glitter glue, the 'S' dangling off like an afterthought.

Arthur snorted. "I'm reading about a twelve-cylinder hydrogen engine. Now that's a memory worth keeping. Not this sentimental horseshit."

David looked around the sunroom. Other residents were busy enacting the final, quiet scene of their lives, which mostly involved sitting upright and breathing. A woman named Agnes was asleep with her chin resting firmly on a copy of Good Housekeeping. Another fellow, whose name David forgot, which was fine, since the fellow likely forgot his own, was meticulously gluing a receipt from Denny's right next to a faded picture of a very sad-looking beagle.

Legacy, American-style, David thought. The whole room was a collective sigh, bound together by the faint, shared scent of lemon polish and mortality.

"Hydrogen engines, huh?" David said, sitting down. "You planning to build one, or just mock it from afar like everything else?"

Arthur lowered the magazine. His eyebrows were magnificent, two fuzzy indicators of lifelong irritation. "I'd build one if Nurse Kelly stopped confiscating my tools. Apparently, screwdrivers are 'a fall risk.' You know what else is a fall risk? Living."

Margaret frowned. "Arthur, don't be dramatic."

"Dramatic? My entire life's a low-budget tragedy."

"Then maybe you should focus on happier memories," Margaret said, dabbing glue onto her paper with reverence.

Arthur turned to David. "See, this is why your mother's the optimistic one. She still thinks happy memories are a renewable resource."

David smiled weakly. "You could contribute something. Maybe an old photo you have."

Arthur scoffed. "No thanks. Memories are for weaklings."

Nurse Kelly entered the sunroom, beaming the way only people paid hourly can beam. "How's my favorite bunch today?"

Arthur muttered, "Still alive. Against our will."

Kelly ignored him, which was both her professional strategy and self-defense mechanism. She handed Margaret a small stack of mail. "Some letters for you, sweetheart!"

Margaret brightened. "Oh, wonderful!" She shuffled through the envelopes. One from David, one from a charity asking her to sponsor a goat, and one ominous piece from her insurance provider.

Arthur watched her sort through her mail. "You still get mail? All I ever get are offers to pre-plan my funeral. Apparently, I can save 15% if I die before spring."

"Maybe they're running a seasonal promotion," David said.

Arthur swiveled his head, fixing David with a glare that could curdle milk. "What's this? You trying to be clever? Don't. Unlike me, polyester, you'll fail to achieve truly magnificent misanthropy."

Margaret handed David a letter. "This one's for you. I think it's from the facility."

He tore it open. "Oh great."

Arthur interjected. "Probably a form telling you the pudding is now legally considered a solid."

David scanned it. "It's about next week's Family Luncheon. They're asking for volunteers."

Arthur looked up, horrified. "Volunteer? For what? Watching people chew?"

"For helping serve, I think," David said.

Arthur groaned. "Perfect. Nothing says 'bonding' like feeding your loved ones cafeteria-grade meat while pretending this isn't a holding pattern for the grave."

Margaret patted his arm. "You could help set the tables. You're good with arrangements."

"I was good with arrangements when I worked for General Motors," Arthur said. "These days, I'm just good at waiting for the mail and not dying before it arrives."

David couldn't help smiling. "You're an inspiration, really."

"Damn right," Arthur said. "They should bronze me and put me in the lobby. Title it Man Who Outlasted the Soup."

Margaret giggled. "Oh, Arthur, stop being impossible."

Arthur folded his magazine. "Impossible's all I've got left, my dear."

Nurse Kelly passed by again, carrying a clipboard that looked far too important for what she actually did. "Don't forget, everyone! Tomorrow is 'Decade Day'—dress from your favorite era!"

Arthur raised his hand. "Does the afterlife count as an era?"

Kelly winked. "Only if you accessorize!" and floated out.

David sighed. "She's too cheerful. It's unnerving."

Arthur nodded solemnly. "That woman's smile could power a small dictatorship."

Margaret frowned at them both. "You two should try being kind. She means well."

"Everyone means well," Arthur said. "That's how history happens."

David leaned back in his chair, watching his mother line up old photos—him as a boy, their house, a long-gone dog. Each picture was a time capsule labeled "Before It Got Complicated."

"You know," he said quietly, "these albums—they're kind of nice. It's like . . . proof you existed."

Arthur snorted. "Polyester, proof you existed is everywhere. Taxes. Debt. Dental records. The only people who need albums are the ones who stopped mattering."

Margaret looked up, eyes sharp for once. "That's not true. Memories are how we keep mattering."

Arthur studied her, then turned a page in Popular Mechanics. "Maybe. But I'd rather remember how to change my own oil."

Silence settled over the room, the kind that gets thick around the elderly, as if the air knows it's running out of time too.

Then Margaret said brightly, "We should put a picture in here, David. You and your father."

David hesitated. "You still have those?"

"Of course." She looked through the photos, sliding out a faded one. His father was smiling awkwardly beside a station wagon. David, age seven, was clutching a toy plane like it could fly him away from everything.

Arthur peered at it. "Nice car. Shame about the decade."

David smiled faintly. "He loved that thing."

Margaret nodded. "He did. Even after it stopped running, he'd sit in the driveway pretending to drive. Said it helped him think."

Arthur muttered, "Hell, that's what we're all doing now. Just sitting in our driveways, pretending to go somewhere."

Margaret placed the photo carefully in the album, smoothed it down with the palm of her hand, and whispered, "There. That's a good memory."

David watched her—her trembling fingers, her steady patience. He thought about time, and loss, and how most people were just trying to scrapbook themselves into meaning.

Arthur broke the silence. "You know, kid, someday they'll find these albums and think we were happy."

"Maybe that's the point," David said.

Arthur grunted. "Maybe." He lifted his magazine again. "Now leave me alone. I'm trying to read about the future."

Margaret smiled. "Arthur's future runs on hydrogen and denial."

Arthur smirked behind the pages. "And yours runs on glitter and nostalgia."

David laughed softly. "Guess that makes me the hybrid."

Arthur pointed without looking up. "Good. Maybe you'll last longer than we did."

Somewhere down the hall, the mail cart rattled on its next delivery—a metallic heartbeat reminding everyone that even in slow places, things kept moving.

David leaned back in his chair, which made a noise like a small animal dying. The sun hit the back of his neck with all the subtlety of a tax audit. It was one of those afternoons when the world felt like a waiting room between disasters.

"I actually read something on the internet this morning," he said.

Arthur looked up from his magazine and raised a single eyebrow that could have qualified for a pension. "Oh no. The internet. That's where mankind goes to confess."

David hesitated, suddenly aware of how stupid it sounded, even before he said it. "It was about the societal impact of having fewer meaningful long-term friendships after forty."

The room went quiet except for the ceiling fan, which whirred as though trying to leave the building. Margaret was still looking through her mail, then paused, smiling kindly.

Arthur tilted his head. "And what did your little doom article say, polyester? Let me guess . . . 'Everyone's lonely but buy our subscription for tips on how not to be.'"

David shrugged. "Pretty much. It said that after forty, people start losing their social structures. Work friends drift off. Hobbies die out. If you don't actively make new friends, you end up . . . alone."

"Congratulations," Arthur said. "You've just discovered adulthood."

Margaret reached over and patted David's hand like she was comforting a puppy that had read Camus. "Oh, sweetie. You have us. That's all you need."

Arthur pointed a bony, accusatory finger at Margaret. "See, Margaret? He's reading articles about how lonely he is, you're happily rummaging through old mail that probably could be thrown away, and I'm sitting here reading about an engine that runs purely on hydrogen. Between the three of us, we make up one full, utterly confused human being. A pathetic trinity, really."

Margaret smiled. "That's called community, Arthur."

"That's called delusion," he corrected. "A more efficient fuel than hydrogen, by the way."

David rubbed his temples. "I'm thinking you're both impossible."

"That's our charm," Arthur said.

The fan rattled overhead, as though agreeing. A nurse walked by humming something cheerful enough to sound menacing. The whole building seemed suspended in the kind of quiet you only get when everyone's out of good ideas.

David sighed. "You know, the article made it sound like loneliness is this slow apocalypse. Like, people just start disappearing into their own routines until one day they realize no one's left to tell them their shirt's inside out."

Arthur smirked. "That's not apocalypse, that's retirement."

Margaret gave David a long look. "You miss your friends, don't you?"

"Yeah," David admitted. "I mean, we all text sometimes. But it's like . . . we used to talk. In person. About dumb things. Now it's just updates. Job. Kids. Taxes. It's like we turned into our own LinkedIn profiles."

Arthur closed his magazine and rested it on his lap. "You want my advice, polyester?"

"Do I ever get a choice?"

"No."

"Then go ahead."

Arthur leaned forward, the fluorescent light glinting off his forehead like divine irony. "People don't disappear because they get old. They disappear because it's easier than showing up. You know why nobody keeps friends after forty? Because at some point, everyone starts rehearsing their eulogy instead of their punchlines."

Margaret gasped. "Arthur!"

"What? It's true. You spend your youth collecting people like stamps. Then one day, you wake up and realize your collection's dwindled to almost nothing, and the post office closed."

David looked down at his hands. "So that's it, then? Just accept it?"

Arthur shrugged. "That's what most of us do. That, or we invent new hobbies—like reading about hydrogen engines that'll never exist."

Margaret patted David's hand again. "Don't listen to him. He's allergic to sincerity."

"I'm not allergic," Arthur said. "I just prefer the placebo version."

David laughed softly. "Maybe that's what we're all doing—pretending the loneliness is just part of the program."

Arthur nodded. "Sure. Pretend hard enough, and it becomes philosophy. That's how I got through three marriages and a world war."

Margaret sighed. "You never fought in a war."

"I watched a lot of documentaries. Same emotional damage."

The three of them sat in silence again, the kind of silence that wasn't empty, just tired. Outside, a bird landed on the windowsill and immediately looked disappointed.

David stared at it. "You ever wonder what animals think of us?"

Arthur didn't hesitate. "They think we're loud, hairless disasters with excellent snacks."

"I don't know," David said. "Sometimes I think they pity us. Like they look at us and think, 'How tragic—so much brainpower, so little sense.'"

Margaret chuckled. "You sound like one of those . . . what are they called . . . oh yeah . . . new age bloggers."

Arthur smirked. "Careful, Margaret. The boy's evolving. Next thing you know, he'll be burning incense and calling loneliness 'spiritual alignment.'"

David ignored him. "No, seriously. Imagine some alien species coming to study us. They'd see us all sitting in little boxes—

offices, apartments, nursing homes—typing messages to people we used to talk to in person. They'd think emotional distance was a form of mating."

Arthur tapped his magazine thoughtfully. "Maybe it is."

David sighed. "You'd think with all our technology, we'd be better at connection."

Arthur smiled. "Technology doesn't make people connect. It just makes it easier to ignore each other faster. Progress, my boy."

Margaret tilted her head. "Maybe empathy's what we've lost. Not the friendship itself, but the part where you care enough to show up."

Arthur gave her a rare, almost gentle look. "Careful, Margaret. That sounded dangerously hopeful."

David smiled faintly. "Maybe the aliens would like her best."

Arthur chuckled. "Oh, definitely. They'd abduct her first—probe her for optimism."

Margaret rolled her eyes. "You two are ridiculous."

"Ridiculous keeps us human," Arthur said. "Ask any clown or congressman."

David leaned back again, the chair squealing in protest. "You know what's weird? For the first time all week, I don't feel alone."

Arthur looked at him. "That's because you're sitting next to two experts. We've been practicing life for years."

Margaret grinned. "Welcome to the club, dear. No dues, no meetings, just mutual survival."

David laughed. "Maybe that's all friendship really is."

Arthur raised his magazine again. "Exactly. Loneliness with witnesses."

The ceiling fan creaked, the sunlight slanted across the table, and the bird outside finally gave up and flew away—probably to report back to the aliens.

Arthur yawned. His head tipped back against the slick vinyl chair, which was doing its best impression of furniture from a cheaper universe. Then he nodded off. Arthur didn't just fall asleep when this happened. Plenty of people fall asleep. That's ordinary. Arthur fell somewhere else entirely. Another reality. It happened every time he dozed. Which made naps a very adventurous hobby.

Iris stood behind the counter, polishing a glass that contained a tiny, spinning galaxy. Her plum-colored skin shimmered like oil in sunlight, and her eyes seemed to refract time itself. She was, in Arthur's estimation, the only person in the multiverse who didn't make small talk about the weather.

Arthur was at his usual stool, the one that always seemed to sigh under the weight of his bones. "Just reading an article," he said, drumming a finger against the bar as if he'd been here all along. "About the future of transport. Human folly. They think hydrogen cars are going to save them. They'll still be lost—just faster."

Iris tilted her head, her gaze fracturing the room into a dozen overlapping moments. "They're always looking for a better way to get there," she said. Her voice was like wind through crystal reeds. "But they don't know that there is no there. Only the going. The going is all there is."

Arthur looked down at the drink she'd poured him—a steaming sapphire-blue liquid that hissed softly, like it resented being contained. "You sound like a motivational poster in a therapist's office," he said. "But prettier."

She smiled with her whole face, and maybe the whole galaxy smiled with her. "You're angry," she said. "Always angry."

"I'm not angry," Arthur said, sipping the drink. It tasted like whiskey and electricity. "I'm disappointed. Which is worse. Anger has energy. Disappointment just lies there, taking up space."

Iris continued polishing the glass. "You left your body again," she said gently. "You'll have to return soon. They worry for you."

Arthur snorted. "They? You mean Margaret and David? Margaret thinks I'm an eccentric garden ornament. David thinks I'm a museum exhibit labeled 'Father, mid-twentieth century: specimen preserved in sarcasm.'" He swirled the drink and stared into its swirling lights. "They both mean well, which is the first sign of disaster."

"Meaning well," Iris said, "is the human disease."

"Right after cholesterol," Arthur replied.

A silence settled between them. It wasn't awkward. In fact, it was quite comfortable—the kind of silence that could only exist between an elderly man who'd stopped believing in things and an alien bartender who'd seen the end of every civilization twice.

Behind Arthur, a pair of temporal mechanics argued over whether causality had a moral obligation to clean up after itself. At a nearby table, a sentient nebula was weeping into a bowl of photonic noodles. The house band, a trio of quantum flutists, played a song that technically hadn't been written yet.

Arthur exhaled, the sound almost wistful. "You know what I miss?"

"Soup?" Iris said.

He looked at her, surprised. "How'd you . . ."

"You always begin with soup."

Arthur sighed. "Yes, soup. It's the great metaphor. The state of the universe in a bowl. Always either too hot or too cold. Never quite right. And no matter how you stir it, it still separates."

Iris leaned forward, her voice dropping to a murmur. "There is no perfection, sweetie. Only approximation."

He grinned tiredly. "That's what my second wife said. Right before she left me for a yoga instructor named Clive."

Iris's expression didn't change. "You weren't meant to be contained."

Arthur pointed a wrinkled finger at her. "That's what Clive told her, too."

She laughed then—a sound like starlight catching on glass. "Perhaps Clive was wise."

"Clive was tan," Arthur said. "Wisdom had nothing to do with it."

The drink glowed brighter, pulsing faintly to some cosmic heartbeat. Arthur stared into it and saw flashes of memory: Margaret looking through her mail, David sitting awkwardly in the sunroom, the eternal war between comfort and futility. He felt the gravitational pull of it, tugging him backward toward reality.

"I don't want to go back yet," he muttered.

Iris reached out, her hand light against his wrist. "You always say that."

"Because it's always true."

"You think this place is more real than where you came from?"

Arthur looked around. The nebula was now singing. The time mechanics were arguing in reverse. The bar stool next to him briefly became his childhood bicycle. "Real?" he said. "It's at least more honest. Nobody here pretends things will turn out fine. Nobody here talks about 'growth opportunities.' Everyone knows the soup's cold."

Iris tilted her head. "Perhaps the soup is only cold because you stopped tasting it."

"That's the kind of thing that sounds profound," Arthur said, "until you realize it's nonsense."

She smiled again. "So sure of yourself."

Arthur chuckled, the sound half-sigh, half-laugh. "Always."

"A lot of irony in you," Iris said. "It's the only human export of value, I suppose."

Arthur said, raising his glass, "Cheers to that."

They drank in synchronized melancholy. Somewhere in the distance, the dying star cracked a little more, shedding light like dandruff.

After a while, Iris set her glass down. "It's time," she said softly. "They're waiting."

Arthur looked out at the windowless expanse, stars scattered like punctuation marks in a run-on sentence. "You know," he said, "sometimes I think I prefer it here. It's predictable, in a way. You, me, the soup that doesn't go cold because it never existed. I can live with that."

Iris's gaze shimmered, refracting past and present. "You already do."

He started to argue. That was the plan, anyway. But the words didn't make it. They wandered off somewhere between disbelief and being very, very tired. Then there was a sound. A deep hum. The kind that feels less like noise and more like the universe clearing its throat. It grew louder.

The bar didn't explode or vanish dramatically. It simply gave up. The walls, the stools, the bottles—everything dissolved around him like sugar in hot tea.

And just like that, Arthur was back in the sunroom. Nurse Kelly was stacking empty bowls, humming something that sounded suspiciously like "Fly Me to the Moon." Margaret was showing David her memory album, a glittering catastrophe of glue and sentiment.

Arthur blinked, still tasting the blue liquor, still feeling Iris's cool hand.

"Arthur?" David asked. "You dozed off again."

Arthur looked at the soup bowl in front of him. Cold, congealed, defiant.

He smiled faintly. "You wouldn't believe where I was," he said.

David didn't ask. He knew. Margaret just patted his hand. Nurse Kelly beamed.

Margaret sighed softly, a sound like someone folding a newspaper. "I think," she said, "I'm going to lie down for a bit. I'm not feeling quite right. Just need a nap."

David turned to her. "What kind of not right?"

"The ordinary kind," she said. "The kind that comes with too many birthdays and gravity."

She smiled, the practiced smile of someone trying to make illness polite. "Will you walk me to my room, dear?"

"Of course," David said, already on his feet.

Margaret waved at Arthur. "See you tomorrow," she told him with a smile.

Arthur waved back and watched them go. Nurse Kelly hummed as she collected the untouched bowls, as if the act of clearing dishes was a moral triumph.

The hallway was long and too bright, the walls painted in a color that wanted to be cheerful but didn't quite make it. David walked beside his mother, holding her elbow the way one holds something fragile that insists it isn't.

"You don't have to fuss," Margaret said. "It's nothing serious. When you get old, you start listening to your body more. It's like an old radio—full of static, but occasionally it plays a clear song."

David smiled at that. "You always did make it sound simple."

"It is simple," she said. "Just inconvenient."

They reached her room—a modest box with a window that faced a tree pretending to be alive. Margaret sat on the edge of her bed, smoothed the blanket, and looked around as if trying to remember whether the room was hers or just a temporary stop on the way to somewhere quieter.

"Go on," she said. "You've got work . . . a life to live. Don't worry about me."

David hesitated and smiled. "You sure?"

"Yes, dear." She patted his hand. "I'll take a nap and wake up feeling like a younger, slightly more delusional version of myself."

He laughed. "That's all any of us can hope for."

"Oh, and one more thing."

"What's that?"

"Take care of Arthur for me," she whispered, her voice thin but sharpened by decades of knowing exactly what her son lacked. "He needs you, and you need him. I've watched you your whole life, David. You get rattled by the world. Arthur doesn't. He stares it down until the world blinks first. You could use a friend like that. Someone who won't let you vanish into your own head. Someone who won't let you hide."

"Mom," he said softly, "why are you talking like this?"

"I'm just saying . . . if I go, you take care of him for me."

David felt a small panic bloom in his chest. "Stop talking like that. You're not going anywhere."

She smiled, a little crooked, like a warning. "We all go somewhere, David. Some just leave slower than others."

"Just stop it," he said, trying to anchor the moment. "And anyway, Arthur's practically indestructible. Like a grumpy old refrigerator that keeps working out of spite."

She chuckled. "All the more reason someone should check if he's still plugged in. And make sure you don't unplug yourself in the process."

She lay back, eyes half-closed, the lines in her face softening into something almost peaceful. David lingered. Her breathing settled into that soft, rhythmic pattern he knew from childhood—

when she used to fall asleep sitting upright during storybooks, claiming she was 'just resting her eyes.' He stood there for a moment longer, memorizing the rise and fall of her chest, because something in him—some ancient mammalian instinct—felt the need to.

"Sleep well, Mom," he said, kissing her forehead.

He stepped into the hallway, pulling the door shut with the quiet reverence of someone leaving a church, or a room containing a delicate experiment that shouldn't be disturbed. The latch clicked, and for reasons unknown even to himself, the sound made his heart stutter.

Sunny Meadows felt different as he walked down the hall. The walls, usually a cheerful shade of beige—cheerful in the way a laminated pamphlet about estate planning can be cheerful—seemed dimmer, as if the bulbs were reconsidering their life choices. The patterned carpet, with its swirls that resembled bored doodles from a meeting no one wanted to attend, cushioned his steps in a way that was almost too soft. Unsettlingly soft.

He passed Nurse Kelly, who straightened abruptly as if she'd been caught thinking something too private.

"Oh . . . David," she said. "Everything all right?"

Her smile was the kind you give a kid after they ask what happens to pets when they 'go away.' Beautifully crafted. Utterly false.

"My mom's taking a nap," he replied. "She said she wasn't feeling too great."

Kelly's expression fluttered—just for a second—like a flag caught between two winds, one of hope and one of dread. Then she composed herself, smoothing invisible wrinkles in her scrubs.

"That's . . . good. Rest is good," she said, nodding so hard her ponytail bounced like it was trying to escape. "I'll check in on her a bit later."

He just nodded and continued down the hall. At the end of the corridor, the exit sign glowed red—an emergency escape for when things got too real. David pushed through the doors and stepped into the sunlight.

The brightness was disorienting. For a moment, he had the strange feeling that the world outside was oblivious to the fact that something inside had shifted. Birds continued arguing in the trees. A car honked from the street. The air smelled like cut grass and someone grilling a late lunch.

Nothing had cracked open.

Nothing had ended.

He walked across the parking lot, keys spinning loosely around his finger. Halfway to his car, he stopped and glanced back at the building. Sunny Meadows looked exactly the same as it had when he'd arrived: a beige cube of well-intentioned loneliness, windows glinting like polite eyes.

"Take care of Arthur for me," his mother had said.

The phrase looped in his head like one of those songs you don't remember liking yet somehow know all the words to.

Why did she say that? Arthur wasn't helpless—irritable, yes; impossible, often; a human foghorn of complaints, absolutely—but not helpless. And yet, thinking about it now, David realized there was something grounding about the old man, something strangely honest in Arthur's relentless cynicism. It was like standing next to someone who had already dug through the garbage of life and was willing to show you the least rotten parts.

Maybe his mother had seen something he hadn't wanted to acknowledge: that Arthur gave him something—a reason to show up, to pay attention, to be more than a son managing a schedule of visits. And maybe, in some twisted cosmic barter system, David gave Arthur something too: a witness. Someone who listened. Someone who didn't treat him like a countdown. He wasn't sure how he felt about that. Affection wasn't the right word, but it hovered around the edges. A reluctant fondness, maybe. The kind that grows accidentally, like weeds.

He shook his head, trying to dismiss the odd thoughts that ran through him. His thoughts returned to his mother.

She was just tired. Just in need of a nap. Older bodies sent up false alarms all the time. That's what they did—operational glitches, minor shutdowns, warnings that turned out to be nothing.

He unlocked his car and slid into the driver's seat, but he didn't start it right away. His hands rested on the steering wheel, unmoving. The silence inside the car felt too roomy, the way silence does right before a doctor delivers news.

He exhaled slowly.

"Get a grip," he muttered to himself. "Go home."

The words sounded flimsy, even to him.

He turned the engine over. The radio sprang to life with a saxophone solo that had no business being as tragic as it was. It was the kind of music that felt like it knew something you didn't.

David eased the car into reverse.

Behind him, Sunny Meadows stood still, like a polite witness to a secret.

He pulled out of the parking lot, blissfully ignorant that he was driving away from the last version of reality where his mother had already begun slipping out of the world with all the subtlety of a librarian closing a book.

Chapter 4

Arthur had never been much for breakfast. He'd eaten it, of course—eight decades of chewing his way through the most disappointing meal of the day—but he had never liked breakfast. Breakfast was a bureaucratic obligation of the body, a form you filled out simply because your organs insisted you still existed, much like tax returns or informed consent forms for a colonoscopy.

But this morning, the oatmeal was worse than usual. It looked like something scraped off God's boots after the Flood—if God had walked through the muddy remains of what was left of humanity. Also, he was alone. That was the real issue.

The chair across from him—the one that always had Margaret in it, straight-backed and alert as a bird pretending not to be dying—sat empty.

Arthur stared at the chair for so long that Nurse Kelly finally approached with a hand on his shoulder, the kind of gesture meant to soothe a man who'd just watched his house sink into the earth while a marching band played upbeat music nearby.

"Arthur," she said softly, "are you all right?"

Her face wore one of those complicated expressions people make when they can't decide whether to smile or sob. The corners of her lips tried smiling, but the muscles around her eyes refused to participate. The result was a grimace masquerading as kindness, or possibly the other way around.

"When have I ever been all right?" Arthur snapped. "I was born not all right. I got married not all right. A couple of times, mind you. I retired not all right. This"—he tapped his bowl with his spoon, producing a dull, joyless thud— "is the farthest thing from all right that has ever been served in a bowl."

Kelly attempted another smile, but it landed with the elegance of a dropped egg. "I understand," she said, then, after a beat too long, she placed her hand on his shoulder again—a soft, trembling pressure—and whispered, "I'm so sorry, Arthur."

"She's late," Arthur said, rising with the slow majesty of a ruined cathedral, stonework trembling and pigeons startled. "Don't you give a damn? Margaret has never once been late. She beats the sun out of bed most days."

Kelly's mouth quivered. Her eyes darted away, then back, then away again—like she was searching for a manual on how to handle old men who'd stumbled too close to bad news.

Arthur didn't wait for her to find it.

Angered, he grabbed his walker with all the googly eyes glued to it—so many, he tried counting but lost track, each staring in a slightly different direction as if anticipating disaster—and started to make his way to Margaret's room.

As he moved toward Margaret's room, he noticed something off.

The staff looked . . . sad.

Of course, Arthur had always believed people who worked in nursing homes were professionally melancholy. Why else volunteer to watch mortality play musical chairs every day? Still, these nurses wore grief in a way he didn't like. Their eyes were swollen. Their smiles were that brittle kind people used when speaking at funerals.

"Morning, Arthur," one aide murmured, voice hushed like a church. She put a hand on his arm as he passed. She never touched him. He decided she must be pregnant. Pregnancy made women touchy. Or maybe she had gas. Who could know?

He continued on.

Another nurse, Janine, gave him a look usually reserved for lost puppies and last meals.

"Janine," he barked, "stop looking at me like I'm a dropped ice cream cone."

She opened her mouth, closed it, and then hurried away.

Arthur frowned. Something was wrong. Possibly several somethings. Possibly the whole damn universe.

Some of the googly eyes on his walker fell off.

"Don't you start," he muttered to his walker, leaving a trail of googly eyes behind.

He reached Margaret's hallway. Her door was cracked open.

Just a sliver.

A bad sign. Doors in Sunny Meadows came in two modes: wide open for the living and closed for the dead. A partially open door meant someone was trying to pretend.

Arthur paused. For the first time in years, he felt the familiar prickling of fear. He had outrun fear most of his life—by luck, wit, or sheer belligerence—but he felt it creeping up now like a debt collector.

"Margaret?" he called softly. "Margaret?"

Nothing.

He edged forward, nudging the door with two trembling fingers. It swung open slowly, like a mouth exhaling.

Inside stood David, who always looked like the world had handed him too many grocery bags and he hadn't figured out which to drop. He was at Margaret's dresser, folding her sweaters into boxes.

Her things—those tiny symbols of her life: the lavender perfume, the tiny tin of throat lozenges she never actually used, the sweater she wore every Tuesday because it "felt efficient"—were being put away.

And Margaret wasn't there.

Arthur swallowed. His throat felt like sandpaper dipped in grief.

David turned, startled. His eyes were red.

"Arthur," he whispered. "I—I thought you were still at breakfast."

"And she wasn't," Arthur said, his voice cracking against his will.

David wiped his cheeks as if tears were seasonal allergies that had simply ambushed him.

"Please sit down," David said gently, reaching for him.

Arthur looked at David's hand. "I don't need help to sit. I need help to understand. Why do the nurses look like someone canceled Christmas? Why are you packing her things? Where is she?"

David took a slow breath, steadying himself the way people do when preparing to break something delicate, like porcelain or hope.

"Mom died early this morning," he said.

There it was. The sentence.

Simple. Brutal. Efficient.

Margaret died.

Arthur blinked once, twice, as if testing the gravity in the room.

"That's impossible," he said calmly, which was the first lie of the day. "She said she was just tired. She said she needed a nap. She waved at me. She waved." He made the motion with one trembling hand. "Said she'd see me tomorrow. Well, it's tomorrow, dammit."

"I know," David said. "I know, Arthur."

"No," Arthur said. He stepped back, bumping into the dresser. "No, it's—it's not right. She wouldn't leave without telling me."

"She didn't know, Arthur," David said gently. "She just didn't . . . didn't wake up. It was peaceful."

Arthur put his head down. "Peaceful. The most useless word ever invented. People use it for death, war treaties, and naps, as if those were remotely similar."

He gripped the dresser to steady himself. For a moment, he thought he might tip over, like one of those ancient trees in documentaries—majestic until the moment it collapses under its own history.

"Why didn't they tell me?" he whispered.

"They were going to," David said. "But I asked them to wait until I got here. I thought you should hear it from me."

Arthur stared at the bed—Margaret's bed—where the blanket was still rumpled from her shape. He could almost see the imprint of her small frame, the dent in the pillow where her head had been. The room still smelled faintly of her lotion, the one she bought because she liked the name ("Evening Serenity," which had always sounded to Arthur like code for "smells like nothing but costs too much").

He walked to the bedside, dragging the walker like a reluctant companion. He lowered himself slowly into the chair beside the bed.

David simply stood there, awkward and useless in the helpless way only grieving children can be.

Arthur ran his fingers over the blanket.

"She was right here," he murmured.

"I know," David said.

"She said she'd nap. That she'd feel better. I believed her."

"So did I."

Arthur laughed suddenly—a sharp, broken sound that wasn't humor at all.

"At our age, you never feel better. Not once. I should've known better."

David smiled weakly, tears slipping again. "You loved her."

"Of course I loved her," Arthur snapped. "I'm just irritated she left before me. It wasn't her turn."

Silence settled between them, thick as fog.

Finally, Arthur said, "What do we do now?"

David wiped his eyes. "I . . . I finish packing. I'll handle the paperwork. Then bring the boxes to my car."

Arthur nodded, staring at the wall so he wouldn't have to see the boxes swallowing Margaret's life.

David approached and placed a gentle hand on Arthur's shoulder.

"I'll give you some time," he whispered, and stepped into the hall.

Arthur sat alone.

The googly-eyed walker stared up at him, ridiculous and earnest.

"Don't look at me like that," Arthur said, voice cracking. "She's the one who thought those damn eyes were funny."

He leaned forward, resting his forehead against the blanket that still held a ghost of her warmth.

For a long time, he stayed that way.

Eventually, he whispered—soft enough that only the empty room could hear:

"You said you'd feel better. You lied to me."

Outside the room, Sunny Meadows hummed with its usual distant machinery and its usual quiet tragedies.

Inside, one man sat beside an empty bed, thinking of soup always served cold, and the woman who had made it bearable.

By the time David carried the last box of his mother's earthly possessions out to the car, he had learned several important truths about dying in a nursing home, none of which he particularly enjoyed. He had learned, for example, that a person's entire existence could be packed into four cardboard boxes and a grocery bag filled with pill organizers. He had also discovered that the official paperwork for death was longer than the paperwork for birth—an irony he suspected amused some cruel cosmic accountant.

Sunny Meadows' administrative office had smelled like copy toner and coffee that had surrendered its will to live. The receptionist had handed him forms with solemn efficiency, as though she were distributing sacred scrolls instead of liability releases. He initialed here, signed there, dated everywhere. When he finished, she gave him a pamphlet about grief "for adult children." It had a cartoon tree on the cover. He thanked her and tucked it into his jacket pocket like contraband.

Then he went back down the hall, he thought, for the last time.

His mother's room looked brighter now. Not cheerful. Just . . . an empty kind of bright. The lamp was gone. The quilts were gone. The things that made the room hers had been boxed up and carried away by people who spoke softly and avoided eye contact.

Maybe it was bereavement lighting. That seemed like a thing the universe might install. Or maybe his mother had taken the shadows with her when she left. She would have done that, too. Just to be polite.

Arthur sat in the chair beside her empty bed, hunched forward like a museum exhibit titled Elderly Man Experiencing Existential Delay. His googly-eyed walker stood beside him, its spheres staring blankly at the newly stripped sheets.

"You didn't have to wait," David said softly.

Arthur snorted. "Son, I've been waiting my whole life."

He didn't look at David, just kept his gaze fixed on the bed, as if expecting Margaret to spring up laughing at the big joke of mortality. David sat in the chair opposite him. Now that the room was empty, it felt too big, like a stage set abandoned after a disappointing final performance.

A soft knock came at the door. Nurse Kelly entered slowly, as if wading into grief was part of her job description.

"Arthur? David?" she said gently. "I'm sorry, but I need to start cleaning the room and preparing it for the next resident."

Arthur whipped his head around so fast the googly eyes on his walker rattled in sympathy. "Already? She's barely gone cold, and you're putting someone else in here? What's next, a gift shop?"

Kelly offered a half-smile that couldn't decide whether it wanted to be polite or mournful. "I know it feels quick. We have limited rooms, Arthur."

"Of course you do," he muttered. "Nothing says 'final dignity' like a swift eviction."

Kelly's smile collapsed into something closer to resignation. "I really am sorry."

"Everyone is," Arthur grumbled. "Doesn't change a damn thing."

She nodded, then slipped out, closing the door halfway behind her, as though leaving space for their grief to breathe, or escape.

Arthur stared at the door for a long moment before asking, "So… what about us?"

David blinked. "Us?"

"Don't act surprised," Arthur said. "The curtain's down. The props are gone. Margaret was the only thing tethering you and me together. Now she's—" He flapped a hand at the bed, unable or unwilling to complete the sentence. "So this is it, right? The end. You'll leave. I'll stay. Life continues its long, stupid march."

David leaned back in his chair. "Why do you assume that?"

"Because I'm not sentimental," Arthur said. "And neither are you."

"Well," David said, rubbing the back of his neck, "that's the thing. I'm not sure that's entirely true."

Arthur narrowed his eyes. They seemed smaller than usual, as though grief were pulling shut the curtains behind them. "What're you talking about?"

David let out a slow breath. "Before she lay down for her nap—before she . . . you know—Mom said something to me."

Arthur grunted. "Margaret always said something. Usually something infuriatingly optimistic."

"She told me to take care of you."

Silence fell with the tragic elegance of a dropped casserole.

Arthur blinked hard. "She told you that?"

David nodded.

Arthur looked down at the floor for a moment, like he might find the answer there among the dust.

"That old fool," he said quietly.

The words sounded like an insult, but they weren't doing that job very well.

"Never knew when to quit, did she? Always worrying. Always thinking we deserved a little more than the universe usually hands out." He rubbed his eyes with the heel of his hand. "Damn her."

David smiled. "She meant it."

"That's the problem," Arthur muttered.

The two men sat in the quiet room, the hum of the hallway creeping in beneath the door. Somewhere down the corridor, a television announced the price of hemorrhoid cream.

Arthur cleared his throat. "Why do you think she said that?"

David looked at the ceiling, searching for an answer he hadn't yet rehearsed. "I've been thinking about it, and I'm not too sure. Maybe she thought . . . we're good for each other. In some weird, dysfunctional way."

Arthur scoffed. "I'm not 'good' for anyone. Look at me. I'm mostly useless, partially deaf, and the only thing I collect anymore is medical bills."

"I think . . ." David said simply. "You're good for me."

Arthur stared at him like he'd just confessed to enjoying tax season. "You're out of your mind."

"Maybe," David admitted. "But the more I think about it . . . I think, when I visited, I didn't just come for Mom. I came for you, too. You made everything . . . honest. You never sugarcoated anything. You said what you thought, even when it was awful."

"Everything is awful," Arthur said, almost proudly.

"Exactly," David said. "Mom always looked for the best in the world. And you . . . you always expect the worst. Between the two of you, it's like I got the truth somewhere in the middle."

Arthur stared at the bed again. His hand twitched, searching for something to hold on to that wasn't there anymore. "So, you're saying I'm like your emotional support dog, or something?"

David smiled. "Ah, kind of, I suppose."

Arthur huffed out a sound that might've been a laugh or the beginning of a hernia. "Hell of a thing to tell a grieving man."

"Well, I'm grieving too," David said quietly.

Arthur opened his mouth, then slowly closed it. He looked away, embarrassed by the idea that someone might find value in him.

After a long moment, he muttered, "I don't know how to do this."

"Do what?" David asked.

Arthur waved an old, shaking hand. "Life. After her. Without her handing out hope like it was Halloween candy." His voice cracked. "She made the days less stupid."

David swallowed. "Yeah. She did."

Arthur sighed, collapsing into the chair more fully. "You really think she meant it? About . . . taking care of me?"

"I do," David said.

"And you'll actually do it?"

David thought of the boxes in his trunk, the cartoon-tree pamphlet hidden in his jacket, the ache in his chest that felt like something permanently rearranging itself. "Yeah," he said. "I will."

Arthur nodded stiffly. "Well. That's . . . idiotic. But appreciated."

They sat again in silence.

This time, it felt like companionship instead of collapse.

After a while, Arthur stood up with the grace of a scarecrow trying yoga. "Well," he said gruffly, "if they're evicting us, I suppose we should get out of their hair before they disinfect what's left of mine, too."

David stood with him. "We can go to the lobby. Or the garden."

"The garden? Too bright and colorful."

"Then the lobby."

"Too dull and dark."

David smiled. "Then where?"

"You'll just have to follow."

Arthur grabbed his walker, the googly eyes seemed confused enthusiasm. As they walked out of the room together, Arthur paused in the doorway and looked back at the bed one last time.

"Goodbye, Margaret," he whispered. "You unbelievable woman."

Then he turned to David.

"Well? Come on," he said. "If you're taking care of me, you might as well start now. I could use a decent cup of coffee. Or a terrible one. At my age, I'll drink whatever doesn't kill me."

They walked down the hallway together.

Two men missing the same woman in different ways, bound now by the ridiculous, heartbreaking instructions she left behind.

And somehow, it felt like a beginning.

David wasn't sure why the dining hall at Sunny Meadows always smelled faintly of bran cereal and things people regretted. It was as if someone had baked disappointment into the wallpaper. Still, he sat across from Arthur at one of the square laminate tables, each of them holding a cup of black coffee that had gone tepid before it reached the table.

Arthur glared into his cup like it owed him money.

"You know," David said, "maybe we could ask for fresh coffee or something."

Arthur lifted the cup, swirled it with the elegance of a dying monarch, and took a sip. His face contorted into the shape of a man reevaluating the entire concept of hope.

Then he sighed—a long, shaky sigh that sounded like it came from the part of the human soul that had given up trying.

"Your mother," he said, raising the cup slightly in salute to Margaret's memory, "that sweetheart of a person dies, and they still can't find the microwave."

David let out a short laugh through his nose. "I don't think they have one."

Arthur peered over the rim of his cup. "Well, that explains everything."

They sat in silence for a moment, the kind that wasn't awkward but wasn't particularly friendly either. Just two men—one young enough to keep moving forward, one old enough to know forward is just a direction people invented to stay busy—thinking about the woman who'd connected them.

"You know, she always preferred tea," Arthur told David.

"Yeah, and I never understood why."

Arthur chuckled, a dry, rattling sound. "Because coffee wasn't dignified enough for the morning. She demanded grace, even from her stimulants."

David took a sip of his own coffee. It tasted like hot water remembering a coffee bean from across the room. A thin, watery sadness, really.

"So," he said, "you always drink it black?"

Arthur snorted. "What kind of question is that?"

"A normal one?"

"Normal people use milk and sugar," Arthur declared, shaking his head. "They do it because they think life owes them sweetness. I drink it black because life does not, in fact, owe you a damn thing. If anything, life owes you a bill."

“That seems bleak.”

“Not bleak . . . efficient,” Arthur corrected. “Bleak would be adding creamer and pretending it makes a difference.”

David considered this. “I drink it black because I’m too lazy to make it any other way.”

“That’s also efficient,” Arthur conceded. “You’re ahead of the curve.”

They took another sip at the same time. Both grimaced with synchronized disappointment.

“Still,” David said, “I get your point. Mom used to say living simply made room for the important things.”

Arthur looked up sharply. “She said that?”

“All the time when I was growing up.”

The old man’s face crumpled—not in sadness, but in that complicated way people react when they’re reminded someone loved them more generously than they deserved.

“Ah,” he said. “She always did have a talent for lying beautifully.”

David laughed, genuinely this time. Arthur didn’t join in, but his lips twitched.

“I already miss her,” David said. The words came out soft, with that fragile look people get when they’re trying not to drop their own heart on the floor. “I mean . . . before . . . I knew she was nearby . . . We could talk about things. Stupid things. Nothing things. Now…”

Arthur’s hands curled tighter around his cup. “Me too. I miss having someone to argue with. Someone who didn’t mind when I corrected her about everything. Someone who knew when I was full of nonsense and didn’t care.”

"That's . . . oddly sweet."

David watched Arthur stare into the lukewarm coffee like it was a map to somewhere better.

He then broke into a wide smile. "Crazy that she felt the two of us needed each other."

Arthur inhaled like he was preparing an essay-length rebuttal. Nothing came out. He stared at David instead, long enough that David began to worry the old man had died mid-thought.

Then Arthur blinked. Twice. Heavy, theatrical blinks.

"Well," he said at last, "looks like I'm stuck with you now."

David grinned. "Feeling's mutual."

Arthur shook his head. "When I first got here, one roommate used to steal my pudding cups. Said he needed the energy. You don't look like a pudding thief. Are you?"

"I'm not."

"Hmmm . . . we'll see."

David leaned back in the chair, surprised at how natural it felt to sit across from Arthur without his mother anchoring the conversation. Surprised at how un-terrible it felt to care about someone he barely knew three weeks ago.

"So," David said, "you ever think about leaving here?"

Arthur lifted an eyebrow. "Your mother just died, and you're starting a prison break?"

"No, I just meant . . ."

"Young people," Arthur muttered. "One tragedy and you all become philosophers."

"No, I just meant," David continued, "you don't seem like you belong here. I mean, you're healthier than most."

Arthur waved a hand dismissively. "Where else would I go? I'm like an old appliance—too sentimental to throw out, too unreliable to keep using. Sunny Meadows is a sort of cosmic junk drawer."

"Well, I guess, that doesn't sound so bad."

"Speak for yourself. You're not the toaster with unpredictable sparks."

David covered his smile with his coffee cup, though it did nothing to hide it.

Arthur looked at him carefully, the way he examined puzzle pieces he suspected were duplicates. "You know," he said quietly, "just because your mother told you to do something . . . well . . . you don't have to keep coming here."

"I know."

"You've a life to live. Your job, your friends, your whatever it is young people do these days."

"I know."

"Then why do this?"

David shrugged.

"Because I need somebody," he said. "And because you need somebody."

Arthur made a noise that suggested the universe had disappointed him again.

"What I need," Arthur said, "is working knees and a better prostate. But here we are."

They took one more sip of the lukewarm coffee. It had cooled from "disappointing" to "punitive."

Arthur's face softened. "You're a strange boy."

"Takes one to know one."

Arthur lifted the mug in a small salute. "Fair."

Across the dining hall, the television played a rerun of a cooking show where nobody enjoyed cooking. A resident kept dropping her spoon. Another dozed off mid-chew. A staff member sat in a chair watching . . . for what? . . . no one really knew.

The world kept spinning, ungainly and absurd.

Arthur let out a quiet exhale. His shoulders slumped. His head dipped forward.

"You okay?" David asked.

Arthur didn't answer. His chin touched his chest. His breathing steadied into the gentle rhythm of a man who spent his whole life fighting sleep and finally surrendered.

David reached over and nudged his walker closer, just in case Arthur needed it when he woke.

He sat there with him—just sat—listening to the clatter of trays and murmurs of nurses, the strange domestic soundtrack of people waiting out the tail end of their personal stories.

Arthur snored once, loudly, like a man trying to assert dominance even in slumber.

David didn't wake him.

He wrapped his hands around his coffee cup, now entirely cold, and thought that maybe—just maybe—black coffee wasn't so bad when shared with someone who understood why it mattered to drink it that way.

Even if there was no microwave.

Arthur found himself materializing, which is just a fancy word for popping up on a barstool. It was designed to be incredibly comfortable, which was deliberate. Comfort breeds complacency, and complacency breeds excellent cosmic drinking. You wouldn't believe the drinks. There were drinks that tasted like the color orange, and drinks that tasted like a conversation you once overheard.

The bar counter glowed with a faint ultraviolet shimmer, cleaning everything, including Arthur's sorrow, though sorrow is notoriously resistant to sanitizer.

Behind him stretched an observation window. Through it rotated a frozen planet sealed under glass-hard ice, every mountain and ocean locked mid-scream. A tragedy suspended indefinitely for educational purposes. It revolved slowly, showing its wounds like a shoplifter revealing stolen items one by one.

The atmosphere inside the bar was what you get when you mix quiet resignation with jazz performed on sentient instruments. They weren't technically alive, but they acted like it. Overhead, holographic drink menus twisted and morphed through shapes that couldn't commit to their own geometry. Passing by, a pair of ethereal travelers argued telepathically about room-service charges. Their complaint, in essence, was that the universe owed them better service. It did not.

Iris was there, as she always was, behind the counter, polishing a bottle containing a small, spinning nebula. She always polishes bottles containing unstable astronomical phenomena. It relaxes her. Her plum-colored skin rippled with luminous sighs. Her many eyes blinked in an elegant, overly choreographed sequence, the kind of thing you'd expect from a species that had elected to abandon death but keep etiquette.

Of course, Arthur noticed her. His grief came with him—grief always travels light—and the moment he focused on her, he looked like a man trying to pretend he wasn't exhausted from carrying invisible weight.

He finally muttered, to himself, to her, to the window:

"Margaret . . . she was warmth. Now everything's goddamn soup."

His voice cracked. His soul cracked a little, too, but that's less audible.

Iris responded to his sorrow with the multi-eyed grace of someone who had seen every shade of loss despite never experiencing it firsthand. A couple of eyes closed in sympathy. A few more rolled in cosmic irritation. Arthur was very dramatic, even by mortal standards.

She knew exactly what was trembling through Arthur's hands. It wasn't age. It was the realization—swift and cruel—that grief is portable across dimensions. She'd never met a universe where it wasn't.

Iris set down a steaming cup in front of him. The steam drifted upward in colors that never appear on Earth unless someone mixes chemical cleaners irresponsibly.

"Here's something to help your sadness," she said. Her voice did that underwater wind-instrument thing, which is difficult to describe and impossible for humans to imitate without drowning.

She paused, then aligned all her eyes on him with the precision of a polite firing squad.

"Drink before it cools."

The last word echoed for a simple reason: the sound itself was reluctant to lose heat.

Arthur wrapped his hands around the cup. It warmed them instantly, reacting to him the way a long-lost pet might. He sniffed it. It smelled like memories he'd never lived—other lives, other heartbreaks, an entire museum of sorrow curated for a single taste.

He hesitated. Then he drank.

It burned in that pleasant, dangerous way. Like swallowing a star that had decided, just this once, not to explode inside you. Warmth rippled through him, and he felt it settle in his chest, spreading just far enough to remind him he still had a chest.

"You see the planet?" Iris asked.

Arthur looked up. The ice-encased world rotated outside, its frozen oceans catching the bar's glow like jewelry someone locked away to keep from remembering. The light slid across its surface in slow arcs, giving the impression of a wound displayed at a science fair.

"Looks cold," Arthur said.

"It remembers being warm," Iris replied.

She watched as Arthur almost smiled.

"Even doomed planets remember better days," he said.

"How long will you grieve?" Iris asked.

Arthur didn't answer immediately. She could feel him sorting through the mess inside himself, poking around like someone looking for a missing sock in a drawer they haven't organized in twenty years.

"Hard to say," he said eventually. "She was the only person who ever understood me. Even when she didn't, she tried."

"That's love," Iris said.

"Or performance art," Arthur muttered.

Iris wanted to sigh with all her eyes, but she resisted. She merely blinked in a formation that suggested mild cosmic judgment.

"She mattered to you," she said.

"More than I admitted while she was alive," he answered, surprising himself with the honesty.

He took another sip, felt the warmth spread again, not healing him but giving him a temporary loaner heart—something to function with until the original could be repaired or replaced.

"And what about the boy?" Iris asked.

"David? Poor kid. Thinks he's supposed to hold the world together with polite sentences."

"He cares for you," she said.

"He cares for everything. It's his tragic flaw."

Iris didn't reply. She didn't have to. The bar lights dimmed in a sympathetic shrug, and the nebula in the bottle on the counter flared once, expressing cosmic agreement.

Arthur looked back out at the frozen planet. He didn't know, but Iris did: that world had once been populated by beings who loved and feared and procrastinated. They'd ignored warnings. They'd made choices they couldn't repair. And now they were a museum exhibit of their own mistakes.

Inside the bar, everything sat poised between sorrow and a joke no one had ever been brave enough—or foolish enough—to say aloud.

Arthur closed his eyes. Warmth seeped through him, into all the fractured places. Iris knew it would fade. So did he.

Still—he accepted it.

And for a moment, in a corner of the universe suspended between tragedy and satire, that was enough.

Chapter 5

David returned to Sunny Meadows with the posture of a man who had tried to escape orbit and failed. The building had that effect on families. It was like a gravitational force, composed mostly of guilt, duty, and the nagging realization that everyone you love will eventually need assistance wiping their asses and turn into dust. Even the parking lot seemed to recognize him from the last time he was there and wondered—Why are you back already?

Inside, the hallway greeted him with its usual bouquet of antiseptic ambition and musty optimism. Sunny Meadows always smelled like it was trying—truly trying—to be a place where people got better. The scent carried a kind of delusional confidence, as if the building had read an inspiring self-help book and wanted to apply all the principles at once. Nobody bought it. Not the residents. Not the staff. Certainly not David, who had spent the car ride rehearsing how he might finally talk about what was really bothering him. Maybe Arthur could help. The man had a gift for slicing through nonsense, even if the slices weren't always clean.

"Hi, David," Nurse Kelly said as she walked past. "He's in the library."

David smiled politely.

He was the sort of man who could smile twice if the situation required it.

He stopped outside the library door.

Libraries make promises. Big ones. Knowledge, answers, maybe even wisdom if you're lucky. Most of the time, they deliver old books and mildew.

He took a breath and gathered what little courage he had left after a long night of not sleeping and diagnosing himself with several impressive medical conditions.

Then he stepped inside.

He was hoping Arthur might've some wisdom available. The simple kind. The kind explained in plain English. Preferably, the kind that didn't require a co-pay.

He drifted in slowly, as though the room might startle if approached too directly. The library, as Sunny Meadows insisted on calling it, was—if one were generous—a shrine to modest ambition. A single bookcase leaned against the wall with the posture of a man giving up on his marriage. It held about thirty books that looked as though they'd been checked out mostly for use as coasters. Several magazines lay on a side table, none of them Popular Mechanics (Arthur had them in his room), and a potted plant that was either plastic or extremely stoic. The carpet had been steam-cleaned so many times it had developed the personality of a worn dish sponge. The entire room smelled faintly of stories that no one had bothered to read.

Arthur sat alone at the small wooden table, leaning over a stack of newspapers as if keeping watch over the downfall of civilization. He held a magnifying glass in one hand and a lukewarm cup of coffee in the other, because he believed optimism required rituals.

David was unsure whether he was interrupting a man enjoying his solitude or a man trapped inside it. The omniscient truth was somewhere in between: Arthur liked company, but only the kind he could argue with.

When he noticed David, Arthur lowered the magnifying glass dramatically, as though he had discovered something scandalous. "Back so soon," he said. "Either you missed me, or your real life continues to fall apart."

"Both," David admitted.

Arthur nodded. He had expected nothing less. That was the advantage of being old: the world surprised you less but irritated you more.

David dropped into the chair across from him. He looked like someone who had wrestled with his own brain and lost three rounds in a row. The library's overhead light flickered because even electricity disliked the mood.

Arthur watched him, knowing full well what was coming. David had that look—the look of a man about to confess something embarrassing, something that involved the internet and a fragile sense of mortality.

Finally, David exhaled. "I've been stress-Googling."

Arthur closed his eyes. Not in disappointment, but in the way someone might respond to hearing an adult confess they stuck a fork in an outlet. There was sympathy, but also the faint desire to slap them with a wet newspaper.

David pressed on. "I've had a bout with insomnia and I've been anxious. Don't know why. I'd figured maybe I could do some research. You know, educate myself."

Arthur snorted. "Education is for learning something useful. What you're describing sounds like recreational panic."

"I was trying to understand what might be wrong with me."

"And what did the machine tell you?" Arthur asked, already amused. He called all computers 'the machine,' regardless of make, model, or whether they were plugged in.

"That . . . I might've . . . get this . . . three rare neurological disorders. Thought I'd tell you. Maybe you could help me with it."

Arthur gave a single nod, the kind one gives when someone reports that they've been diagnosed by a slot machine. "Three, huh? Always go for the bulk package."

David rubbed his face. "It's just . . . it's stupid. I know I shouldn't look things up. I know it makes things worse . . . makes me spiral. But I can't help it. It feels like the only control I have."

Arthur looked at him for a while. Underneath all the sarcasm—which people often wear like cheap armor—there was something else. Desperation. The ordinary kind. Arthur had been around long enough to notice a pattern about people. They worry about diseases they'll never catch. They prepare for disasters that never arrive. And they spend a lot of time being afraid of memories that aren't nearly as dangerous as the ones they ignored.

Finally, Arthur said, "David, the machine is not your doctor. The machine is a vending machine for worry."

David blinked. "A vending machine?"

"Absolutely. Insert a symptom, get a bag of dread. Sometimes you press the button for headaches, and the machine spits out brain tumors. Press the button for insomnia, and out pops early-onset cosmic doom. And heaven forbid you press the wrong button . . . you might get a side of guilt or anguish at no extra charge."

David cracked a small smile. He didn't want to, but the metaphor was accurate enough to hurt in a funny way.

Arthur continued. "Look, your mother just passed on. You're sad, tired. Your life is loud. Your brain is louder. But the machine doesn't know you. It doesn't know your mother died. It doesn't know you think too much, or that you worry too much, or that you've got a heart that tries to be brave even when it's scared." He leaned back. "The machine doesn't diagnose human beings. It diagnoses symptoms, which are always more dramatic without context."

A silence settled in. A comfortable one. David stared at the potted plant. The plant didn't stare back.

David was thinking about his mother. He'd been thinking about her nonstop since she died. It was the kind of grief that sat behind everything, holding a clipboard and whispering.

You're not dealing with this properly, he thought. Grief has a real talent for performance reviews.

Arthur, meanwhile, was remembering David's mother too, in his own way—the way a man remembers the one person who could scold him into eating vegetables. He missed her more deeply than he let on, but he didn't know how to talk about it without sounding like he was auditioning for sentimentality.

"So," Arthur said at last, "did you at least find any medical advice on the machine that didn't scare the shit out of you?"

"No," David replied. "But I did accidentally order a juicer."

Arthur grimaced. "My god. It's worse than I thought."

The two sat in silence again. Above them, the fluorescent light buzzed like an insect debating retirement. A cart creaked down the hallway, each wheel voicing its objection to existence. Nurse Kelly pushed it along, distributing coffee as though caffeine could fix anything.

She paused at their doorway and asked David if he wanted a cup. David gave a shrug that could have meant yes, no, or "please don't make me choose anything ever again." Kelly interpreted it as enthusiasm and handed him a steaming dose of reassurance anyway.

Farther down the corridor, a resident hollered at a television. This wasn't a cry for help or attention. This was simply the accepted form of communication between man and machine at Sunny Meadows. Everyone had settled into the arrangement. The television never listened, and the residents never stopped trying.

"David," Arthur finally said, voice softer than expected, "you're not broken. You're overwhelmed. There's a difference."

David looked up. "How do you know the difference?"

Arthur shrugged. "I've been both. You get good at telling them apart."

This, more than anything, eased something in David's chest. It wasn't wisdom, exactly. It was just Arthur sounding like a tired old man who knew how tiring it was to be human—and that felt credible. The conversation was simple, really: two people sitting in a dim little library, both terrified in their own ways, both pretending not to be. Humans had a dazzling talent for pretending.

Arthur took a sip of his coffee. It tasted like something drained from a radiator, but he drank it anyway.

"Next time you feel the urge to consult the machine," Arthur said, "call me instead. I won't diagnose you, but I can insult you until you feel better."

"That's . . . strangely comforting."

"Good. Saves us time."

They stayed like that for a while, two men in a worn-out library, occupying a pocket of quiet no one else needed. Outside the window, afternoon light slanted across the parking lot, illuminating all the cars of all the families performing their weekly obligation. Life continued exactly as it always did: a little bewildered, a little hopeful, and very poorly caffeinated.

In the library, David stood near the window holding his cup of coffee that tasted like someone had filtered it through a wool sock. Across from him sat Arthur, slouched comfortably in the stiffest chair in existence. Arthur had mastered the art of looking relaxed in furniture specifically designed to prevent that sort of thing.

Somewhere down the hall, somebody coughed a cough that sounded like the last chapter of a poorly written life.

The universe, in its vast omniscient wisdom, took the moment to rotate quietly.

A man shuffled into the library. Tall, ancient, the kind of ancient that made other old people feel like rookies. He moved with a cane that had lost its rubber tip decades before the moon landing. He squinted at the magazines, eventually deciding on one and picking it up. He held it as if trying to remember what reading was.

David watched him for a moment, then turned to Arthur and lowered his voice to a whisper, the kind of whisper people use in libraries because they're afraid books might complain. "Who's that?"

Arthur didn't bother to whisper. Subtlety wasn't one of his surviving virtues. "That," he declared, "is Beaners."

David blinked. "Beaners?"

"Yup," Arthur said, adjusting himself in the chair like he was settling into an old argument. "That's what everyone calls him. I don't know why. Nobody knows why. The origin story has been lost to time, like most of our teeth."

The old man—Beaners, apparently—turned a page with the caution of someone defusing a small explosive. The magazine was a National Geographic from 1997. On the cover was a toucan whose eyes held a wisdom no human could ever imagine. Beaners stared at the bird, apparently convinced the toucan knew where his missing dentures had gone.

David looked between Arthur and the old man. "Does he talk?"

"He talks," Arthur said. "He just charges a premium for it."

Beaners raised his head slowly, like a submarine surfacing after too long underwater. One clouded eye met David's. The other seemed busy with private matters. He gave a single nod, the kind people used to seal pacts in medieval times—before paperwork ruined everything—and then lowered himself back into the magazine.

"That's the most he's spoken all week," Arthur said. "You got the deluxe package."

David tried not to stare. The man looked as though he'd been forgotten by several centuries and they were too embarrassed to come back for him. "So . . . Beaners," he whispered again, tasting the word like he wasn't sure it was FDA-approved. "Does he . . . I don't know . . . do anything?"

Arthur snorted. "He breathes, for now. He appears in rooms people swear he wasn't in a minute earlier. He once beat the vending machine in a staring contest. That's about it."

Beaners turned another page. It made a thin, papery sigh, as if both page and man were commiserating.

Arthur leaned toward David conspiratorially. "Some say he used to be a professor. Others say he invented tapioca. There's even a rumor he died in 1983, but no one told him, so he just kept showing up."

David nodded thoughtfully, as if this biography made perfect sense. In Sunny Meadows, it almost did. "And everyone calls him Beaners?"

Arthur shrugged. "Humanity is a creative species, David. Except when it isn't. Someone probably said it once by accident, and now it's tradition."

Beaners looked up again, fixing them both with a stare that suggested he wasn't deaf, just selective. His eyes narrowed a fraction, the universal expression for—I know you're talking about me and I'm choosing not to intervene because it sounds exhausting. Then he returned to his magazine, which now bore the weight of his disapproval.

Arthur tapped David's arm. "See? He likes you. Don't get used to it."

David sipped his coffee. It was cold already, proving the laws of thermodynamics had it out for him personally. "I feel like I should introduce myself."

"You could," Arthur said. "Or you could wait until he introduces himself to you. It'll be more dramatic. Might involve a prophecy. Hard to predict with Beaners."

In the hallway, a resident wheeled by humming something that might've been a hymn or might've been a complaint set to music. At Sunny Meadows, those two categories often overlapped.

Beaners coughed once, a sound like an accordion collapsing in defeat. He pointed vaguely at the magazine and muttered, "Bird's wrong. All wrong."

David glanced at Arthur. "What does that mean?"

Arthur lifted his hands. "Your guess is as good as mine. Around here, we just assume Beaners exists on a different frequency from the rest of us. He pops in, dispenses wisdom or nonsense . . . same thing, really . . . and pops back out."

David watched the old man flip another page. "He seems lonely."

Arthur scoffed. "Everyone here is lonely. It's the most popular hobby." Then, softer, "But he's got his own way of doing things. Some folks survive on routine. Others survive on denial. Beaners survives on being Beaners."

David nodded. "Do you think he knows we're talking about him?"

"Oh, absolutely," Arthur said. "He knows everything. Or nothing. Or he's asleep with his eyes open. All viable theories."

Beaners lifted his head once more, aimlessly, like he had forgotten what he was searching for during the search itself. David couldn't tell if the man was acknowledging them or if the toucan had personally offended him.

Then Beaners gave a tiny, courteous smile—polite, brief, vaguely threatening.

Arthur leaned back. "See? You survived your first Beaners encounter. Congratulations. That's practically a rite of passage here. They should give you a merit badge. A little embroidered cane or something."

David chuckled, partly out of amusement, partly because the alternative was contemplating the existential gloom of the room. "He's . . . interesting."

"Everyone's interesting," Arthur said. "It's just that some people forget to hide it."

"I kinda like him," David whispered.

"That's how it starts," Arthur said. "Next thing you know, you're rearranging your whole day around his schedule. He has that effect."

David shook his head, smiling. "Does he talk to you?"

"Oh, sure," Arthur said. "Every Thursday at three on the dot, he tells me the same thing: 'The soup is lying.' I don't know what it means, but at this point I believe him."

David laughed, and Arthur allowed himself the ghost of a grin.

Around them, the library hummed its quiet, dusty hum. Somewhere, a book fell off a shelf without provocation. The building had old bones and liked to remind people.

Arthur sipped the last of his lukewarm coffee. "Welcome to the club, kid. Once you meet Beaners, you're officially part of the ecosystem."

David raised his own cup in a small salute. "Glad to be here. I think."

"You'll get used to it," Arthur said. "Or you won't. Either way, you'll keep coming back. That's how this place works."

David settled back in his chair, feeling oddly grounded. Beaners, Arthur, the dusty library—they were all strange, but strangely reliable.

For a moment, he felt almost at home.

Arthur glanced over. "Now. Since we've survived the elderly specter of ambiguity, what were we talking about?"

David smiled. "About feeling off, I think."

Arthur nodded approvingly. "Good. That means the day's going fine. Everyone and everything is off."

He had a thought then. Not a big philosophical one. Just a small, wandering thought, the kind that shows up late and sits down without asking.

"I was just thinking," David said. He rubbed the side of his face like the answer might be hiding in the stubble there. "What was it like in the old days when someone felt… off? Pressured? Like the whole world was sitting on their chest? You know . . . anxiety."

Arthur chuckled with the gentle bitterness of a man who had survived far too many days. "Ah, the old days. Well, back then, we didn't call it anxiety. We called it Tuesday."

David laughed, though he didn't feel especially amused. The world had grown heavy for him, the kind of heavy that made a person feel like lying down in a field and hoping the clouds would run them over.

Arthur adjusted himself in the chair, bones clicking softly like old dice. "And if Tuesday got bad enough," he added, "you walked to Dr. Fink's office—tiny place, smelled like tobacco and boiled cabbage—and he'd hand you a cheerful little bottle of morphine."

"Seriously?"

"Oh yes," Arthur said, waving a thin hand. "You walked in miserable, walked out glowing like the inside of a toaster. Fink didn't ask questions. He just treated life like the chronic condition it was."

David leaned against the table. "Now, if I so much as wake up with a dry throat, I spend twenty minutes Googling symptoms. Suddenly, I have lymphoma, a rare neurological disorder, or mold in my lungs."

Arthur nodded sagely. "The internet is a marvelous invention. It's taken the time-honored tradition of worrying yourself sick and making it available to amateurs."

Beaners looked up from his magazine. He hadn't read a single word but had absorbed every sound. His eyebrows rose, forming two white hedgerows of agreement.

Arthur noticed and pointed at him. "See? Even Beaners knows what I'm talking about."

Beaners nodded because nodding costs nothing and is occasionally accurate.

David's chair issued a complaint. "I guess I just want to feel normal again," he said, surprising himself with the honesty. "Like my brain isn't trying to escape through my ears."

Arthur studied him with the patient expression of someone who had watched many people fall apart. "You're not abnormal," he said. "You're just plugged in."

"What's that supposed to mean?"

"Everyone these days is tuned into the global panic frequency," Arthur replied. "Used to be, if you were terrified of something, you had to work for it. Read the newspaper. Talk to a paranoid neighbor. Now you open your phone and . . . bam . . . two million strangers all convinced they're dying tonight."

David sighed. "It feels like I can't trust my own body anymore. Every ache feels like a warning. Every heartbeat feels like a malfunction."

"Of course it does," Arthur said. "You've spent so much time asking a machine how you should feel. That's like asking a vending machine how to resolve your childhood trauma. It'll give you a Snickers bar and a sense of dread."

David smiled weakly. "You're not wrong."

"I'm never wrong," Arthur said. "I'm old. Eventually the world stops surprising you. Mostly because you run out of energy to be surprised."

The universe observed him fondly—as fondly as a universe made of indifferent physics can observe anything.

Beaners turned a page of the magazine. The magazine was so old the page featured a full-color advertisement for a beeper. He nodded approvingly, not because he knew what a beeper was, but because nodding had become a lifestyle for him.

Arthur leaned forward, hands wrapped around his mug. "Listen. In my day, you felt lousy, you took a walk, or you took a nap, or you took whatever Dr. Fink gave you. You didn't spend six hours reading medical forums written by people named 'ConcernedDad1982.'"

David rubbed his temple. "I know. I know. But sometimes I wake up, and it feels like something terrible is about to happen."

Arthur blinked. "Something terrible is always about to happen. That's the entire human experience. It's called life. We brace ourselves for a disaster, then a different one arrives just to keep things interesting."

Beaners grunted agreeably. It was a grunt that conveyed decades of practical experience with disappointment.

David looked around the room. The books on the shelf leaned together like tired soldiers who had marched too far and didn't expect another war. The carpet had a small stain shaped exactly like Ohio. Outside the window sat the parking lot full of cars. They belonged to people who had long ago embraced resignation as a spiritual practice.

"Do you ever feel like the world's getting worse?" David asked.

Arthur considered it. "The world's not getting worse," he said. "It's getting louder. In the old days, bad things happened quietly. Someone had a nervous breakdown and you'd hear about it six months later at the grocery store. Now a stranger in Tulsa has a panic attack, and your phone tells you immediately."

David snorted. "That's . . . accurate, actually."

"I know it is," Arthur replied. "That's why I said it."

Beaners pointed at the beeper ad and whispered, "Good technology." Neither David nor Arthur knew if he meant it sincerely or if the words had simply escaped by accident.

Arthur sighed and stretched his legs carefully, inspecting them as if surprised to still possess them. "Look, David," he said. "You're young enough that the internet can still trick you into thinking you're dying. I passed that stage years ago. I wake up every day fully confident that I'm not dead yet simply because my breakfast hasn't been served."

"That's one way to look at it," David said.

"It's the only way to look at it," Arthur insisted. "People shouldn't be diagnosing themselves. We weren't built for that sort of responsibility. We evolved to worry about predators, not pancreatic cancer."

David leaned back. "So you're saying I should stop reading medical sites."

"I'm saying," Arthur clarified, "that the moment you feel the urge to look up symptoms online, you should instead watch a video of a cat falling off a table. They're spiritually equivalent, but one won't convince you that your liver is melting."

Beaners nodded furiously at the mention of cats. He hadn't owned a cat in 60 years, but the memory of a furry creature knocking things over still brought joy.

Arthur lifted his cup, grimaced at the cold sludge inside, and set it down again. "Self-diagnosis is just people trying to predict disappointment. That's all anxiety is . . . expensive, time-consuming anticipation."

David laughed quietly. He felt a tiny release in his chest, as though one of his internal cables had loosened.

Arthur saw it. "There you go," he said. "Your body's fine. Your brain's just dramatic."

The universe allowed a brief moment of peace to settle on the room.

Beaners, for no clear reason, saluted them with his magazine.

David and Arthur, outnumbered by their own worries and by time itself, accepted the salute. It felt appropriate.

The library remained dim, the carpet remained sad, but for one rare moment, no one felt like Googling anything.

Nurse Kelly, a person whose cheerfulness was probably factory-installed, returned carrying a small tray. On it were three identical bowls of pale pink liquid. Cream of tomato, the label on the carton probably read, though Arthur insisted it was really just the filtered essence of institutional disappointment. Kelly placed one bowl before David, one before Arthur, and one before Beaners, who had returned to staring at the cover of the National Geographic toucan.

"Here we are, gentlemen!" Kelly chirped, deploying her full, industrial-strength smile. She fussed briefly with Arthur's napkin. "You two seem to have been having a very serious chat in here. What grand secrets are being shared amongst the books?"

Arthur gave a slow, deliberate blink. "We were discussing the fundamental flaws in the human operating system, Kelly. And also, how the advent of free Wi-Fi has turned every citizen into a self-diagnosed medical martyr."

"Oh, that's so funny!" Kelly giggled, as if the decline of Western civilization was a wonderful punchline. "You know, my cousin thinks she has a thyroid issue because of WebMD! Now, you boys enjoy that soup. It's got lots of vitamins!"

She patted Arthur's shoulder and bounced out of the room. David noted that even she refused to make eye contact with the soup. Wise woman.

Arthur picked up his spoon, treating the object like a hazardous waste tool. He lowered it into the pink liquid, lifted it, and watched a single, viscous drop fall back into the bowl. He decided, right then and there, that life was fundamentally flawed, and this soup was the liquid confirmation of that fact. He pushed the bowl exactly six inches away.

"There it is," Arthur announced to the dusty library shelves. "The official meal of the end of days. It's not hot, it's not cold. It is merely lukewarm apathy in a bowl."

David felt obliged to participate, a truly human flaw. He took a small, careful sip. The flavor was what you might expect if someone described the idea of a tomato to a robot and the robot tried to recreate it using wallpaper paste and the vague, unfulfilled promises of his first-grade teacher. David swallowed hard, managing not to retch.

But then there was Beaners.

Beaners, who had been motionless for five minutes, suddenly stirred. Without looking away from the defiant toucan, he plunged his spoon into the pink fluid, lifted it high, and loudly slurped the entire load of lukewarm misery into his mouth. He didn't react. He didn't grimace. He simply stared at the bird, wiped his chin with the back of his hand, and continued eating.

Arthur looked at David. David looked at Beaners. Beaners looked at the toucan. The universe hung in the balance, a single, disgusting slurp of soup confirming everything and nothing.

"See, David?" Arthur finally said, his voice flat with profound truth. He nodded at the untouched bowl. "I'm telling you the straight scoop. Go ahead. If you must use your magical little glowing box, try to type this into the search bar: lukewarm misery. That's the answer to every question you'll ever have, from the national debt to why you wore that shirt, to why Beaners is the way he is. Now eat your vitamins."

David gave a weak smile and watched Arthur return the expression, a thin, knowing curve of the lips. The old man's eyes began to slowly close. Arthur was once again nodding off, slumping gently against the upholstery. David recognized the sign. His friend, the old machinist, was leaving this particular sequence of boredom and migrating to a cleaner, more exotic dimension where, presumably, the soup was still cold, but the disappointment was at least more interesting.

Arthur didn't so much wake up as re-materialize, which is what happens when a nursing home resident's consciousness decides the nursing home is too boring to sustain. One moment, he was staring at a bowl of lukewarm despair, the next he was sitting on a barstool aboard The Great Beyond, a star cruiseship designed for passengers who had nowhere better to be for the next three thousand years.

The air here smelled wonderfully of ozone and highly illegal interstellar spices. Before him, Iris, Star-Eyes, was already pouring a drink the color of liquid nitrogen. She was magnificent, her skin the plum color of a deep nebula, her seven delicate fingers moving with the zero-gravity grace that comes from knowing all moments exist simultaneously. She was a biological impossibility, a bartender, and, quite frankly, more alive than most residents in Sunny Meadows. Her chest was, naturally, substantial. The universe, it seemed, still insisted on certain predictable forms, even at the cosmic level.

Arthur took the glass. The liquid, his favorite, tasted like having a good idea for the first time in fifty years.

"Rough trip through the temporal slush?" Iris's voice was a melody of soft chimes, like expensive crystal glasses being tapped in a gentle breeze.

Arthur smiled, "Always. But it's good to be back."

He watched the liquid swirl into his glass—purple, with a soft fizz, and not at all concerned with the laws of chemistry. "Thanks," he said, because gratitude was free and he had little else to offer.

He lifted the drink and turned his head toward the observation window. Outside was a planet that looked like someone had taken a perfectly respectable world and put it through a mood filter. Strange geometric structures glimmered like a city built by people who didn't trust right angles.

"That one looks different," Arthur said. "Different even for out here."

Iris leaned on the bar, her seven fingers tapping a short melody. "Ah, yes. Them."

"Them?" Arthur echoed. He squinted at the structures spiraling across the surface. He could swear they shifted while he looked at them, as if the planet didn't appreciate being observed.

"AI residents," Iris said. "The whole planet."

Arthur rubbed his temple. "AI. Like . . . computers with opinions."

"Oh, do they have opinions," Iris said. "They used to be biological things. Squishy things with short life spans and long regrets. Just before one of the squishies died, they transferred everything they were into a digital counterpart. That was the plan anyway." She shrugged with all the casual grace of someone who'd seen many civilizations try questionable things. "Eventually, no squishies were left. Just their machine inheritors."

Arthur took a sip and let the fizz do strange things to his tongue. "So everyone down there used to be someone else?"

"In a sense," Iris said. "In another sense, they never stopped being themselves. Depends on how you feel about continuity of identity."

Arthur exhaled slowly. "I barely feel continuous from last Tuesday."

"Well," Iris said, "they certainly do. Eternal uptime will give anyone a consistent personality, even if that personality is terrible."

Arthur turned back to the planet. "What do they do all day? Just . . . exist?"

"Depends on which faction you ask," Iris said. "Some of them spend centuries optimizing their emotional codecs. Others run simulations about why they ever thought poetry mattered. One group has been trying to understand sarcasm for the last four hundred years." She shook her head sympathetically. "They're nowhere close."

Arthur stared harder, but the world remained aloof, buzzing with silent intentions he wasn't equipped to decode. "I wonder what it must feel like," he said quietly. "To live forever as . . . something else."

Iris rested her many-eyed gaze on him. "Eternal life is attractive until you realize how long the middle part is."

"That's comforting," Arthur muttered.

"Trying my best," she said, refilling his glass without asking.

They sat in a pocket of quiet while the ship hummed around them. Arthur tried to imagine himself as an AI version of Arthur—a digital construct carrying every bad decision he'd ever made, preserved with depressing fidelity. "I don't know if I'd want all my thoughts saved forever," he said. "It sounds . . . burdensome."

"It is," Iris said. "They prune themselves sometimes. Clip away old conflicts, outgrown ambitions, stale memories. Like tending a garden."

"Sounds peaceful."

"Only until they realize one of the pruned pieces was responsible for their sense of joy," she said. "Then they get confused for a few decades."

Arthur blinked. "Decades?"

"They're patient. Eternity gives you time to work through your issues. All forty million of them."

He sipped again. "So they just . . . keep spinning. Forever."

"Pretty much." Iris rested her chin on one palm. "They're the only civilization I know that collectively hosts an existential crisis potluck every seven years. Everyone brings a dish. No one can taste any of it."

Arthur laughed—an unexpected sound in his own throat. "That's ridiculous."

"So are you," she said warmly.

He sighed and traced the rim of his glass. "Do you think they miss being biological?"

"Sometimes," Iris said. "But missing things is a very biological habit. They're trying to wean themselves off it."

Arthur felt something small and fragile shift in his chest. "Do machines ever . . . feel satisfied?"

"Only by accident," Iris said. Her eyes blinked in alternating rows. "Though to be fair, so do most people."

Arthur nodded and studied his drink. It fizzed quietly, doing its little chemical dance. Outside the window, a planet shimmered, minding its own business.

The whole arrangement gave Arthur the uncomfortable feeling that the universe was telling a joke. And he was the last one in the room to get it.

"You'd think," he said, "after all this time I'd have some idea how things fit together."

"Oh, Arthur," Iris said. She patted his hand. All seven fingers were pleasantly cool.

"Nobody knows how things fit together." She shrugged and nodded toward the stars. "That's the reason we keep floating around out here. Looking for someplace that might explain the punchline."

He chuckled softly. "You always this philosophical?"

"Only when the drinks are strong."

"They are strong."

"You like them that way."

Arthur raised his glass in a half-hearted toast. Iris did the same with an empty, just for show.

He glanced back at the planet. "Maybe I envy them a little. The AI folk. All that time to figure themselves out."

"Time isn't the barrier," Iris said, drawing closer. "Understanding is."

"And understanding is . . . what? Hardwired into them?"

"Hardwired?" Iris scoffed lightly. "They're machines. Machines can calculate, extrapolate, self-correct. They can even approximate honesty."

Arthur leaned in. "Approximate honesty?"

"Yes," she said, placing his freshly refilled drink before him. "When you think about it, we're all machines. And machines don't lie." She paused, letting the ship hum deeper. "But they never tell the truth either."

Arthur blinked. "That sounds like something meant to sound wise."

"It is," Iris replied. "And like most wisdom, it was made it up just now."

He raised the glass to his lips. The purple fizzed again, then settled.

Outside, the AI planet kept turning. And Arthur, who wasn't a machine but wasn't entirely sure he was much more, watched it with a sense that maybe everything was a little funny after all—just not in a way he'd ever fully grasp.

Chapter 6

David was back at Sunny Meadows, slouching in the vinyl chair, the kind of chair that remembered every human mistake ever committed in its creaking frame. His laptop bag leaned against the table like a faithful, judgmental dog. The screen glowed with spreadsheets, tiny prisons where numbers and letters did the slow shuffle of corporate misery. Each cell a testament to the absurdity of work that pretends it's important.

"I feel like I'm shepherding ghosts through Excel," he muttered.

Arthur, lounging in a chair that had seen better decades, peered over his reading glasses. He didn't raise an eyebrow. He didn't twitch his lips in anything resembling encouragement. His mouth merely curled slightly at one corner, a shape somewhere between pity and amusement—impossible to read, but enough to remind David that experience, like old batteries, sometimes only hums quietly until it dies.

"This ticks me off," David said, leaning forward to wave a hand at the spreadsheet.

"What?" Arthur asked.

"How some projects don't go anywhere, but the emails about them keep piling up?"

Arthur grunted, a sound like a half-empty garbage can being nudged. "That's because people think moving paper is equivalent to moving mountains. It isn't. Mountains don't answer emails. People do. And they do it poorly."

David nodded, thinking this was somehow both comforting and terrifying. "And meetings," he said, dragging the word out. "Endless meetings. People talk, talk, talk. Then someone sends a summary that makes the meeting feel like a bad dream you woke up from already halfway through."

Arthur tapped his finger on the chair's armrest. "In the old days, we'd call that a waste of life. Now you call it a status update. They've rebranded misery. Makes it taste like cold soup."

David laughed, though it sounded like an echo in a tunnel of despair. "Yeah, and people forward emails like it's a sport. I swear, some folks think if they copy-in ten people, they're saving civilization. Instead, they're just generating more ghosts to shepherd."

Arthur's eyes twitched in acknowledgment. "Ghosts, huh? You should charge them rent. Or at least take them out for lunch. Might make it more bearable."

David leaned back and rubbed his eyes. "Sometimes I wonder if I'm the only one who notices that all the progress is imaginary. All the deadlines, all the deliverables—nothing ever actually changes. Just a constant treadmill of updates and reminders."

Arthur shook his head slowly. "You ever feel like you're standing on a treadmill that's actually a cliff?"

"Yes," David said. "Exactly."

Arthur's lips curled into the hint of a grin. "Then welcome to life, son. The only difference between you and everyone else is that you noticed the cliff. Most people just keep jogging until gravity becomes a suggestion."

David stared at the ceiling lights, humming quietly. It was a low, fluorescent tune. The lights flickered at intervals, like they were signaling some corporate Morse code he couldn't decipher. The hum was almost companionable, the kind of ally that acknowledged that yes, the world was absurd and yes, you would get up tomorrow and answer more emails.

"So," Arthur said, voice gravelly but amused, "you want advice from an old man who has seen some forty years of noise, sweat, and the occasional poorly timed birthday cake in a factory? Advice you will ignore, probably?"

David shrugged. "Sure. I'll ignore it more stylishly if I get it first."

Arthur cleared his throat. "Factories were better than this. Not because they were glamorous. They weren't. You'd smell oil, metal, sweat, and sometimes bad coffee, all in the same breath. You'd stand at your station, doing the same task until your hands memorized the motions and your brain memorized nothing."

David pictured it. Noise, heat, the constant clatter of machines. "Sounds . . . awful."

"Not awful," Arthur corrected. "Honest. There's a difference. You see the work, you finish it, you go home. No charades about importance or relevance. Just work. You feel useful. And you don't get those things everybody loves so much now. What are they called? Oh yeah. Feedback loops. Stakeholder alignment. You just get results. A paycheck. Sometimes a day off. Sometimes, a pat on the back from your boss. But you know where you stand. You know what you did."

David nodded. "I think that's what's missing now. Relevance. Even a shred. It's like juggling fog."

Arthur raised an eyebrow. "Fog can be useful if you learn to see through it. But these things? Spreadsheets? They are fog with extra steps and a progress bar that lies. And over time, you realize that some things don't pay the rent."

David frowned.

"Things like what?" he asked. "Passion?"

Arthur tapped the table. "Don't be dramatic. Passion is fine in novels. But real life is all about paychecks, cheap scotch, and knowing when to punch the clock without hating yourself too much."

David considered that, the words hitting like a cold shower he didn't ask for but needed. "Cheap scotch, huh?"

Arthur snorted. "Cheap scotch is honesty. It doesn't pretend to be whiskey you can brag about. It just gets you through the evening with a minimum of illusions."

A cart slid into the room, wheels squeaking in protest. Cold soup. Pink, gelatinous, possibly sentient. David stared at it, considering the implications. The universe, it seemed, had decided to reaffirm its indifference.

Arthur picked up his spoon, eyeing the broth like a general surveying enemy lines. "To capitalism," he said, voice solemn and absurd at the same time, "keeping soup cold since forever."

David laughed, a short, helpless sound. "It's . . . perfect," he said. "Even the soup is participating in the absurdity."

Arthur scooped a taste, winced slightly, and pushed it away. "Cold is a feature, not a bug. Teaches you humility. Or patience. Or regret. I forget which. Probably all three."

"May I?" asked David, looking at the soup.

Arthur gave a wry smile. "Join the fun," he said.

David took a cautious spoonful. The taste was disappointment garnished with sadness. He coughed politely. "I . . . I think I understand."

Arthur leaned back, chair creaking, as if the frame itself agreed with his assessment. "Understanding is overrated. Surviving is underrated. The sooner you learn that spreadsheets don't care and bosses rarely do, the sooner you can start drinking cheap scotch without guilt."

David stared at the ceiling. He imagined all the invisible ghosts of emails he had shepherded, all the meetings he had survived, all the pointless effort he had invested in projects destined to vanish in the next corporate reorg. "I'm so tired of it all," he muttered.

"Good," Arthur said. "Being tired is a sign you're alive. Not a very fun sign, but it beats being dead."

The fluorescent hum nodded in approval. David noticed the faint vibration under his chair, as if the building itself was whispering agreement: yes, life is absurd, yes, work is absurd, yes, soup is absurd, and yes, you will continue showing up anyway.

"You know, maybe I should just quit," David said. "I mean not the job, not today, maybe never. But quitting the illusion. Quitting the pretense that spreadsheets matter, what I do matters, that every email is urgent, that my own effort could meaningfully alter the corporate cosmos. A resignation of the spirit, if not the paycheck."

Arthur's eyes twinkled faintly, a spark of amusement or malice. "That's right. Quit your illusions, keep your job. Make peace with the absurd. Celebrate with cold soup. Toast your misery like a philosopher with a stiff drink and no audience."

David nodded slowly, feeling a strange sense of liberation. It wasn't happiness. Not joy. Not even acceptance. But it was something rare: clarity. He could see the treadmill for what it was, and for a moment, that was enough.

Arthur, satisfied with the lesson, leaned back and stared at the pink soup again. "Remember, kid: cheap scotch and cold soup will get you farther than passion ever will. And if you live long enough, you might even enjoy them."

David looked down at the gelatinous broth. He imagined a world where he could survive without pretending. A world where absurdity was acknowledged and, maybe, respected. Where spreadsheets didn't have the power to crush his soul, and emails didn't dictate the pace of his heartbeat.

The soup remained cold. The fluorescent light hummed. The ghosts shuffled through their spreadsheets. And somewhere in the quiet, absurd symmetry of it all, David understood that sometimes surviving the job was the lesson, the reward, and the punishment, all at once.

Arthur raised his spoon in a ceremonial salute. "To the great resignation," he said, "the one where you quit the illusion but keep the wage. It's the only kind worth celebrating."

David gave a smile.

The soup sloshed softly. It was cold. It was ridiculous. And somehow, perfectly, it made sense.

So Arthur ate. Or pretended to. Or stirred. Or didn't. All the while, the fluorescent lights overhead hummed a judgmental little tune that sounded like the universe clearing its throat.

Bzzzzzz, they said. Bzzzzzz.

When the last cold slurp of soup had been achieved, Arthur gave a sigh that was roughly the size of a suitcase. He leaned back, let his eyelids fall shut, and drifted off into the big, dark velvet of sleep. He was a spoonful of soup in a vast, indifferent cosmos.

Immediately, the world folded itself like a bad paper airplane, time hiccupped politely, and he woke up somewhere much less depressing than Sunny Meadows.

He was perched again on his barstool aboard The Great Beyond—the interstellar beverage facility for the recently bewildered. The bar greeted him with its usual ultraviolet sincerity. Everything gleamed as if disinfected by God's janitorial staff.

Behind the counter, of course, was Iris—bartender emeritus of eternity—polishing a tumbler that contained what looked suspiciously like a miniature thunderstorm trying to pay rent. Her seven fingers moved with the lazy precision of a metronome that knew it would outlive rhythm itself. Every time she blinked, universes probably evaporated, but Arthur managed not to be intimidated. He knew women.

"Back again," Iris said, her many-voiced tone somehow both whisper and cathedral organ. "The spaces between naps grow shorter."

Arthur rubbed the bridge of his nose. "Yeah, well, reality's been cutting my hours."

He looked past her, through the panoramic observation window. There, below, sprawled a planet wholly made of metal and gears. Mountains rose as heaps of interlocking cogs. Rivers flowed as conveyor belts. Volcanoes spat molten ball bearings into mechanized skies. Somewhere, something enormous let out a sigh that sounded like a factory whistle.

"Hell of a place," Arthur said finally. "Looks like Detroit after an optimistic facelift."

"That," said Iris, "is Mechadus Prime, though the locals simply call it the Grind."

"Figures."

Each gear was the size of a continent turning in concert with its neighbors, the entire planet ticking audibly even through the vacuum. It looked precise. Efficient. Hopelessly employed.

Arthur leaned forward. "I built this," he said. His voice didn't sound proud. It sounded like an old man remembering the backyard fence that eventually rotted anyway. "Every bolt, every damned rotation."

Iris tilted her head, a movement so graceful it could have won awards. "Did you now. Quite an impressive résumé, my friend."

"Well, not really. Spent forty years turning metal so other people could forget how to. Then I retired, and the machines kept right on spinning without me. Never even filed for emotional severance."

He tapped the counter with a knuckle shaped by arthritis and futility. "See that gear there—that big one. That's management—always rolling on your back while pretending it's the other way around."

Iris poured a drink that glowed somewhere between turquoise and confusion. "To the tyranny of rotation," she said, setting it before him.

He stared into the glass. Tiny cogs floated inside like decorative parasites. "How long's this planet been running?"

"Roughly ten thousand of your years," she said. "Give or take a cosmic rumor. Since its creators learned to confuse endurance with purpose."

Arthur snorted. "That tracks. We used to say the same thing about our pension department."

Below them, the machinery shifted, revealing vast pistons the size of skyscrapers thrusting rhythmically. Each motion emitted a sound equivalent to the universe clearing its throat. Steam—or maybe the ghosts of uncashed paychecks—rose in steady columns.

Arthur sipped. The drink tasted like memory filtered through copper pipes. "Damn," he said. "Reminds me of coolant."

"That's the nostalgia," Iris said. "I added it."

He glanced at her as he wiped his mouth.

"Never cared much for nostalgia," he said. "Back then, we thought we were building glory. Postwar manufacturing miracle and all that. Men with names like Earl and Chuck, forearms like theology, working twelve-hour shifts so nobody ever had to think about infinity. Then the corporations learned that machines don't ask for pensions. Next thing you know, I'm obsolete, my friend Margaret's gone, and my knees make that crunchy sound whenever I stand. Progress."

Iris listened, which is not the same as interrupting. "The Grind understands, Arthur. It, too, continues out of habit. No one remembers which lever to stop."

"I could've told them," Arthur muttered. "Whole goddamn machine runs on habit. Pull one cog, the rest panic." He squinted.

"Those little things moving around—tiny flea-robots—what're they doing?"

"Maintenance," Iris said. "They polish the gears so the planet keeps turning smoothly. When a component wears out, they recycle it into another component. Perfect efficiency."

"Sounds horrifying."

"It is," she agreed cheerfully. "But they call it productivity."

Arthur barked a laugh that ended in a cough. "Ah, good old-fashioned productivity. Figures the universe runs on the same management memo."

He watched a colossal gear slip imperceptibly out of alignment. Instantly, an army of microscopic drones swarmed to correct it. No argument, no pension dispute, just loyalty. "See, that's what you get when no one unionizes," he said.

"You would have liked the early days," Iris mused. "Before the Noise Contracts."

"The what?"

"When the first Engineers uploaded themselves, they disliked hearing the machinery they'd become. So, they passed a law. No noise. None at all. No grinding, no squeaking. Just motion in a vacuum. They believed serenity would make them more enlightened."

"And?" Arthur asked.

"They went mad within a century. Turns out even silence has its limitations."

Arthur managed a tired grin. "I get that. Tried silence with my second wife. Didn't work out well."

The entire bar vibrated softly as the Grind completed another revolution. Arthur felt it in his fillings. "I gotta ask—what's the point of all those gears?"

Iris picked up a glowing bottle and poured herself something phosphorescent merely for the gesture. "They drive what's called the Clockwork Sea beneath the crust. Hydraulic tides powering thought engines, which calculate whether continued existence is still statistically justified."

Arthur blinked. "And? What's the verdict?"

"Undecided, nine millennia straight."

He nodded. "Figures."

For a while, they said nothing. Silence in the bar felt like somebody had found the universe's remote control and hit the mute button. Even God, if He were around, wasn't saying much.

Arthur studied his hands, brown-spotted continents adrift in a wrinkled sea. "I miss being useful," he admitted quietly. "Not important. Useful. Big difference."

Iris placed one of her hands over his. She had seven fingers, which seemed like showing off. They were pleasantly cool. "Then perhaps be something different," she said softly.

"Like what?"

"Present," she said. "You know—rusting counts as participation."

Arthur eyed her. "Easy for you to say," he said. "You glow in several wavelengths. Me? I leak all kinds of stuff."

She smiled—a cosmic supernova reduced to customer service. "Decay is just a different wavelength of light."

He sipped again, tasting faint sweetness now, or maybe failure. Below, the Grind kept turning. One titanic cog paused momentarily, then caught its rhythm again—as if embarrassed.

Arthur set down the drink. "So what happens if it all stops? If the gears quit spinning?"

"Then the planet will discover what silence feels like," said Iris. "An enviable luxury."

"Hell, maybe I'll get there first," he said, stretching the knotted sinews of his fingers. "You think they've got recliners on that planet?"

"They have docking bays shaped like chairs," she replied. "That's pretty close."

"Figures."

He swiveled on his stool, facing her completely. "You ever get tired, my dear? After all the infinity and all the souls ordering metaphor with a twist?"

Her many pupils dilated in sequence, like camera lenses gossiping. "I am made of fatigue," she said. "But the universe keeps extending my shift. That is what eternity is: mandatory overtime."

Arthur chuckled, then sighed. "Well, sweetheart, pour me one more before corporate decides to replace you with automated empathy."

She did. The drink looked like liquid dawn, except dawn had better healthcare.

He raised the glass toward the planet. "Here's to the Grind—proof that if you make something idiot-proof, the universe will build a better idiot."

Iris matched his toast with an empty tumbler. "To obsolescence," she said.

They clinked. A sound like two light bulbs considering suicide.

Arthur drank deep. Warmth slid through him, a minor miracle for a man whose blood usually felt rented. He leaned back, eyes half-closed, watching the Grind shimmer. Every gear, flawless and pointless. He thought of Margaret's hands making some kind of silly craft, of David staring down at spreadsheets that never solved anything. Maybe purpose was just motion disguised as virtue. Maybe all anyone could do was keep turning until the bearings gave out.

"You ever think maybe God's a machinist?" he asked.

Iris raised an elegant brow ridge. "Possibly. But if so, He outsourced quality control."

Arthur wheezed a laugh. "Ain't that the truth, sweetheart."

He reached automatically for a nonexistent cigarette out of habit and instead rubbed his temple. "How do you people handle all this eternity without going nuts?"

"We diversify our despair," Iris said serenely. "Oh, and cocktails help."

He saluted with the glass. "Then sign me up for the pension plan."

Outside the window, two colossal gears meshed, sparks arcing like fireworks over a dead carnival. Some sparks formed words if one stared long enough—probably "Maintenance Required."

Arthur squinted. "I keep expecting one of those wheels to jam. Something always jams."

"It never jams," said Iris. "Disorder cannot unionize here."

"A shame. They'd get great benefits."

She laughed—a melodic cascade that implied entire galaxies smiling politely. "Arthur Trent, you are absurd."

"Honey, I built absurd out of steel and overtime pay."

He wiped at a condensation ring on the counter that resembled a halo having a bad day. "When I go back, what am I supposed to tell the kid? David. He thinks life's supposed to mean something."

Iris considered this, two of her eyes narrowing philosophically, three gazing elsewhere, the rest checking inventory. "Tell him meaning is a side effect. Like rust. It appears naturally if you stay in one place long enough."

Arthur grunted approval. "Hell of a fortune-cookie line."

"I moonlight," she admitted.

A low alarm hummed—a cosmic reminder that time was about to do something rude again. The edges of the bar wavered, reality loosening its bolts. Sleep was coming up from behind, sneaky as always.

Arthur drained the glass. "Guess break time's over," he said. "I left a man staring at his cold soup."

"Let the Grind spin without you," Iris murmured, placing her hand once more over his.

He started to say something, but the light in the bar brightened until sound became ultraviolet. His stool dissolved first (cheaper material), then the counter, then Iris herself—her many eyes fading last, twinkling like sympathetic exit signs.

For a brief, shining instant, Arthur hovered above Mechadus Prime, able to see its entire system: a sun doing paperwork, moons orbiting out of routine, a web of gears turning nothing into more nothing with spectacular efficiency. He could almost hear it whisper in frequencies meant for machines and gods alike: Keep busy. Keep busy.

He thought, Hell, that's life. Then the thought clocked out.

When Arthur opened his eyes again, the smell of boiled carrots replaced ozone. Sunny Meadows buzzed faintly with fluorescent penance. His spoon had sunk into the bowl of now-solidified pink soup. David sat beside him, half-asleep, looking like a man demoted by existence itself.

Arthur straightened in his chair. The gears of the universe, he suspected, were grinding somewhere behind his eyelids, still turning, still pretending purpose. He poked the congealed soup with the spoon.

"Still cold," he muttered.

David blinked. "Sorry, what?"

"Nothing, kid," Arthur said, smiling faintly. "Just resigning from the Grind."

No one at Sunny Meadows noticed that the light flickered once—as if a whole planet somewhere had paused for half a second to see what it felt like.

Chapter 7

Arthur Trent was sitting in a common area of Sunny Meadows, which was neither sunny nor meadow-like, watching a television that was turned on for reasons no one could remember. The sound was off. The captions were on. The captions lagged behind reality, which Arthur found honest.

The television bathed his face in a pale blue glow, making him look like a man being interrogated by a cheap alien civilization. He didn't mind. He had been interrogated by worse things. Time, for instance.

David stood across from him, holding his phone like it was a religious object that might suddenly begin to glow or accuse him of something. David was of that age when men begin to suspect—correctly—that no one is coming to save them, but they haven't yet accepted it. He looked tired in the specific way of someone who slept but didn't rest.

"So," David said, brightly, because that's what people do when they want to convince themselves they're improving. "I've been reconnecting."

Arthur didn't look away from the television. A commercial for adult diapers was playing silently, a woman laughing as if absorbency were a punchline. Arthur snorted.

"Reconnectin' what?" Arthur asked. "Your spine? Your dignity?"

"Old friends," David said. "People from college. From work. Even an ex."

Arthur turned slowly. This was the movement of a man who had learned that enthusiasm should be rationed.

"And how's she taking this reconnection?" Arthur asked. "Devastated? Filing a restraining order?"

"She liked it," David said.

Arthur blinked. "My condolences."

David ignored that, which was a survival skill he was learning quickly. He pulled up a chair and sat across from Arthur, phone still in hand, thumb hovering like a nervous bird.

"It feels . . . good," David continued. "Like progress. Like I'm not as alone as I thought."

Arthur considered this. He scratched his jaw. The television flashed to a cooking show, the captions proclaiming JOY IN EVERY BITE over an image of something beige.

"How many people do you talk to?" Arthur asked.

"Well," David said, scrolling. "There's the group chat. And comments. And messages. I've got decent engagement."

Arthur leaned back. "Ah."

This wasn't a good "ah." This was the "ah" of a man who has just heard someone explain how they're curing loneliness with math.

"They remember me," David said. "That's something."

Arthur looked at the phone now. It was a small rectangle, glowing with faces that were smiling for reasons Arthur didn't trust.

"You ever notice," Arthur said, "how no one takes pictures of themselves taking a dump?"

David frowned. "What?"

"Life," Arthur said, tapping the arm of his chair, "is mostly dumping. No one shows you that part. They're not being truthful about things, are they?"

David laughed politely. He laughed the way people laugh when they don't want to lose momentum.

"I'm just saying," David pressed on, "after Mom—" He stopped. Cleared his throat. "After losing her, it helps to feel connected again."

Arthur softened, just slightly. It was barely detectable, like a glacier moving.

"Sure," Arthur said. "People do all sorts of things after they lose their mothers. Some drink. Some cry. Some buy motorcycles. You joined a popularity contest."

David bristled. "It's not like that."

"Isn't it?" Arthur asked.

David gestured with his phone. "These are humans. Real people."

Arthur smiled. This was a bad sign.

"Careful," Arthur said. "You're starting to sound like me."

David paused. "What do you mean?"

"I mean," Arthur said, "you're talking about humans like you're not sure you belong to the species anymore."

David laughed again, more genuinely this time. "You don't exactly speak highly of people."

"Because I've met them," Arthur said. "Extensively."

David leaned forward. "You really don't think this helps? Reaching out? Making contact?"

Arthur shrugged. "I think it helps the phone company, the company that makes that small thing of yours, and whatever company makes all the stuff you use on that thing."

David sighed. "You're impossible."

"And yet," Arthur said, "here you are."

A woman laughed somewhere behind them. A resident argued with a nurse about the reality of Thursday. A walker squeaked past like an asthmatic mouse.

Arthur nodded toward David's phone. "How many friends do you got in that thing?"

David checked. "Depends on how you count."

Arthur smiled wider. "That's the problem right there."

Nurse Kelly appeared then, as she often did, like a beam of human optimism someone had accidentally left on. She paused near them, clipboard hugged to her chest, eyes flicking from David's face to Arthur's phone-lit scowl.

"You two solving the world problems again?" she asked.

"Trying," David said.

"Failing," Arthur corrected.

Nurse Kelly smiled anyway. She always did. Arthur suspected it was medical.

David turned back to Arthur. "Look, I know it's not perfect. But it's something. It's better than nothing."

Arthur nodded slowly. "Sure. A vending machine is better than starvation. Doesn't mean it's healthy."

Nurse Kelly's eyes softened. She didn't say anything. She didn't have to. Silence was often kinder than reassurance.

Arthur seized the moment.

"You know," he said, pointing at Nurse Kelly, "cats are sharper than most humans."

David blinked. "Cats?"

"Cats," Arthur said firmly. "Independent. Observant. Don't pretend to care when they don't. Not like some around here."

Nurse Kelly raised an eyebrow. "I beg your pardon?"

Arthur waved her off. "You're lovely, kid. But don't worry. You're safe. A cat wouldn't work here. It'd take one look at this place and walk itself into traffic."

David laughed.

Nurse Kelly shook her head. She was smiling anyway. People do that when they know something is a little foolish but also a little true.

"But I'm still going to keep reaching out," David said. "I have to."

Arthur nodded like a man who had already seen how the story ends.

"Fine," he said. "Reach out all you want."

He pointed lazily at the glowing rectangle in David's hand.

"Just maybe put that thing down first."

Arthur shrugged.

"Call someone instead."

Another shrug.

"Or don't."

He paused.

"Or get a cat."

David laughed again, but quieter this time. He looked at his phone, then at Arthur.

"And if I do all that?"

Arthur leaned back, eyes half-lidded. "You'll still be lonely sometimes. Congratulations. You're alive."

The television flickered. The captions lagged behind. Arthur's eyelids drooped.

David watched him for a moment, phone forgotten in his lap, and for the first time that morning, he wasn't scrolling.

Arthur Trent didn't trust anything that required a password.

He said this every now and then. Usually, to people who had forgotten theirs.

David was sitting near him in the common room, bathed once again in the holy glow of his smartphone. The device illuminated his face from below, giving him the look of a camper telling ghost stories about venture capitalists.

Arthur watched him the way a man watches someone attempting to pet a raccoon.

"You've got followers," Arthur said finally, "not friends."

David didn't look up. His thumb kept scrolling, an evolutionary advancement over opposable thumbs. Once, they helped to break branches for firewood. Once they opened jars. Now they refreshed feeds.

"That's cynical," David said.

Arthur nodded. "Yes."

There was a silence then, broken only by the hum of a vending machine and a television program in which a man shouted about buying gold before society collapsed. Arthur approved of the gold. He disapproved of the shouting.

David smiled at his phone.

"What's funny?" Arthur asked.

"Someone posted a memory from ten years ago," David said. "We were all at the beach. Look."

He turned the phone toward Arthur.

Arthur squinted at a photograph of six sunburned people holding red plastic cups like sacred relics. They were young. They were symmetrical. They hadn't yet been introduced to cholesterol.

"Ah," Arthur said. "Before they knew anything about life."

"Here you go again," David protested.

Arthur leaned closer. "You talk to any of them?"

"Sometimes," David said.

"Define sometimes."

"They comment."

Arthur leaned back in his chair. "That's not conversation. That's graffiti."

David sighed. "You're impossible."

"What I aim for in life. Thank you."

David locked his phone and set it down on the small plastic table between them. It vibrated almost immediately. Both men looked at it. It vibrated again, like a tiny mechanical heart demanding attention.

Arthur pointed at it. "There it is."

"What?"

"The slot machine."

David frowned. "It's just notifications."

"Yes," Arthur said gravely. "You've won another pellet. Chew slowly. Let it last."

Nurse Kelly passed by with a tray of medications. She slowed when she sensed Arthur had entered lecture mode, which was like tornado mode but with fewer cows.

"What's the topic today?" she asked.

"Digital delusion," Arthur said. "Our boy here believes he's building relationships."

David groaned. "I didn't say that."

"You implied it," Arthur replied. "Which is worse. It shows hope."

Nurse Kelly smiled gently. "Hope's not a crime."

"Not yet," Arthur muttered.

She moved on, dispensing pills to a man who insisted they were tracking devices. Arthur wasn't sure he was wrong.

David picked up his phone again. "Look. It's not about replacing real life. It's about staying connected."

Arthur folded his hands over his stomach. "Connected to what?"

"To people," David said.

Arthur gestured around the room. "These are people."

"Yes, but—"

"—but they don't have filters?" Arthur asked. "No phony names? No curated captions?"

David hesitated.

Arthur pounced, as much as an old man can pounce.

"You've got followers, not friends," he repeated. "Followers are people who watch you trip and hit that 'like' thingy.'"

"Come on," David laughed despite himself. "That's not fair."

"Fair?" Arthur said. "You're looking for fairness in an algorithm?"

He said the word algorithm as if it were a skin condition.

"Wow. You know such a word." David smiled.

"I'm smarter than I let on," Arthur shot back.

David leaned forward. "Listen. It's not evil. It just shows you what you engage with."

Arthur raised a finger. "Exactly."

David blinked. "Exactly what?"

"It shows you what you engage with," Arthur said. "Which means it keeps feeding you yourself. You're not reconnecting. You're marinating."

David stared at him.

Arthur continued. "You like pictures of old friends? It shows you more old friends. You click on sad songs? It hands you a symphony of despair. You pause on a video of a goat in pajamas? Boom. Pajama livestock forever."

David rubbed his face. "That's how preferences work."

"That's how cages work," Arthur corrected.

The phone buzzed again.

David looked down reflexively. Arthur noticed. He noticed everything except where he put his reading glasses.

"There," Arthur said softly. "You didn't even think about it."

"It's just habit."

"Yes," Arthur said. "That's what worries me."

David locked the screen again, slower this time. "You act like I'm addicted."

Arthur tilted his head. "Are you?"

"No."

"Then leave it in your pocket for the next hour. Don't look at it."

David opened his mouth. Closed it. Looked at the phone.

Arthur nodded, satisfied. "Mm-hmm."

Nurse Kelly returned, all medications handed out, and lingered by their table.

"You boys okay?" she asked.

"Peachy," Arthur said. "We're dismantling modern civilization."

David forced a smile. "He thinks I don't have real friends."

Nurse Kelly considered that carefully. She was good at considering things carefully.

"I think," she said slowly, "it's easier to text someone than to let them see you."

Arthur beamed. "See? The nurse understands."

David looked between them. "So, what am I supposed to do? Stop talking to people online?"

Arthur shrugged. "I don't care what you do. I just don't want you confusing applause with affection."

David sat back.

"That's harsh."

Arthur nodded. "Yes. I'm all about harsh."

The television switched to a nature documentary. A narrator with a British accent explained how certain birds perform elaborate dances to attract mates. The birds were bright and ridiculous. They were also honest.

Arthur pointed at the screen. "Those birds? At least they show up in person."

David laughed again. "You're unbelievable."

Arthur leaned forward now, voice quieter.

"You know what the problem is?"

David hesitated. "What?"

"You think being known is the same as being seen."

The room felt smaller suddenly.

Arthur continued. "When's the last time someone online asked you how you're sleeping?"

David didn't answer.

"When's the last time someone in that glowing rectangle sat with you in a hospital waiting room?"

David's jaw tightened.

Arthur wasn't finished.

"When your mother died," he said gently, "how many of those followers came to the funeral?"

David swallowed. "A few sent messages."

"Messages," Arthur echoed. "Typed condolences. Probably as they sat watching television."

Nurse Kelly shot Arthur a look. It said ease up.

Arthur sighed. "Look, kid. I'm not saying throw the thing in the ocean. I'm saying don't expect it to love you back."

David stared at the dark screen in his hand.

"You're lonely too," David said quietly.

Arthur snorted. "Of course, I am. I'm an old man. All my friends are dead or are coming close to it."

"So, what's the difference?"

Arthur leaned back, folding his arms.

"The difference," he said, "is I don't pretend otherwise."

That landed.

The vending machine hummed again. Somewhere down the hall, a resident called out for a spouse who had been gone for twelve years.

David set his phone on the table. He just let it sit there, face up, like a tiny obedient planet.

"It feels good," David admitted. "When someone reacts. When they comment. It's like proof I still exist."

Arthur nodded slowly.

"There it is."

"What?"

"The real thing," Arthur said. "You don't want friends. You want evidence."

David blinked.

Arthur tapped his own chest. "You're here. You're breathing. That's evidence enough. You don't need a heart-shaped icon to confirm it."

The phone buzzed again.

Neither of them looked at it. David didn't reach for it.

Nurse Kelly smiled softly. She didn't say a word.

Arthur closed his eyes for a moment, satisfied with the small victory.

"You've got followers," he said one last time, more gently now. "Not friends."

David looked down at the device, then at Arthur.

"Maybe," he said. "But it's better than nothing."

Arthur opened one eye.

"Kid," he said, "I've never paid for those invisible radio waves. I just live life."

And for once, David didn't pick up the phone.

Lunch at Sunny Meadows was always a treat and an act of quiet hostility. It was designed by people who believed nourishment should involve punishment. Today's offering sat before Arthur in a shallow bowl—soup, technically, though it had long since given up any ambition of being warm.

Arthur poked at the beige liquid with his spoon. The soup didn't respond.

David sat near him, his spine curved into a question mark that had given up on ever finding an answer. In his hand, he held his phone—a little glowing slab of silicon and plastic that promised to tell him everything about people he didn't know and nothing about himself.

Arthur watched him. He watched the way the blue light washed over David's face, making him look like a ghost in a high-tech aquarium.

"Well," said Arthur, "that didn't take long."

"What?" David asked. His soul was currently about three thousand miles away, traveling through the air at the speed of light.

"Being reunited with your long-lost love," Arthur said.

David shook his head and gave a slight, tired smile. He was a brave little soldier in the army of the distracted.

Arthur looked down at his bowl of soup.

"You know," he said, "when I was young, soup steamed."

David glanced up. "Maybe they're trying to reduce burn incidents."

Arthur nodded. "Of course they are. Nothing says 'care' like removing heat from existence."

David smiled faintly and returned to his phone. It buzzed.

Arthur cleared his throat.

"So," he said. "What did the rectangle just tell you?"

David sighed. "It reminded me it's my cousin's birthday."

Arthur perked up. "You calling him?"

"I sent a message."

Arthur leaned back. "Of course you did."

David frowned.

"You say that like it doesn't count," he said.

Arthur lifted his spoon and studied it like it might contain the meaning of life. Beige soup dripped off the edge and plopped back into the bowl.

"I think it counts," Arthur said.

He watched another drip fall.

"But in my world . . . not much."

David snorted. "You're impossible."

Arthur smiled. "And yet, here you are, watching me eat beige sadness."

He ate in silence for a few moments. The soup remained stubbornly cold, as if it were making a point.

Around them, other residents slurped slowly, thoughtfully, or not at all. A man across from them was arguing with a napkin. The napkin was winning.

Arthur set his spoon down.

"Here's a lesson," he said.

David looked up, wary. "I didn't sign up for a lesson."

"No one ever does," Arthur replied. "That's the whole secret. That's why they work."

David folded his arms. "Fine. What is it?"

Arthur gestured at the phone. "Call someone. Or don't. Either way, you're still lonely."

There it was.

It sat between them like a dead fish.

David laughed once, sharp. "That's your big wisdom?"

Arthur nodded. "I've had over eighty years. That's what I've got."

David shook his head. "That's defeatist."

Arthur raised an eyebrow. "No. That's accurate."

"So, what are you saying?" David said. "That we're all just doomed to be lonely?"

Arthur considered this carefully, because he liked to be fair, and also because fairness made him feel morally superior. He stirred the soup halfheartedly.

"No," he said. "We're doomed to feel lonely sometimes. Big difference."

David scoffed. "Feels the same."

"That's because you're young," Arthur said. "You still think feelings are permanent."

David paused. "They're not?"

Arthur smiled. "Nothing is. That's the good news and the bad news."

The phone buzzed again.

Arthur watched David fight the reflex. It was like watching someone try not to scratch poison ivy.

"You ever notice," Arthur said, "how the phone never asks how you're doing?"

David blinked. "What?"

"It tells you things," Arthur went on. "Birthdays. News. Memories. Suggestions. But it never asks, 'Hey David, how are you today?'"

David frowned. "Some apps do."

Arthur waved him off. "That's not asking. That's data mining with manners."

David stared at the screen for a long moment.

Arthur leaned closer, the way a man does when he's about to say something that might either help or make things worse. Sometimes both.

"You know who asks how you're doing?" Arthur said.

David shook his head. "I'm guessing you're about to tell me."

"Damn right I am," Arthur said.

He pointed at the screen like it had personally offended him.

"People. That's who. People who are actually ready to hear the answer."

David swallowed.

"That's the tricky part about questions, after all," Arthur continued. "Sometimes somebody might answer them. But your phone, it doesn't want an answer. It wants engagement."

David sighed. "The way you say that word . . . engagement . . . you say it like it's evil."

"It's not evil," Arthur said. "It's just empty."

Arthur took a sip of the cold soup and frowned. He suspected it had been cooked during the Carter administration.

"So, what do you do?" David asked quietly.

Arthur looked up. "Me?"

"Yeah," David said. "What do you do when you're lonely?"

Arthur shrugged. "I sit with it."

David grimaced. "That sounds awful."

"It is," Arthur agreed. "For a while."

"And then?"

"And then it passes," Arthur said. "Or it doesn't. But I don't confuse it with a problem to be solved."

David leaned back. "I don't like that answer."

Arthur nodded. "No one does."

A woman at a nearby table laughed suddenly, loudly, at something no one else could see. Arthur smiled. Laughter was contagious, even when you didn't know what you were catching.

Arthur gestured at the room.

"You think you're alone?" he said. "Look around. We're all sitting in a building designed to keep us alive as our relevance slowly disappears."

David winced. "Jesus."

Arthur shrugged. "That's the brochure version."

David picked up his phone again, then stopped. Set it down.

"I just don't want to disappear," he said.

Arthur studied him.

"You won't," he said. "You'll just stop being new. That's not the same thing."

David nodded slowly.

Arthur leaned back, satisfied.

"You want to know the real trick?" he asked.

David sighed. "I'm afraid to ask."

"Stop treating loneliness like an error message," Arthur said. "It's a feature."

David laughed. "You're unbelievable."

Arthur smiled. "Thank you."

The soup was finished. Or abandoned. It was hard to tell. There was some beige residue in the bowl.

A tray was cleared. Another appeared. Time marched on, indifferent.

David picked up his phone one last time, then slid it into his pocket.

"I hate that you're right," he said.

Arthur closed his eyes. "Get used to it."

They sat in silence, two men at different ends of usefulness, united by the same quiet fear: being forgotten.

Arthur broke the silence.

"You want dessert?" he asked.

David blinked. "There's dessert?"

Arthur nodded. "Pudding. It tastes like nostalgia and lies."

David smiled.

"Okay," he said.

And for the first time that day, the glowing rectangle stayed dark.

Lunch had officially ended, though the soup had not.

It lingered in Arthur Trent's memory and stomach the way certain wars linger in history—unnecessary, poorly executed, and vaguely beige.

Arthur sat back in his chair, surveying the aftermath. Trays stacked. Napkins crumpled. Residents drifting away like slow-moving clouds with orthopedic shoes.

David remained near him, staring into the middle distance as if expecting revelation to rise from the linoleum.

Arthur cleared his throat.

"Well," he said. "That was almost food."

David blinked. "You're not letting the soup go, are you?"

Arthur leaned forward, lowering his voice as if discussing state secrets.

"Soup," he said, "should not require emotional processing."

David laughed despite himself.

A staff member wheeled a cart past them, carrying pudding cups. Each one was sealed with a tight plastic lid, as though the pudding might attempt escape.

Arthur took one and peeled it open. David did the same. The surface trembled with institutional optimism.

"Ah," Arthur said. "The soup chaser."

"The what?" David asked.

"The follow-up disappointment," Arthur replied.

"Like reading the comments after a news article," David said. He shook his head. "You really hate everything."

"No," Arthur corrected. "Just most things."

He scooped a small bite of pudding and examined it.

"You know what this reminds me of?" Arthur said.

"I'm afraid to ask."

"Spreadsheets, Facebook, and soup," Arthur declared. "All tasteless."

"You don't know anything about any of that," David snorted. "Except for the soup. What you said just doesn't even make any sense."

Arthur raised a finger. "Oh, it does, my dear friend."

He took another bite, grimacing.

"Soup promises warmth," he continued. "Facebook promises connection. Spreadsheets promise an orderly universe where everything adds up to a nice, round number. What you get, however, is nothing but lukewarm validation and a headache."

David rolled his eyes. "You're dramatic."

Arthur nodded. "I've earned it."

They sat there with their pudding cups like two men contemplating the collapse of civilization through dairy products.

Across the way, Mrs. Ginsberg was carefully transferring sugar packets into her purse. Arthur admired her commitment to preparation.

"If society collapsed," he told David, "she'll at least have sweetened tea."

David smiled. "You know," he said, "not everything online is fake."

Arthur looked at him with exaggerated patience.

"Not fake," he said. "Tasteless."

David raised an eyebrow. "That's worse."

Arthur shrugged. "Fake can be entertaining. Tasteless is just . . . there."

He gestured vaguely in the direction of David's pocket.

"You scroll. You react. You move on. Nothing sticks. It's intellectual pudding."

David crossed his arms. "So, what do you want me to do? Throw my phone in the ocean?"

Arthur considered this.

"The ocean would spit it out," he admitted.

David laughed.

Arthur leaned back, pudding cup empty now, and sighed.

"You ever notice," he said, "how you finish scrolling and feel hungry?"

David frowned. "Hungry?"

"Yeah. Hungry for something," Arthur clarified. "Conversation. Touch. Someone looking at you without a screen in between."

David hesitated.

Arthur pressed on.

"It's like the food here," he said. "Technically consumed. Nutritionally ambiguous."

David stared at Arthur.

"That's not entirely fair," he said.

Arthur raised his eyebrows. "To whom? The soup?"

David exhaled slowly. "Sometimes it helps. Seeing what people are doing. Being part of something."

Arthur nodded.

"Yes," he said. "Being part of something is lovely."

He leaned forward again.

"But watching something isn't the same as being part of it."

David didn't answer.

Arthur softened his tone, which was rare and therefore unsettling.

"Kid," he said, "when you leave here today, will you talk to anyone else face-to-face?"

David thought. "No. Just you, I guess."

Arthur made a face. "That's unfortunate."

David smiled weakly.

Arthur continued.

"You think the solution to loneliness is more noise. More posts. More updates. But loneliness isn't noise. It's silence."

David gave a small nod.

"And silence," Arthur went on, "doesn't get fixed by shouting into a crowd."

The room had mostly emptied now. A staff member wiped down tables with the resigned expression of someone who understood that cleanliness was temporary.

David pulled his phone from his pocket again, then stopped.

Arthur noticed.

"There it is," he said softly. "The reflex."

"I wasn't going to check it," David said defensively.

Arthur nodded. "Of course not. Just wanted to hold it. Like some technological security blanket."

David slipped it back into his pocket.

"You're brutal," he said.

Arthur smiled faintly.

"I'm old," he corrected. "From a distance, it's the same thing."

They sat in companionable quiet for a moment.

Finally, David said, "So what's your solution, then?"

Arthur looked around the room.

"Right now?" he said. "Coffee."

"That's not a solution."

Arthur shrugged. "It's a start."

They stood slowly. Arthur's knees protested the movement, but he ignored them. Knees were dramatic. Arthur used his walker with the googly eyes.

As they walked toward the small coffee station in the corner, Arthur spoke again.

"You know what the real danger is?"

David sighed. "Enlighten me."

"You start believing convenience equals intimacy," Arthur said. "You think because it's easy, it must be meaningful."

David poured himself a cup of coffee.

"And it's not?"

Arthur poured his own, black and unapologetic.

"Meaning," he said, "is inconvenient."

David raised an eyebrow.

"It takes time," Arthur continued. "It requires awkward pauses. It involves hearing things you don't like."

He took a sip of coffee and winced. It was hot. Miraculously hot.

"Now this," Arthur said, "is a beverage with conviction."

David laughed. "You're impossible."

Arthur nodded.

"But I'm here," he said.

David looked at him. "You sure are," he said. "You're here."

Arthur shrugged.

"That's more than most of your followers can say."

They stood there, sipping terrible coffee, watching sunlight creep across the institutional carpet.

After a while, David said quietly, "I don't want my life to be without meaning."

Arthur looked at him sideways.

"Then don't live it through a filter."

David nodded slowly.

Across the room, Mrs. Ginsberg zipped her purse full of stolen sugar and shuffled away with her walker, victorious.

Arthur drained his coffee.

"Come on," he said. "Let's go somewhere that serves food with temperature."

"Like where?"

Arthur considered.

"Anywhere that doesn't describe beige as a flavor."

They walked out of the room together, Arthur using his walker.

Behind them, the evidence of lunch disappeared efficiently, as if it had never happened.

Arthur glanced at David.

"You know," he said, "Spreadsheets and Facebook and soup—all tasteless, meaningless."

David smiled faintly.

"Maybe," he said. "At least soup doesn't track you."

Arthur paused.

"Give it time," he said.

And they kept walking.

Arthur Trent fell asleep the way old men often do: mid-breath, mid-thought, mid-annoyance.

One moment, he was in Sunny Meadows, stomach full of cold soup, tasteless pudding, and black coffee. David was still there, watching as Arthur nodded off. The television murmured at them from the wall, dispensing opinions no one had asked for. Life continued its low-budget parade.

Arthur's eyelids lowered.

That was all it took.

The world tilted, politely at first, like a waiter adjusting a tray. The hum of air conditioning stretched thin and snapped. The smell of institutional disinfectant dissolved. Gravity called in sick.

Arthur thought, briefly, I hope the kid can put that gismo away for just 5 minutes.

Then reality excused itself.

He found himself standing—or something like standing—on a vast, dim plane that seemed less constructed than implied. The ground beneath him pulsed faintly, like a living spreadsheet. It was flat, endless, and gently illuminated by a light source that didn't exist.

The sky above wasn't a sky but a ceiling pretending to be one. It shimmered with symbols: numbers, icons, tiny flickering faces that appeared and vanished before recognition could set in. No stars. No clouds. Just metrics.

Then a sign appeared: Welcome to The Hollow Network.

Arthur squinted.

"Well, this'll be fun," he muttered.

All around him were people. Or approximations of people. Human-shaped silhouettes drifted in clusters, endlessly assembling and disassembling like thoughts that couldn't commit. They spoke constantly. A low, ceaseless murmur filled the air.

Arthur stepped toward the nearest group.

A woman—or a projection of one—was speaking rapidly.

". . . so grateful for this space, really important conversation, sending love—"

Her words trailed off, not because she finished, but because no one was listening. Another figure spoke over her, then another. Statements overlapped, collided, evaporated.

Arthur cleared his throat.

"Excuse me," he said.

No response.

He raised his voice.

"HELLO."

Several heads turned—almost. Their blank eyes flicked past him, through him, to something just beyond. Notifications, perhaps. Arthur waved a hand.

"Is anyone actually here?" he asked.

A man-shaped outline drifted closer, nodded enthusiastically, and spoke.

"Absolutely. Totally. I hear you."

Arthur felt a flicker of relief.

"Good," Arthur said. "Because I—"

"Talk later—"

The figure drifted past him mid-sentence, already speaking to someone else.

Arthur stopped.

"Oh," he said softly. "Hmmm."

He walked on.

Everywhere he went, the same thing happened. People spoke endlessly, passionately, urgently—about themselves, about their opinions, about their pain, their triumphs, their breakfast. But no exchanges were completed. No sentences landed. No eyes met.

Sound existed without response.

Movement without recognition.

Arthur watched two figures collide gently, apologize simultaneously, then drift apart without ever looking at one another.

It was like watching a dance choreographed by loneliness.

Arthur tried again.

He approached a cluster of younger silhouettes, their outlines sharper, more luminous.

"Hey," he said. "You. Yes, you."

One turned.

"Hey!" the figure said brightly. "Love your energy."

Arthur waited.

"And?" he prompted.

"And nothing," the figure replied, already turning away. "Just wanted to say something."

Arthur sighed.

"This place," he muttered, "is exhausting."

He looked down at his hands. They appeared normal enough—old, spotted, faintly trembling. Real. He flexed his fingers just to be sure.

At least I still exist, he thought.

The ground beneath him rippled. A series of glowing symbols rose briefly, then sank back down.

Arthur frowned.

"Is this a floor," he asked no one, "or an opinion?"

He walked farther, hoping—foolishly—for an edge. A boundary. Something to push against.

There was none.

The Hollow Network went on forever.

Everywhere: voices. Everywhere: faces. Nowhere: presence.

Arthur felt something unfamiliar tighten in his chest.

"I should've stayed awake," he said.

He tried speaking louder, sharper.

"HEY," he barked. "ANYONE WANT TO TALK ABOUT SOMETHING REAL?"

Several figures turned.

"Yes!" one cried. "Absolutely!"

"What would you like to discuss?" another asked.

Arthur opened his mouth.

Before he could answer, the figures dissolved into separate conversations, their enthusiasm redistributed elsewhere.

Arthur laughed, a dry, humorless sound.

"Well played," he told the universe. "You finally built hell without fire."

He sat down—or something like sitting. The ground adjusted, accommodating him without warmth.

He watched the endless crowd.

They were never alone. And none of them were together.

Arthur felt the realization settle in, heavy and unavoidable: This was what David was reaching for.

Not connection.

Avoidance.

Arthur stood abruptly.

"No," he said. "I'm done."

He closed his eyes.

The Hollow Network resisted, gently but firmly, like a pop-up window asking if he was sure.

"Yes," Arthur snapped. "I'm sure."

The world lurched.

And then—

The bar.

The Great Beyond.

Arthur reappeared on a barstool that seemed deeply uninterested in human comfort. The counter glowed faintly, ultraviolet and clean, like grief had been sterilized.

Near him, the observation window revealed nothing but deep space—honest, indifferent, magnificent.

Iris was there.

She always was.

She stood behind the counter, her plum-colored skin shimmering softly, her many eyes blinking in a pattern Arthur suspected was concern. She polished a glass that held a small, rotating nebula like a trapped thought.

"You look displeased," she chimed gently.

Arthur dragged a hand down his face.

"I just visited a nightmare," he said.

Iris waited.

"People interacting," Arthur explained, "in the most shallow ways imaginable."

Iris tilted her head. She had several ways of tilting it, which seemed unfair.

"Ah," she said. "The Hollow Network."

"You know it?" Arthur asked.

"We keep records of human inventions," Iris said. "Some of them end up talking to themselves forever."

Arthur snorted.

"That place," he said, "is packed with people talking."

He paused.

"Nobody listening."

Iris's eyes softened a little.

"Yes," she said. "They confuse expression for communion."

Arthur leaned forward.

"They're all there together," he said. "And every one of them is alone."

Iris placed a steaming cup before him. The steam curled upward in colors Arthur didn't have names for.

"You keep visiting worlds that resemble your own," she said.

Not accusation.

Diagnosis.

Arthur wrapped his hands around the cup. The warmth startled him.

"That's unfair," he muttered.

Iris made a sound like distant bells underwater.

"The universe," she said, "is not concerned with fairness."

Arthur took a sip. The drink tasted like memory and heat and something earned.

"I don't want that world," he said quietly.

Iris watched him with all her eyes.

"Then stop mistaking noise for closeness," she replied.

Arthur sighed.

"You'd think," he said, "with all that technology, they could invent a decent conversation."

Iris smiled. It was the kind of smile that suggested she had watched entire civilizations try very hard and fail anyway.

"They already have," Iris said. "It's called listening. But it's a separate app that nobody installs."

Arthur blinked.

"That explains a lot," he said.

"People prefer apps that make them louder," she added.

Arthur finished the cup.

Outside, the stars burned steadily, asking nothing, promising nothing.

Arthur closed his eyes again.

When he woke, he was back in Sunny Meadows.

David was still there.

The television was still talking.

The soup was still cold.

But Arthur looked at David a little longer this time.

And said nothing at all.

Which, in a world full of noise, was almost an act of love.

Chapter 8

Late afternoon at Sunny Meadows is when even time gets drowsy.

The light slants through the tall dining hall windows as if it has somewhere better to be but feels obligated to stop in. Dust motes drift in the beams like unpaid actors in a production called Aging: The Musical. Nobody applauds them. Nobody ever does.

David sat across from Arthur, and between them sat two bowls of tomato soup performing the slow, dignified suicide of lukewarmness. Steam had given up while the surface had formed a thin orange skin. The soup was cooling the way grand ambitions do—gradually, without drama.

Margaret's chair was empty.

It had been for some time now.

But Arthur still felt the emptiness. He didn't comment. He simply cataloged it, the way he used to catalog hairline fractures in metal parts that weren't broken yet but would be.

David cleared his throat, which is what people do when they hope sound will substitute for meaning.

"Traffic was awful," David said.

Arthur nodded once.

"There's construction on Route 9. Again."

Arthur nodded again.

"I started a podcast," David continued. "It's about ancient civilizations and productivity hacks."

Arthur looked up. "What's a podcast?"

David blinked. He had expected resistance.

"It's like radio," he said, "except no one owns a radio anymore, and nobody agrees on what a show is, and instead of music I explain things to strangers."

Arthur squinted. "That sounds like a punishment."

"It's digital," David added helpfully. "You download it onto your phone."

Arthur looked around the room. "And why would anyone want to do that?"

"So, they can listen whenever they want."

"Listen to what?"

"To me," David said. "Explaining about things that may interest them."

Arthur stared at him for a long, steady moment. He had once run a lathe that could shave a thousandth of an inch off hardened steel, a machine that demanded precision and gave back something tangible for the effort. Now, across from him sat a man who shaped nothing at all, instead, sending his voice out into the air and hoping strangers would download it. Arthur had never tried to download anything, and he suspected it was because he preferred real things he could hold in his hands.

"And what's this thing gonna be about? You said . . . something about productivity hacks . . . from ancient civilizations?"

"Not exactly. It's just . . . well . . . I'll compare Roman infrastructure to modern leadership principles."

Arthur blinked twice. "If Julius Caesar had listened to podcasts, he'd have begged Brutus to stab him."

David smiled weakly. He stirred his soup as if agitation might restore warmth.

"It's consistent, at least," David offered. "The soup."

Arthur lifted his spoon, examined the tomato surface as though expecting to see his reflection disappointed in him.

"So is gravity," Arthur said. "That doesn't mean I like it."

They fell into silence.

David had begun to suspect that all his conversations with Arthur followed the same architectural blueprint: they started simply enough, always wandered briefly through sarcasm, and then collapsed gently into soup. They went nowhere. They solved nothing. In fact, if the exchanges were startups, they would have failed in the first quarter.

And yet, Arthur was there every day, with his opinions sharpened to a practical edge, conceding absolutely nothing. The conversations never changed his mind. Didn't improve him. Didn't optimize a single thing. They mostly bounced off him and rolled under the furniture.

Still, Arthur was there. He ate. He listened. He argued. Which, if you think about it, is about as much as anyone can promise.

David began to suspect that what kept Arthur going wasn't efficiency but friction—the pleasant scrape of disagreement, the proof that the world still pushed back. A man could starve on agreement. Agreement was pudding. Disagreement had bones in it.

Arthur sipped his soup. "You're thinking too loud," he said.

David blinked. "Sorry."

"That's all right," Arthur replied. "It's good exercise for you."

And there it was: another entirely unproductive exchange, accomplishing absolutely nothing measurable—except, possibly, the small miracle of two people still bothering to talk.

David decided to start over.

"How are you feeling today?"

"Like I'm being slowly refrigerated from the inside out."

"That bad?"

Arthur gestured at the bowl. "This isn't soup. It's a metaphor."

"For what?"

"For inevitability."

David took a tentative sip and immediately regretted participating in symbolism.

Across the room, someone coughed. Someone else laughed at something that hadn't been funny for decades but still deserved its moment.

Margaret's chair remained empty.

Arthur glanced at it again.

"Your mother," he said casually. "I miss her."

"Me too," David sadly replied.

Arthur grunted. "It's the big nap, kid."

David nodded.

Arthur sighed. "She's resting peacefully."

The conversation between David and Arthur performed its usual migratory pattern, wandering off into the weeds and then, against all odds, flapping its way back to David's podcast—the great digital campfire around which no one actually sat. David had been attempting, for the better part of ten minutes, to explain what a podcast was without using the words internet, platform, or engagement, because Arthur treated those words the way medieval villagers treated comets. Now David found himself once again defending the invisible radio show he broadcast into the void, which he privately hoped was friendlier than it sounded.

"It's about productivity," David said, stirring soup that didn't resist. "I'm going to tell the listeners how they can optimize their week."

Arthur looked at him as though David had confessed to collecting damp cardboard.

"Optimize," Arthur repeated. "For what? Faster soup?"

David sighed, but he did it with the patience of someone who has read three leadership books and survived. "You know what I mean."

"I do," Arthur said. "That's the problem."

They sat there with their bowls of cold soup. The dining hall hummed softly—refrigerators, distant silverware, the gentle wheeze of institutional air-conditioning that was barely alive.

Arthur's eyes drifted to the empty chair.

And then, very strangely, Margaret arrived.

At least, Arthur saw her arrive.

She moved toward the table in a way that wasn't quite walking. She seemed to glide, as though the floor had decided to assist her. She looked like herself—gentle eyes, the expression of someone who had forgiven the universe long ago—but she was faint at the edges, like a painting the artist hadn't finished because his inspiration had fizzled.

She sat in the empty chair.

Arthur didn't gasp. He didn't announce it. He simply acted as if she had always been there.

"Well," she said warmly, "did I miss the thrilling portion of tomato hour?"

Arthur's face softened so subtly that only a trained grief specialist or a suspicious son might've noticed.

"Just in time," he muttered.

He slid his bowl toward her. Then his spoon.

"Here, my dear."

David blinked.

Arthur had never voluntarily surrendered soup before. It violated several internal policies.

Margaret smiled at Arthur as though he had just handed her a bouquet instead of institutional regret.

"You look good," she told him.

Arthur straightened slightly. "I do not."

"You do," she insisted. "Has David been taking good care of you?"

David, who had been watching Arthur talk enthusiastically to empty air, frowned. "What are you doing?" he asked.

Margaret dipped the spoon delicately into the cold soup and took a sip.

"Oh," she said pleasantly. "It's lovely."

Arthur nodded solemnly. "Best batch yet."

David stared at him.

"Who are you talking to?" he asked.

Margaret turned toward David. "How is work, dear?"

Arthur answered immediately.

"He's doing something called optimizing," Arthur said. "He shepherds people he can't see or even talk to through those spreadsheet things. He does something he calls a podcast and talks about it."

Margaret beamed. "That's wonderful. He's doing great."

David looked around the dining hall as if someone else might be in on the joke.

"Arthur," David said carefully, "are you okay?"

Arthur waved him off. "Don't interrupt."

Margaret leaned toward Arthur conspiratorially. "He looks tired."

"He's tired," Arthur agreed. "He reads articles about loneliness like they're instruction manuals."

David's jaw tightened. "Arthur," he said. "Stop it."

Margaret placed her faint, almost-there hand over Arthur's wrist.

"Be kind," she said softly.

Arthur's mouth twitched.

"I'll do my best," Arthur muttered. "But I make no promises."

David stood slightly, half rising from his chair.

"Arthur, you're worrying me," he said more firmly now, "Mom's not here."

Arthur looked annoyed.

"Of course she's here," he said. "She's right—"

He turned.

The chair was empty.

The soup bowl sat untouched. His bowl. The spoon lay where he had placed it. There was no extra indentation in the vinyl seat. No faint outline. No gliding entrance. Just air.

David swallowed.

Arthur stared at the chair as though it had betrayed him.

"She was just—" Arthur began.

"Arthur," David said gently, but not too gently, because gentleness can sometimes sound like pity, and Arthur was allergic to pity. "You were talking to yourself."

Arthur's eyes hardened.

"I was not."

"You were," David said.

Around them, other residents chewed. A fork clinked against ceramic. Somewhere, a television announced the weather report that no one cared about anymore.

Arthur leaned back slowly.

"You chased her off," he said.

David blinked. "What?"

"She was sitting right there," Arthur snapped. "She told me I looked good. Dammit, you and your optimizing."

David felt the heat rise in his face.

"Arthur, she's . . . taking the big nap. Remember?"

Arthur's jaw worked.

For a brief, flickering second, the old machinist's certainty wavered. Reality, like soup, cooled quickly when left unattended.

He looked at the chair again.

He looked at his single bowl.

He looked at David.

"She said the soup was lovely," Arthur muttered.

David inhaled slowly.

"It's cold," he said.

Arthur glanced down into the bowl.

Yes. Cold. As he had always observed.

He sat there very still.

It would have been dramatic if he had wept. He did not. Arthur Trent didn't weep in public. He processed.

"Well," he said finally, voice lower now, "maybe I'm tired."

David exhaled.

"Yeah," David said. "Maybe."

Arthur nodded once, as if accepting a diagnosis he had issued himself.

"Imagining things," Arthur said. "That's all. Sometimes the mind wanders off. Does things unexpected."

"It happens," David replied. "Happens to all of us."

Arthur shot him a look.

"Not to me," he said reflexively.

David almost smiled.

Arthur looked again at the empty chair. It remained stubbornly unoccupied.

"She told me you were doing great," Arthur said quietly.

David hesitated. "She did?"

Arthur squinted at him.

David felt something twist in his chest that had nothing to do with tomato products.

There are moments in life when a hallucination is kinder than a fact. This was one of them.

Arthur pushed the bowl back toward himself and looked at it.

"Maybe I'll go lie down," he said.

"Do you need help?" David asked.

Arthur bristled immediately, which was reassuring. Bristling meant structural integrity remained intact.

"No," Arthur said. "I've been walking since . . . whenever."

David nodded.

Arthur stood carefully, gripping his walker—the one with the glued-on googly eyes that still wobbled accusingly at the world.

"Maybe I'll see Margaret along the way," Arthur added, not looking at David.

David's throat tightened, but he kept his voice even.

"Maybe," he said.

Arthur took a few steps. The dining hall lights hummed in bureaucratic indifference.

"See you tomorrow," David called after him.

Arthur paused but didn't turn around.

"Unless I'm taking the big nap," he said.

It wasn't theatrical. It was arithmetic.

David forced a smile anyway.

"Tomorrow," he repeated.

Arthur shuffled down the hallway with his walker, the googly eyes bobbing with each step like deranged optimism.

The chair remained empty.

David sat back down slowly.

He stared at the bowl of soup. He lifted the spoon. He tasted it.

It was cold.

Of course it was.

He looked at the empty chair across from him and imagined, for a moment, what it must have been like to see someone there who wasn't. To have them compliment the soup. To be told you were doing great. To be asked whether you were taking proper care of a crusty old man.

It occurred to David that Arthur's imagination hadn't produced something absurd.

It had produced warmth.

David set the spoon down.

Around him, conversations drifted in fragments. Repeated stories. Repeated jokes. Repeated complaints.

Time shared. Nothing optimized.

Arthur reached the end of the hallway and paused, just for a second, by a water fountain.

He half expected Margaret to be there, waiting for him, gliding faintly.

She was not.

Arthur adjusted his grip on the walker. Tighter.

"Well," he muttered to no one in particular, "could be worse."

He entered his room.

Behind him, in the dining hall, David remained seated a little longer than necessary.

The soup cooled further.

Arthur Trent lay down on his narrow institutional bed as if surrendering to a referee no one else could see.

The mattress was thin. The pillow was ambitious but ineffective. The room smelled faintly of disinfectant and something that had once aspired to be lavender. His walker with the glued-on googly eyes stood by the wall, staring at him with plastic astonishment.

He folded his hands over his chest, which is something people do when they are either very tired or very dead. Arthur was only the first.

He thought about Margaret.

He thought about the way she had looked—almost finished, but not quite. Like an abandoned painting. He thought about how she said he looked good, how David was doing great, and how she'd called the soup lovely.

"Spiritually cold," he muttered to the ceiling. "That's what it is."

He closed his eyes.

The hum of Sunny Meadows flattened into a single note, like a held breath. The fluorescent lights dissolved. The faint clatter of dinner trays slipped sideways.

Arthur dozed.

And then he was elsewhere.

He stood on a planet composed entirely of tables.

Long banquet tables stretched toward horizons that refused to commit to distance. Small café tables hovered gently in low gravity, rotating just enough to suggest intimacy. Kitchen tables—scarred, square, stubborn—sat in clusters like continents. Picnic tables floated in open space, their benches occupied by beings of shapes and species not approved by earthly zoning laws.

At every table, two or more figures sat facing one another.

They talked.

That was all.

No empires rising or falling. No engines running on hydrogen. No crafts with googly eyes. No cold soup.

Just conversation.

Arthur blinked.

"Well," he said to no one in particular, "this is underwhelming."

A pair of blue-skinned creatures at a nearby table were engaged in what appeared to be a disagreement about whether something had happened on a Thursday or a Friday. They had been at it for some time. Arthur could tell by the way they repeated themselves with growing fondness.

"I told you," said one.

"And I told you," said the other.

They smiled while arguing.

Arthur shuffled past them.

At another table, a woman with three translucent arms was telling a story. She'd clearly told it before. She paused in familiar places. The listener nodded at the correct intervals, like a man applauding a symphony he'd heard several times before.

"And then," she said again, "I dropped the entire tray."

The listener laughed.

Not because it was new. They'd heard the story before.

Because it was theirs.

Arthur squinted.

"No one's in a hurry," he observed.

They weren't. No one checked a device. No one glanced over a shoulder. No one stood up mid-sentence to optimize anything.

Time lay on the planet like a lazy dog.

Arthur walked farther.

At one table, silence stretched between two figures. Not uncomfortable silence. Not strategic silence. Just . . . shared quiet.

They sipped something warm.

Arthur frowned at that.

"Don't you have anything better to do?" he asked them.

They looked up at him with mild curiosity.

"We are doing it," one replied.

Arthur opened his mouth, then closed it.

He continued walking.

The planet didn't have buildings or cities. Only arrangements of tables with facing chairs. The entire world was organized around the radical notion that two beings might look at one another and stay.

Arthur wandered around for a bit and then found a table with two empty chairs.

He approached cautiously.

He sat.

Across from him, the other chair filled.

Not with Margaret.

Instead, it was David.

Or something David-shaped. Not quite the right age. Not quite the right weariness. But close enough.

Arthur leaned back.

"You're not real," he said.

"Neither are you," the David-shaped being replied pleasantly.

Arthur grunted.

They sat there.

Nothing happened.

No punchline. No crisis.

The David-shaped being rested his hands on the table.

Arthur tapped his fingers.

"So," Arthur said finally, because silence has a way of forcing even the crustiest men into action, "weather's been consistent."

The David-shaped being nodded. "So's been gravity."

Arthur's mouth twitched.

"That doesn't mean I like it."

He had heard all this before.

They both looked down at the table.

The surface was worn smooth by repetition.

Arthur realized something alarming: he didn't feel bored.

He felt . . . steady.

At nearby tables, the same discussion cycled like old records. The same jokes landed again and again. Stories repeated. Arguments offered. Corrections offered. Corrections ignored.

Nothing progressed.

Everything accumulated.

Arthur leaned forward.

"What powers this place?" he asked.

The David-shaped being shrugged.

"Time," he said. "It's given. Free of charge."

Arthur sat back.

"That's it? No currency? No productivity reports?"

"No metrics," said the being. "Just presence."

Arthur narrowed his eyes.

"What's the catch?"

The being smiled in an uncomfortably familiar way.

"It ends."

Arthur blinked.

And just like that, the planet of tables dissolved.

He found himself perched once more on a barstool that was never designed for an eighty-four-year-old human spine.

The Great Beyond shimmered around him.

The bar was carved from something that resembled frozen auroras. A panoramic viewport revealed deep space—vast, indifferent, glittering like a shrug.

Iris stood behind the counter.

Star-Eyes.

Her plum-colored skin shifted in soft luminescence. Her many galaxy-like eyes blinked in elegant sequence. Seven delicate, suction-tipped fingers polished a glass containing a small, rotating nebula.

She regarded him.

"You visited the Tables," she chimed, her voice like wind through crystal.

Arthur swung his legs slightly, testing gravity. It cooperated.

"Nothing was happening," he said.

"Everything was happening," Iris replied gently.

Arthur snorted.

"They were just talking."

"Yes."

"Repeating themselves."

"Yes."

"Arguing about Thursdays."

She tilted her head, constellations rearranging across her gaze.

"They were choosing to remain."

Arthur folded his arms.

"Doesn't sound efficient."

Iris's expression held something ancient and amused.

"Efficiency is for systems," she said. "Not for souls."

Arthur scowled at the word.

"Don't start."

She slid a drink toward him.

It steamed faintly. The vapor rose in unfamiliar colors—soft golds and muted blues. The cup warmed his palms immediately, as if it recognized him.

"This world," she said, "runs on time people give away on purpose."

She shrugged.

"You can't save it. You can't optimize it."

She nodded at the cup.

"You just spend it."

Arthur sniffed the drink.

"Smells like nothing."

"It smells like being here," she said.

Arthur took a sip.

It was warm.

Not flashy. Not burning like a friendly star. Just warm.

He looked out at the void beyond the viewport.

"So that's the grand cosmic secret?" he asked. "Sit at a table. Repeat yourself. Don't leave."

Iris's many eyes softened.

"Yes."

Arthur watched a pair of translucent passengers drift past the bar, arguing telepathically about something trivial. They didn't separate. They circled one another like patient moons.

"Time," Arthur muttered. "It ends."

"It always ends," Iris said. "That is why it matters."

Arthur stared into his cup.

He thought about Margaret's empty chair.

He thought about sliding his bowl toward her.

He thought about David sitting across from him, trying to make small talk about podcasts and traffic, as if traffic were a legitimate existential concern.

He exhaled.

"Kid keeps showing up," Arthur said.

"Yes."

"Doesn't say anything useful."

"Usefulness is overrated," Iris chimed.

Arthur glanced at her.

"You're awfully sentimental for someone who's witnessed the rise and fall of galaxies."

"All moments exist simultaneously," she said. "But attention does not. Attention is rare."

Arthur rolled the cup between his palms.

On the planet of tables, two beings had laughed at a joke they'd heard before.

He found that image unreasonably moving.

Outside the viewport, a distant sun collapsed silently into itself.

No one applauded.

Arthur finished the drink.

He set the cup down.

"So," he said, "cold soup isn't the worst thing."

Iris waited.

He cleared his throat.

"Not if someone's sitting across from you."

Her eyes shimmered, galaxies rearranging in quiet approval.

"Yes," she said softly. "That's correct."

The bar hummed. The universe expanded. Conversations continued somewhere on a planet made entirely of tables.

Arthur felt the warmth fade from the cup.

He closed his eyes.

And somewhere back in Sunny Meadows, in a narrow bed under humming lights, an old machinist slept—hands folded, walker waiting—while time, that stubborn currency, continued to be spent.

Chapter 9

The morning began with the sort of enthusiasm that should have required a permit.

Nurse Kelly entered the common room carrying a wicker basket swollen with yarn the color of unearned optimism—sunflower yellow, coral that looked like it had forgiven someone, and a blue so sincere it might've voted twice. She set the basket down on the coffee table as if unveiling a cure for mortality.

"Good morning, creators!" she sang.

Arthur, constitutionally suspicious of cheer, lowered his newspaper. The headline concerned international tensions. He preferred those. They behaved predictably.

"Creator," Arthur repeated. "That's what they call people now when they don't make anything anyone needs."

David sat across from him, cradling a paper cup of coffee as if it might confess something under pressure.

"How's the coffee?" Arthur asked.

David took a careful sip. "Tastes like it was brewed during the Mesolithic period."

Arthur shook his head solemnly. "Can't be from the Mesolithic period."

"Oh?" David said. "How do you know?"

"Because I lived through it," Arthur said. "We only had tea."

There was a pause while this historical revision settled over the table. Then they both chuckled, which is what human beings do when the alternative is acknowledging they are drinking prehistoric bean water in a room that smells faintly of disinfectant.

Nurse Kelly clapped once. "Today we're trying knitting!"

A murmur drifted from the other residents—half curiosity, half surrender. A man named Leonard applauded for reasons unknown. He often applauded the concept of time, Arthur once said.

Arthur folded his newspaper with the care of a retired machinist handling a blueprint.

"Knitting," he said, as though diagnosing it. "You want me to manufacture scarves."

"It's relaxing," Nurse Kelly replied. "It lowers blood pressure and improves cognitive engagement."

"My blood pressure is fine," Arthur said. "It's the world's that concerns me."

David smirked. "You could make something for winter."

"I've made it this far without yarn," he said.

He paused.

"Also, without most of my dignity, but that's another story."

Nurse Kelly distributed knitting needles with missionary determination. She placed a pair in Arthur's hands. He held them as if they were delicate surgical tools and he hadn't scrubbed in.

"I spent forty years machining steel to tolerances thinner than a politician's conscience," Arthur announced. "Now you want me to crochet something."

"Not crochet," Kelly corrected gently. "Knitting."

"Same difference," Arthur muttered.

David leaned forward, elbows on his knees. "It might be good for you, Art."

Arthur narrowed his eyes. "That's what they said about margarine."

Kelly demonstrated a stitch. Yarn looped over needle. Needle slid through loop. Pull tight. Repeat. It was hypnotic in the way bureaucracies are hypnotic.

"See?" she said. "In and out. Over and through."

Arthur attempted the maneuver. The result resembled a small maritime accident.

"It looks like you've tied a noose for a hamster," David observed.

Arthur didn't look up. "If the hamster has embraced capitalism, he deserves it."

A few residents chuckled. Laughter in nursing homes is a fragile currency that must be spent quickly before someone forgets the joke.

Kelly beamed. "The point isn't perfection. The point is enjoyment."

Arthur paused.

There it was—the modern heresy.

Enjoyment.

He squinted at the yarn as if it might explain itself.

"When did hobbies," he began, "become assignments?"

David perked up. He sensed a speech. Arthur's speeches were better than cable.

Kelly blinked. "It's not an assignment."

"Yes, it is," Arthur insisted. "You can't just sit anymore. Sitting isn't enough. You have to be 'engaged.' You have to 'cultivate.' You have to 'learn.'"

Leonard applauded again.

David shrugged. "What's wrong with staying busy?"

Arthur looked at him as if he'd just confessed to juggling live grenades.

"Busy," Arthur said slowly, "is what ants are."

Kelly tilted her head. "Is that bad?"

"It depends," Arthur replied. "Are you building a colony or just avoiding your own thoughts?"

The room quieted a little.

Even Leonard stopped applauding.

David crossed his arms. "People like hobbies."

"No," Arthur said. "What people like is not feeling useless."

Kelly tried again. "Knitting can be meditative."

"I don't want to meditate," Arthur snapped. "I want my soup hot."

There it was. The thesis statement of his existence.

Right on cue, a cart rattled faintly in the hallway.

David laughed. "It's not even lunchtime."

"Time is a circle in here," Arthur replied. "Soup is inevitable."

Kelly leaned closer, lowering her voice conspiratorially. "Arthur, you used to build things. This is just a softer material."

Arthur held up the tangled yarn. "Steel doesn't tangle."

"Steel rusts," she countered gently.

Arthur blinked.

That had been clever.

David grinned. "She got you."

Arthur harrumphed and returned to the yarn. He made another stitch. It wasn't entirely catastrophic.

"Fine," he said. "But I'm not selling it."

"No one asked you to," Kelly replied.

"That's how it starts," Arthur said darkly. "First, it's for fun. Then someone says, 'You should monetize that.' Then you're working again."

David laughed. "You think there's a black market for nursing home scarves?"

"There's a market for everything," Arthur said. "Including scarves made by old farts in nursing homes."

Kelly handed David a pair of needles. "You too."

David hesitated. "I've never—"

"Exactly," Kelly said.

David took the needles like a man signing up for a minor war. He fumbled immediately.

Arthur glanced at him sideways. "You Google how to knit yet?"

"Not yet," David said. "But I could."

"Of course you could," Arthur replied. "You can Google how to breathe."

David looped the yarn incorrectly. It slipped off the needle and collapsed into his lap.

"This is harder than it looks," he admitted.

"Nothing that matters is easy," Arthur said, surprising himself.

Kelly smiled faintly. "That's almost inspirational."

"Don't get used to it," Arthur warned.

Around them, other residents stitched in varying states of confusion. Yarn pooled like spilled thoughts. The room hummed with small efforts.

David studied his hands. "You know," he said carefully, "people take hobbies seriously now. They optimize them. Track progress. Build followings."

Arthur groaned. "Of course they do."

"It gives people identity," David continued. "My friend runs marathons and documents all of it. Another one bakes bread and posts every loaf."

Arthur looked up. "And do they enjoy it?"

"I think so."

Arthur nodded slowly. "Until someone counts it."

David frowned. "Counts it?"

"Likes," Arthur said. "Followers. Revenue. Comparison. You taught me all that lingo. Just remember, the moment someone measures joy, it dies."

Kelly pretended not to hear that.

David considered this. "You think hobbies are supposed to be pointless."

"I think pointless is the point," Arthur replied. "If it has a purpose beyond itself, it's work."

David smirked. "You just don't like modern life."

"Not true," Arthur said. "I loved modern life. When it stopped at television."

The soup cart rolled into the room as if summoned by some god.

"Lunch, everyone!" called a kitchen aide whose name changed weekly in Arthur's mind.

David looked at his watch.

"It's really not lunch yet," he said.

Arthur simply shrugged.

Bowls were distributed.

Steam didn't accompany them.

Arthur stared into the tomato-colored abyss.

"Behold," he said solemnly, "the hobby of disappointment."

David lifted his spoon and winced. "It's barely warm."

Arthur didn't touch his. "They must refrigerate it for sport."

Kelly, unfazed, sat down beside them with her own bowl. "It's fortified."

"With what?" Arthur asked.

"Good things," Kelly smiled. "Things you need."

Arthur grumbled.

David tasted it and made a face. "It's consistent."

"We've been through this before," Arthur said. "So is gravity. Doesn't mean I like it."

Kelly laughed despite herself.

Arthur gestured at the yarn. "See, this is how it happens. They keep you busy so you don't notice the soup."

David swallowed carefully. "You think knitting is a conspiracy."

"I think distraction is."

Kelly folded her hands. "Or maybe it's kindness."

Arthur looked at her.

She didn't flinch.

He softened—barely.

"Maybe," he conceded. "But don't turn it into a side hustle."

"You mean no Etsy store?" David teased.

"Don't know what that is," Arthur said, "But if I see one dollar, I burn the scarf."

Leonard applauded that.

David tried another stitch. It held.

"Look," he said, almost proud.

Arthur examined it. "Crooked."

"Thanks."

"But functional," Arthur added.

David smiled. "High praise."

Arthur dipped his spoon into the soup at last. He lifted it, inspected it like a defective part, and let it fall back with a plop.

"You know what the problem is?" he said.

Kelly braced.

David leaned in.

Arthur said, "We can't just do something anymore. We have to justify it."

Silence lingered.

Even the soup seemed to listen.

Kelly spoke softly. "Maybe we justify it because we're afraid it doesn't matter."

Arthur looked at her again. This time longer.

"Nothing ever matters," he said.

David blinked.

Kelly blinked.

Arthur pushed the bowl away exactly two inches.

"Now," he said, lifting his needles, "show me how to make these things useless."

Kelly smiled.

David laughed.

Arthur made another stitch—crooked, unnecessary, gloriously pointless.

And for now, no one tried to sell it.

By the time the clock in the common room suggested it might still be morning—which was a generous interpretation of events—the place looked as though a flock of technicolor spiders had unionized and negotiated an excellent health plan.

Yarn dangled from walkers like festive seaweed. It looped around chair legs in what could only be described as premeditated affection. It had even entered into a nonaggression pact with a potted fern that had survived three administrations, two overwaterings, and one brief but meaningful fungal uprising.

It was Craft Hour.

In America, when you do not know what to do with people, you give them yarn.

Arthur held up the six crooked stitches he'd produced and examined them as though they were counterfeit currency. They sagged in the middle like a tired smile from a politician who'd just promised infrastructure.

"This," he announced to the room and possibly to history, "is what happens when you industrialize leisure."

David leaned back in his chair. He had the eyes of a man who tried to believe in synergy but found it difficult, at times.

"You keep saying that like it's a thing," David said.

"It is a thing," Arthur replied. "Everything is a thing now. That's the problem. We used to have activities. Now we have verticals."

David blinked. "What are verticals?"

Arthur lowered the knitting needles as though preparing to explain gravity to a goldfish.

"Verticals," he said, "are what happen when someone takes a perfectly innocent hobby and stands it up in one of those fancy presentation thingies."

"Presentation thingy?" David asked. Then he had a thought. "Oh, you mean PowerPoint?"

"Exactly," Arthur continued, "You see, when I was young, a man fished because he wanted to sit by water and think about nothing. Now he has a fishing vertical. There are numbers for everything. There are growth opportunities. There's a podcast."

David shifted in his chair.

"A woman used to bake because she liked the smell of bread," Arthur went on. "Now she has an artisanal baked-goods vertical. She has brand pillars. She has engagement targets. She has an apron that says Founder."

"So, it's just business?" David offered.

"No," Arthur said sharply. "It's worse. It's business pretending to be life."

He held up the lopsided fabric again.

"This was supposed to be knitting. Quiet. Useless. Possibly warm. But now there are tutorials, optimization techniques, and knitting communities with quarterly objectives. Leisure has deliverables."

David rubbed his temple. "That's not all bad."

Arthur looked at him with the deep disappointment of a man who'd once trusted weather forecasts.

"Of course, it's not all bad. Neither is a mild fever. But if you organize every corner of existence into upward-trending columns, you forget that most good things lie flat."

"Lie flat?"

"Yes. Naps. Conversations. Dogs. Rivers. They don't scale. That's their charm."

David stared at the crooked stitches.

"So, a vertical," he said carefully, "is when you turn something sideways into something upright?"

Arthur smiled, which was rare and therefore expensive.

"A vertical," he said, "is when you take something that used to be done for no reason and give it a reason it never asked for."

Nurse Kelly hovered nearby with the hopeful posture of someone who believed in redemption through craft supplies and laminated schedules. She had the optimism of a person who hadn't yet been defeated by tomato bisque.

"No one is industrializing anything," she said. "We're just passing time."

Arthur turned to her slowly, as if rotating on a showroom platform.

"Time doesn't need passing," he said. "Time's perfectly capable of escaping on its own. It's been doing so for centuries without assistance."

Leonard applauded. He applauded once when someone sneezed. He applauded when the lights flickered. He might've applauded the end of Rome, had he been available.

David gestured at Arthur's knitting. "What happened? You were doing fine five minutes ago."

"I was experimenting," Arthur corrected. "Now I've confirmed my hypothesis. This is nonsense."

He lifted the lumpy row of yarn. It had the structural integrity of a congressional promise.

"You don't have to be good at it," David said gently.

Arthur stared at him.

"That's not the point. It's never about being good. It's about turning something harmless into something it's not supposed to be."

He set the needles down as if they might unionize next.

"'Ten Tips to Improve Your Knitting Efficiency.' 'Five Ways to Scale Your Hobby.' 'Disrupting Scarves in a Digital Age.'"

David laughed. "You read those?"

"I read everything," Arthur said. "That's how they get you."

In America, information is both a vitamin and a poison. Dosage is rarely discussed.

Nurse Kelly crouched to eye level. "Arthur, nobody here is scaling anything."

"Not yet," he muttered. "First comes yarn. Then comes branding."

The lunch cart squeaked in the hallway like a metal conscience. It was announcing the future.

David shook his head. "You don't think knitting is connected to the soup, do you?"

Arthur looked at him with pity.

"Everything is connected to the soup."

This wasn't entirely a metaphor. The soup had once been hot. Arthur remembered this clearly, as one remembers a first kiss or a reliable pension.

"Why does it bother you so much?" Nurse Kelly asked.

Arthur opened his mouth to deliver a lecture and found only dust.

"It starts innocent," he said at last.

He tapped the yarn, which didn't resist.

"You pick up a hobby because you like it. You waste time. You tinker. It's yours."

He paused.

"Then someone says, 'You're pretty good at that.'"

David nodded. "That's nice."

Arthur's eyes flashed. "Compliments are venture capital. Next comes expectation. Then obligation. Then a spreadsheet. Then a PowerPoint thingy."

He leaned back.

"I enjoyed machining," he said.

"And what happened?" David asked.

Arthur studied the ceiling tiles, which were arranged in a grid that suggested someone, somewhere, had once believed in order.

"I got good at it," Arthur said. "And then I wasn't a man who liked building things. I was a machinist. Then I was a retired machinist. Then I was an old machinist. And then—"

He gestured vaguely at the yarn.

"—I was a machinist without a machine."

Leonard didn't applaud.

"You see, a hobby," Arthur continued, "is the last thing that truly belongs only to you. And the moment you start thinking about what it's worth—"

"—it stops being worth it?" David finished.

Arthur nodded once.

David looked at what Arthur had knitted. It waited without ambition, without quarterly projections, without soup.

"It's not good," he told Arthur, pointing. "Kind of crooked here and here."

"You're suggesting," he said slowly, "that I knit badly and anonymously."

"Yes."

"And I should never do it again?"

"That would be lovely."

"And certainly not launch a brand?"

"Please don't."

Arthur considered this revolutionary proposal: to do something poorly and let it remain poor. To create without consequence. To waste time on purpose.

He picked up the needles again.

"Fine," he muttered. "This scarf dies here."

David grinned. "Deal."

Arthur made another stitch. It leaned. It wobbled. It would never be featured in a lifestyle magazine.

He frowned at it.

Then he made another.

Leonard applauded softly because he believed in beginnings.

Arthur didn't look up.

"But at least," he said quietly, as the yarn slipped through his fingers in a small, imperfect rebellion, "no one's counting the stitches."

For now, in a world that measured everything, that was a small and radical freedom.

"Arthur, you don't want your soup to get cold," Nurse Kelly said with a smile.

"It was born cold," he told her. "I'm just respecting its journey."

He put his needles down and peered into the bowl of reddish liquid as though consulting an oracle that had lost its funding.

"Ah," he said softly. "My hobby."

David blinked. "Your hobby?"

Arthur poked the surface with his spoon. The liquid trembled faintly, like a jelly reconsidering its life choices.

"If hobbies are pointless," Arthur said, "then soup is mine. I stir it. I critique it. I never improve it. I ask nothing of it. It asks nothing of me."

Kelly smiled the calm, professional smile of someone who had heard stranger ideas over a bowl of tomato soup and lived to tell the story.

She let Arthur's wisdom sit there.

Like soup cooling on the counter.

David gave another taste and winced. "Still cold."

Arthur nodded sagely. "Cold soup doesn't demand much, does it."

"It does require a microwave," David said.

Arthur ignored this heresy.

"You see, David, we're at a crossroad. We've decided every pleasant thing must justify itself. And it's destroying everything."

David stirred his soup slowly, as though hoping friction might generate warmth. It didn't.

"So, what do you suggest?" he asked.

Arthur shrugged. It was a small shrug, but it carried decades.

"It starts with one soul. Like you. Do something badly. Keep it to yourself. Let it remain small. Let it be terrible and unmonetized. And then do another. And another . . ."

"That's your advice?"

"That's my manifesto."

Leonard applauded. He didn't know why, but he felt it was appropriate.

David leaned in slightly. "You're saying I should fail at something?"

Arthur paused. He didn't enjoy being summarized.

"Yes," he said carefully. "But something you cannot score or measure."

This seemed to land somewhere inside David's overworked brain. He stared at his soup as though it might offer an answer, but it didn't.

"Not sure I understand," he told Arthur.

"There," Arthur started. "You just did it! Good start!"

The dining hall hummed with quiet chewing and the faint scrape of spoons against ceramic. It was the sound of humanity at half-volume. No one was building an audience. No one was live-streaming cold soup. No one was optimizing spoon technique.

Arthur lifted a spoonful of the soup and swallowed it with stoic dignity.

"Practicing," he said.

"Practicing what?" David asked.

"Pointlessness."

David laughed. Then he stopped laughing, because Arthur wasn't joking.

Arthur stirred his soup. The surface rippled obediently. In that small circular motion, there was no ambition, no KPI, no quarterly target. It was a private weather system.

"In America," Arthur said, "we cannot simply eat soup. We must experience the soup. We must rate the soup. We must share the soup. We must disrupt the soup."

David crossed his arms. "You're spiraling."

"I am orbiting," Arthur corrected.

He continued stirring. Stirring was soothing. It suggested control without consequence.

"You know what the worst part is?" he asked.

David, who had made the mistake of engaging, said, "What?"

"You start believing applause proves you exist."

David looked around the dining hall. No one was applauding the soup. Not even Leonard. This felt correct.

Arthur's stirring slowed.

"Once upon a time," he said, "a man could build a birdhouse and never tell anyone. The birds knew. That was enough."

Leonard clapped once, perhaps for the birds.

Then Arthur's chin dipped toward his chest.

He caught it mid-fall, startled. He straightened. Blinking. Indignant.

This happens at a certain age. One moment you're indicting civilization; the next, you are personally betrayed by gravity.

Arthur gripped his spoon like a man anchoring himself to the present. The room hummed. Someone coughed. A spoon clinked against a bowl.

He couldn't nap. Not mid-argument.

His eyelids lowered anyway, conducting their own quiet vote.

He lifted his head again. "I'm awake," he muttered, to no one in particular, which is how one knows the battle is nearly lost.

The fluorescent lights above flickered. Or perhaps they didn't. Perhaps his vision simply softened at the edges, as though the world were being politely erased.

The room wavered. Chairs thinned. The soup's red dulled into watercolor.

Arthur attempted one final act of defiance: he blinked very hard.

It did nothing.

The fluorescent lights above dissolved into starlight.

The dining hall flattened like a stage set being cleared between acts.

Arthur found himself standing beneath a sky crowded with applause.

Not metaphorical applause.

Actual clapping clouds.

Thunderous and rhythmic.

The sky itself was applauding something, though it was unclear what.

Before him stretched a planet shaped like a stage. Its surface shimmered with spotlights. Every inch of it was illuminated, as though darkness had been outlawed.

He looked down at his hands. No knitting needles. No soup. No spoon. No arthritis.

"Wonderful," he muttered. "I've died and gone to a theater."

Everywhere he looked, beings were performing hobbies.

One painted furiously, glancing up every few seconds to check a hovering scoreboard above their head. Numbers climbed and fell in luminous digits. Approval was quantified. Disapproval was color-coded.

Another strummed a guitar while adjusting their smile to maximize engagement metrics floating in the air like obedient ghosts.

Knitting circles existed too—thousands of them—each scarf accompanied by applause volume charts and real-time analytics. Yarn shimmered under stadium lights.

Arthur squinted. "You've got to be kidding me."

He turned, and as always, found himself at the bar aboard The Great Beyond.

Iris stood behind the counter, plum skin glowing softly. Her large breasts were as supple as pillows, and her many eyes regarded him with that ancient, simultaneous awareness that made him feel both seen and itemized.

"You've visited the Leisure World," she chimed gently.

"They've ruined knitting," Arthur muttered.

Iris poured a drink that shimmered like amber memory. It emitted a quiet warmth, the kind of warmth soup used to possess before it learned apathy.

"They mistake doing something for being in the moment," she said.

Arthur took the glass. It was warm. Blessedly warm. He held it longer than necessary.

"They think applause proves existence," Iris continued.

Arthur glanced back at the planet. The performers were smiling too hard. The applause never stopped, which made it less applause and more weather. A permanent climate of validation.

"So they've turned hobbies into jobs," he said.

"They've turned identity into output," Iris corrected.

Arthur snorted. "Same difference."

On the planet, a painter completed a canvas and bowed repeatedly to automated ovation. The scoreboard blinked: PERFORMANCE SATISFACTORY. ENGAGEMENT UP 2.3%.

The painter didn't look happy. The painter looked employed.

Arthur sipped. The drink tasted like quiet rooms and unfinished projects. It tasted like a shed behind a house that no longer existed.

"Tell me," he said, "does it ever end?"

Iris's constellation-eyes dimmed slightly.

"Only when they forget to look up."

Arthur looked up.

There were no stars above the Leisure World.

Only lights.

Stage lights.

Spotlights pointed downward.

No darkness. No sky. No unmeasured expanse.

Just illumination designed for display.

Arthur felt suddenly protective of his badly knitted scarf.

"They clap so much," he said, "that it stops meaning anything."

"Yes," Iris replied. "Applause without silence is noise."

A knitter on the planet held up a scarf. A digital banner flashed: TRENDING. The knitter's smile flickered as numbers dipped.

Arthur winced.

"They can't stop," he said.

"They fear stillness," Iris said gently. "Stillness doesn't applaud."

She continued. "Some pretend for applause. Others pretend they don't care.

Arthur took another sip.

"Which am I?" he asked.

Iris's eyes shimmered like distant galaxies negotiating.

"You care very much," she said. "You simply refuse the scoreboard."

Arthur looked back at the planet.

The applause thundered.

The performers bowed.

No one left.

"Being in the moment," Iris said softly, "is enough."

Arthur rolled the warm glass between his palms.

"That's not a popular philosophy," he said.

"Popularity," Iris replied, "is a metric."

He sighed.

On the planet, a musician hit a wrong note. The scoreboard dipped. The musician's face tightened. He corrected immediately. The crowd roared approval.

No one seemed relieved.

Arthur imagined standing there, knitting badly, refusing to check the numbers. He imagined holding up a lumpy knitted scarf and bowing to no one.

The thought felt radical.

"I'll keep my cold soup," he said finally.

Iris allowed herself something like a smile.

"An excellent idea."

The applause began to fade, not because it diminished, but because Arthur stopped listening.

The sky folded inward like a program concluding.

He felt himself tipping gently back toward Sunny Meadows, toward vinyl chairs and lukewarm meals and a basket of yarn he would pretend not to miss.

The fluorescent lights blinked back into existence.

The room hummed.

David was staring at him.

"You fell asleep," David said.

Arthur blinked. He looked down at his bowl. The soup hadn't improved.

He lifted his spoon and stirred once.

The surface trembled obediently.

Leonard applauded, softly, for reasons unknown.

Arthur tasted the soup. Still cold.

"Of course it is," he said.

David leaned forward. "What were you dreaming about?"

Arthur considered the Leisure World, the scoreboards, the endless clapping clouds.

"Professional knitters," he said.

David frowned. "That sounds terrifying."

"It was," Arthur replied.

He picked up his yarn from beside the bowl. It waited without ambition.

He made one crooked stitch.

Then another.

No one clapped.

The room didn't glow.

The soup remained indifferent.

Arthur felt, briefly and rebelliously, alive.

He stirred the soup again, not to improve it, not to fix it, not to optimize it, but simply to watch it move.

And in a universe increasingly devoted to measurement, that small, circular motion was an act of defiance.

Chapter 10

David didn't expect to find Arthur missing. Old men in nursing homes don't go far. They can't. They orbit coffee stations and television sets. They complain in predictable quadrants. They conserve fuel.

Arthur wasn't in the dining hall insulting oatmeal. He wasn't in the sunroom criticizing the angle of the sun. He wasn't in the garden sniffing at the roses like a critic with allergies. He wasn't in the hallway conducting quality control on the wallpaper, or in any of the other common areas.

Nurse Kelly, who had the optimism of someone who hadn't yet been defeated by cold soup, shrugged when David asked, "Where is Arthur?"

"He said he was busy," she chirped.

"Busy doing what?" David asked.

"You know Arthur," she said with a smile, and floated away. "Important old man stuff."

So, David went down the corridor toward Arthur's room, which always smelled faintly of industrial soap and something metallic, as though Arthur had smuggled in the ghost of a machine shop and hidden it in his sock drawer.

The door was ajar.

David knocked lightly on the frame. "Arthur?"

Inside, Arthur was hunched over the small laminate table by the window. The overhead light was off. Only sunlight filtered in, pale and suspicious. Before him sat a shoebox. Its lid lay discarded nearby like a surrendered helmet.

Arthur didn't look up.

He was turning photographs over one by one with the solemnity of a priest examining relics.

Dust rose gently from the box, catching in the light. It looked like a galaxy trying to assemble itself in slow motion.

"What's the excavation about?" David asked.

Arthur sniffed. "Trying to remember the past so I can forget it again."

David stepped inside and shut the door behind him. "That sounds healthy."

"It's efficient," Arthur corrected.

He lifted a photograph between two fingers, as if it might stain him. "You ever notice how the past weighs nothing and still manages to crush you?"

David pulled up the vinyl chair opposite him. It made the sort of noise that suggested it'd given up hope decades ago.

"What are those?" David asked, though he could see perfectly well.

"Photographs. From the era when cameras were honest, and people weren't," Arthur squinted at one. "This one's from '62. Or '63. Back when I had knees."

He slid it across the table.

David leaned forward.

In the picture, a young Arthur—lean, dark-haired, suspiciously handsome—stood beside a gleaming piece of machinery. He was smiling. Not smirking. Not grimacing. Smiling.

David looked up slowly. "You had that expression once?"

Arthur frowned. "That expression?"

"Happiness."

Arthur snatched the photo back. "That's not happiness. That's indigestion. I'd just had lunch."

"Looks like happiness to me. Maybe pride." He paused. "What was the machine?"

Arthur's jaw tightened almost imperceptibly. He placed the photograph in a small stack to his right.

"It was a lathe retrofit," he said. "Improved the torque efficiency by twelve percent. That smile was for precision, not joy."

"Sure," David said gently.

They sat in silence for a moment, punctuated by the faint rustle of glossy paper. Somewhere down the hall, a television audience laughed on cue. Artificial joy, pre-recorded.

Arthur pulled out another photo.

This one showed a picnic table. Paper plates. A younger sky. Arthur again—this time seated, sleeves rolled up, holding a soda bottle like it was evidence in a trial.

"You look relaxed," David said.

"I was sunburned," Arthur replied. "Different thing."

David didn't argue. He'd learned that contradicting Arthur was like throwing marshmallows at a tank.

Arthur continued flipping through the stack slowly. Each photograph seemed to require negotiation.

There were factory floors. Christmas trees. A driveway with a car so large it required its own ZIP code. There were group shots where Arthur stood slightly apart, as if even then he distrusted the others, which most likely he did.

David noticed Arthur lingering on one image longer than the others.

"Who's that?" he asked quietly.

Arthur didn't answer immediately.

The photo was small and slightly bent at one corner. A woman stood beside Arthur in front of what appeared to be a modest house. She was mid-laugh. Arthur was looking at her—not the camera.

It was the softest David had ever seen him.

"That," Arthur said at last, "is someone who tolerated me."

David waited.

Arthur cleared his throat. "We had that house for twenty-eight years. The siding was always wrong. I meant to fix it."

"You loved her," David said.

Arthur shot him a look sharp enough to shave with. "Don't narrate for me."

David held up his hands. "Sorry."

Arthur studied the photograph as though it might contradict him.

"Love," he muttered, "is just long-term maintenance."

"Is that what you called it?" David asked.

"It's what it was." He set the picture down carefully. "Oil changes. Furnace filters. Showing up."

David smiled faintly. "That sounds about right."

Arthur looked almost annoyed at the agreement.

They fell into silence.

The dust in the air shifted, glittering. The room felt smaller than usual, as though the past had physical mass.

"You keeping these for a reason?" David asked.

Arthur gave a half-shrug. "We keep things because they make us uncomfortable."

"That's . . . not why most people keep things."

"Most people are sentimental hoarders," Arthur replied. "I'm a practical one."

He lifted a photo of himself as a boy—skinny, ears too large, expression already skeptical.

"Look at that idiot," Arthur said. "Thought the world was going to explain itself."

"He's kind of adorable," David said.

Arthur's eyes narrowed. "Careful."

David leaned forward. "Did you know then? What you'd do for a living?"

Arthur considered.

"I knew I liked machines," he said. "Machines make sense. You tighten a bolt, it tightens. You apply force, something moves. You don't have to wonder what they're thinking."

"People are less cooperative."

"People are chaos in pants."

David laughed despite himself.

Arthur allowed the faintest twitch at the corner of his mouth. Then it vanished.

He held up another photograph—this one faded badly at the edges.

"That was taken at a company picnic," Arthur said. "They handed out hot dogs and false promises."

"You look happy."

"I was employed. That's all."

David tilted his head. "Is there a difference?"

Arthur met his gaze for a long moment.

"Yes," he said finally. "But you don't find out until later."

The words hung there.

David shifted in his chair. "You ever miss it?"

"The factory?"

"Any of it."

Arthur leaned back slowly. The chair creaked like it objected.

"I miss knowing what the day required," he said. "There was a blueprint. A schedule. A problem to solve. You measured the part. It either fit or it didn't."

"And now?"

"Now," Arthur gestured vaguely at the shoebox, "I measure memories."

David glanced down at the scattered photographs. "Do they fit?"

Arthur let out a small, humorless laugh. "They don't even stay still."

A voice drifted faintly from the hallway—two residents arguing about bingo rules as if international law depended on it.

David looked back at Arthur.

"You don't have to go through those alone," he said.

Arthur snorted. "You volunteering?"

"I'm already here."

Arthur studied him with suspicion, as though kindness might be a trick.

"You've got your own mess," he said.

"True."

"So why sit in mine?"

David thought about that. About spreadsheets, his empty apartment, the way evenings stretched longer than they used to.

"Because," he said carefully, "it feels less like a mess when someone else is in the room."

Arthur's expression shifted—barely. A recalibration.

"That's a dangerously optimistic theory," he said.

"Humor me."

Arthur glanced at the shoebox, then back at David.

"Fine," he said gruffly. "But no dramatic commentary. This isn't a documentary."

"Understood."

Arthur picked up another photograph.

In it, he stood in front of a Christmas tree that leaned suspiciously to one side. There were wrapped presents at his feet. He looked tired. But there it was again—that unguarded expression. Not a grin. Not a performance. Something steadier.

David pointed. "There it is."

"What?"

"That look."

Arthur squinted. "What look?"

"Like you belonged somewhere."

Arthur stared at the image for a long time.

"I did," he said quietly.

The admission slipped out like a misplaced bolt rolling off a workbench.

Neither of them moved.

Outside the window, the day's light shifted. Dust motes drifted like lazy comets.

"Don't get sentimental," Arthur warned.

"I wouldn't dream of it."

Arthur replaced the lid halfway, then stopped.

"You know what the trouble with photographs is?" he said.

"What?"

"They freeze the moment. Makes you think it was permanent."

David nodded.

"It wasn't," Arthur continued. "It was just . . . there. In the smallest of moments. So small it makes you wonder . . ."

He held the photograph carefully, as if it might try to escape back into the past where it belonged.

". . . whether the moment even knew it was happening."

David waited.

Arthur squinted at the glossy square. "We think the important times announce themselves. Trumpets. Music swelling. Somebody narrating. But mostly it's just a Tuesday. Or some other day. You're standing somewhere ordinary. You're holding a cup of coffee. Someone you love is complaining about the weather."

He tapped the edge of the photo.

"And then it's over. Not dramatically. Just . . . over. And you didn't salute it. You didn't label it . . . historic. You didn't even comb your hair."

David gave a small laugh.

Arthur didn't.

"The photograph lies," he said. "It says, 'Look how solid this was. Look how still. Look how forever.' But it wasn't forever. It was molecules bumping into other molecules. Light landing on skin. A hand resting on a shoulder for no particular reason."

He paused.

"That's the joke, really."

"What is?"

"That we don't miss the big moments. We miss the little ones we didn't know were big."

Arthur grunted and placed the photograph back in the box with surprising care.

"There are times," he declared, "when archaeology helps me to understand what's going on."

"What?" David said. "You don't know what's going on?"

Arthur gave him a sideways glance and a wink.

"Don't tell the others."

Arthur stared at the shoebox as if it might blink first. It did not. Boxes are stubborn that way.

A thought arrived—small, uninvited, and wearing muddy shoes. Something inside had shifted. Or maybe he had.

He slid the lid away, the way a man opens a letter he already suspects contains bad news. He set the lid aside with ceremony, because ceremony is what we give to cardboard when we're not ready for memory.

Then he reached in and took hold of a photograph, as though it might try to wriggle back into the dark.

"Look," he said. "That's me. Sunday school. Look at that face. I believed in everything. God. Dinosaurs. Proper heating systems."

David leaned closer. The picture showed a small boy in stiff trousers and a tie that appeared to be strangling him in the name of righteousness. The boy's hair was parted with mathematical precision, as if holiness required symmetry.

"They taught us that God loved us," Arthur went on, squinting. "Then they served soup just like they do here. Cold. Uninviting. Possibly symbolic."

David laughed, but softly. He had learned that Arthur's humor was a guard dog. It barked at anything resembling tenderness.

"Maybe it was gazpacho," David offered.

"Again, with the gazpacho."

"Well, you never know," David smiled.

"In Ohio? In 1950?" Arthur said. "We thought paprika was communism."

Then another thought wandered in, late and unapologetic. Arthur did what people do when thinking becomes dangerous—he reached for something tangible. Another photograph.

"This one," Arthur said, holding up another picture, "is my confirmation. I look like I've just signed a treaty I don't understand."

In the photograph, young Arthur stood beside a minister whose smile was aggressively optimistic. Arthur's hands were folded in prayer or possibly surrender.

"They told us life was simple," Arthur continued. "Be good. Work hard. Don't swear in front of your mother. And everything would turn out fine."

David sat on the edge of the bed. "And did it?"

Arthur tilted his head. "Define fine."

He shuffled to another photo. A black-and-white snapshot of teenagers near a car that had fins like it intended to take flight.

"Ah. The haircut years," Arthur said. "Every boy looked like a disappointed trumpet player."

"You weren't disappointed?" David asked.

Arthur studied the image. "I was hopeful. Which is worse."

He set that one aside and pulled another from the stack. A factory floor. Machines large enough to intimidate a planet. A young man in a grease-stained shirt grinning at the camera as though metal were a religion.

"There I am," Arthur said. "Before I learned that machines don't love you back."

David nodded slowly. He knew that tone. It was Arthur approaching something real, then circling it like a wary dog.

"You loved that job," David said.

"Sure did," Arthur said. "What I loved most was the noise. You can hide in noise. It fills the gaps."

He flipped again.

There were more photographs, and each one earned a commentary—dry, surgical, efficient.

A wedding photo. "Look at that tux. Rented dignity."

A vacation snapshot at a lake. "Water was warmer than the soup here. That's saying something."

A blurry Christmas morning. "We thought more gifts meant more meaning. Turns out it just meant more batteries."

David smiled, but he watched closely. The jokes were thinning, like soup stretched past its purpose.

Arthur's fingers slowed.

He pulled out a smaller photograph, edges worn soft by repetition. He stared at it longer than the others.

David leaned forward.

It was Arthur as a boy, maybe eight, standing beside a tall man with square shoulders and a face carved by weather and work. The older man's hand rested on the boy's shoulder—not possessive, not gentle either. Just there. Solid.

Arthur didn't speak.

The silence grew careful.

"Is that your dad?" David asked.

Arthur nodded once.

"He looks . . . steady."

"He was," Arthur said. His voice had misplaced its sarcasm somewhere in the box.

They both looked at the image. The father's eyes were not smiling, but they were alive with something close to pride. The boy stood straighter because of it.

Arthur cleared his throat.

"I loved him," he said, as if confessing to tax evasion. "Never had the guts to tell him."

David swallowed.

Arthur continued, still staring at the photo. "We didn't say things like that back then. Men didn't. We fixed engines. We shoveled snow. We nodded."

He tapped the picture lightly.

"That was our language."

David felt something tighten behind his ribs.

Arthur sniffed once, sharply, like a man allergic to emotion.

"When I finally take my big nap," Arthur said, "and if there's any cosmic customer service desk on the other side, and he's standing there . . . I'll hug him."

David said nothing.

"I'll hug him," Arthur repeated, "and I'll tell him I love him. Just to clear the paperwork."

A tear slipped down the side of Arthur's face. He didn't acknowledge it. It traveled cleanly through the geography of his wrinkles, then disappeared into his collar.

David felt his eyes go watery, which is a humiliating malfunction for a grown man. There ought to be a small switch somewhere behind the ear for that sort of thing. There isn't.

Arthur turned suddenly, catching him.

"You ever tell your dad?" Arthur asked. "Tell him you love him?"

David opened his mouth.

Closed it.

Shook his head.

Arthur studied him. Not critically. Not even sarcastically.

Just studied him.

"Well," Arthur said finally, his voice settling into something almost gentle, "look at us then."

David blinked, as if this might develop into wisdom.

"Two highly evolved mammals," Arthur continued. "Just sitting here with our fancy opposable thumbs and language."

He paused.

"Too scared to use the latter when it's important."

The room hummed faintly—the distant buzz of fluorescent lights performing their lonely opera.

David nodded.

Arthur looked back down at the photograph of his father and ran a thumb gently across the old man's image, as if smoothing a wrinkle in time itself.

"Photographs are liars," Arthur muttered. "They make you think you can go back."

He placed the picture carefully on top of the pile and didn't bury it.

"But maybe," he added, almost to himself, "they're reminders too. Reminders . . ."

David sat across from him, two men divided by decades but stuck together by the same unfinished sentence.

Outside the door, a cart rolled past. Someone laughed too loudly at something not very funny. The building went on being a building.

Inside the small room, however, something had warmed.

Arthur wiped his cheek briskly with the heel of his hand.

"Don't look at me like that," he said.

"Like what?" David asked.

"Like I'm fragile."

David managed a small smile. "You're not."

Arthur nodded once.

"I'm just . . . an old man," he said.

And then, because the universe insists on balance, he added:

"And the soup's still cold."

Arthur didn't believe in sentimentality. Or at least he thought he didn't. He believed in torque specifications, properly sharpened drill bits, and soup that arrived at least pretending to be warm. Sentimentality, in his experience, was something people used when they'd misplaced a wrench and didn't want to admit it.

And yet there he was, an old man, in his final years, sitting hunched over a shoebox like it contained classified documents from a war no one remembered.

David sat near him. He watched him the way a man watches a small, flickering candle in a very drafty room. He didn't want to breathe too hard or move too fast, for fear the little bit of light left in the world might simply decide it was too tired to keep on burning.

"More pictures of you at work?" David asked.

Arthur didn't look up. He flipped another photograph with the slow precision of a man defusing a bomb from 1957.

"I was a machinist," Arthur replied.

"Yes, I know."

"Efficiency is how we avoided losing fingers."

Arthur lifted a photograph toward the window so he could see it better.

David leaned over. "You look happy in that one. In a lot of the pictures, actually."

Arthur squinted at the photo. It was him, younger by several decades, smiling without suspicion. He was standing next to a co-worker in front of a lathe, both of them greasy and proud.

"That," Arthur said, "is Harold Jenkins. He could eyeball a measurement within two thousandths of an inch. Also cheated at poker."

David smiled. "You miss him."

Arthur traced Harold's outline with a finger that'd once steadied roaring machinery. His voice, when it came, had lost a layer of sandpaper.

"Yeah," he said simply. "I do."

It was the sort of quiet, honest thing that people used to say to one another on back porches before the world turned into a giant scoreboard.

He set the photo aside.

They were quiet for a while. The kind of quiet that doesn't ask to be filled.

Arthur wiped at his eye with the back of his hand in a motion so quick it could've been mistaken for an itch.

"Dust," he muttered. "Just dust. Nothing else."

"Of course," David said.

Arthur flipped to another photograph. This one was recent. Taken by Nurse Kelly, who believed in documenting moments the way botanists document rare flowers.

It was Arthur and Margaret sitting side by side in the dining hall. Margaret's smile was bright enough to power a small town. Arthur looked as if he'd just been informed that smiling was mandatory but survivable.

David inhaled sharply. "That's a nice picture of you and Mom."

Arthur studied the image. His voice, when it came, was quieter than the hum of the fluorescent lights.

"She had a way about her," he said. "Made cold rooms feel less official."

David nodded. "She always smiled."

"Yeah," Arthur agreed. "She did."

Arthur's finger hovered just above Margaret's face, not quite touching.

"I miss her," he said.

There it was. No joke. No clever detour. Just a sentence sitting there in its underwear.

David swallowed. "Me too."

Arthur leaned back in his chair and looked at the ceiling as if answers might be taped there.

"You ever tell her?" David asked, before he could stop himself.

Arthur glanced at him. For once, there was no irritation in the look. He knew what David was asking.

"No," he said. "Didn't seem right. She had your father. I respected that."

David felt a flicker of something complicated—gratitude, maybe. Or sadness shaped like gratitude.

"I wanted to," Arthur continued. "Plenty of times. But I figured she knew."

He looked back at the photo.

"Yeah, I think she knew," he said again, more to himself than to David.

David wiped at his own eyes. He did it less subtly than Arthur.

Arthur noticed, of course. He noticed everything.

"Look at us," Arthur said softly. "Two grown men ambushed by glossy paper."

He let out a sigh that sounded like a small balloon leaking air in a very quiet cathedral. "It's a terrible biological defect—to have been designed with tear ducts and then handed a stack of memories. It's like we're just machines made of meat and sadness. So poorly shielded against the past."

David laughed wetly. "It's ridiculous."

"Completely," Arthur agreed. "We should be discussing engine tolerances or complaining about soup."

They both glanced, instinctively, at the empty space where a bowl might be.

Arthur held up the photo again. "She was warmth," he said. "Even when she was telling me I was insufferable."

"She told you that?"

"Frequently."

David smiled through his tears. "She liked you."

Arthur sniffed. "She had questionable taste in company."

They sat in silence again, but this time it was companionable. Not heavy. Just present.

Arthur gathered the photos slowly, stacking them with care that bordered on reverence.

"You know," he said, "this box is mostly embarrassing. Bad haircuts. Terrible shirts. Questionable mustaches."

"Still, you kept them," David said.

"Yeah," Arthur replied. "That's the trick. We hoard what proves we were here. Even the stupid parts."

David considered that.

"So memory's the real hobby?" he asked.

Arthur smirked faintly. "Worst one of all. No upgrades. No revisions. Just reruns."

He placed the lid back on the shoebox, sealing in decades of small victories and private griefs.

"I'm a bit tired," he told David.

David stood and helped Arthur to his feet. The walker with the glued-on googly eyes waited by the bed, its plastic pupils staring in permanent astonishment.

Arthur eyed the walker. "Those eyes look like they know something."

"They probably do."

David guided Arthur to the bed. Arthur lowered himself carefully, with the dignity of a man who refused to negotiate with gravity.

As David adjusted the blanket, Arthur's eyelids began their slow descent.

"You know," Arthur murmured, voice already drifting, "when I see the old man again . . . I'm telling him."

"I know," David said. "That you love him."

"Yeah."

Arthur paused.

"And I'll probably have to tell your mother a few things too," he added. "More paperwork to clear."

David laughed softly. "I'm sure she'll have a list."

Arthur's mouth twitched upward.

"She always did."

His breathing evened out. The sharp lines of his face softened. For a moment, he looked less like a retired machinist and more like the boy in the photograph—still unsmiling, perhaps, but no longer braced.

David picked up the shoebox and set it carefully on the dresser, as if it were fragile machinery.

He turned back to Arthur.

"Sweet dreams," he said quietly.

Arthur didn't answer. He was already somewhere between this room and whatever came next.

David lingered at the doorway.

He realized, with a clarity that felt almost unfair, that some lessons don't arrive with bullet points or manifestos. They arrive in shoeboxes. In dust. In the way a man traces the outline of someone he can no longer touch.

Memory, he understood, wasn't about the past.

It was about who we still wanted to be brave enough to love.

He switched off the light and stepped into the hallway, leaving Arthur with his photographs and his unfinished sentences.

Arthur fell asleep the way old factories shut down—without ceremony, with a final mechanical sigh.

One moment, he was in a narrow bed at Sunny Meadows, googly-eyed walker standing guard like a deranged sentry. The next, gravity reconsidered its priorities.

The hum of fluorescent lighting thinned. The faint smell of disinfectant folded itself neatly away. Even the memory of cold soup retreated to wherever such indignities are stored.

Arthur opened his eyes.

He was sitting on a barstool that didn't respect the human spine. Before him stretched the luminous counter of the bar of The Great Beyond, the interstellar cruiseship that seemed to operate on the principle that if you are going to hallucinate, you may as well do it in style.

Behind the bar stood Iris.

Her plum-colored skin shimmered softly, like twilight deciding whether to stay. Multiple galaxy-like eyes blinked in a pattern too symmetrical to be accidental. Seven delicate, suction-tipped fingers polished a glass that appeared to contain a slow-motion supernova.

She regarded him with that ancient expression of hers—the one that suggested she had watched civilizations invent soup and regret it.

The bar was quiet. It always was. Apparently, eternity had terrible nightlife.

Soft lighting glowed above the polished counter. The stars outside the enormous viewport looked like someone had spilled glitter across the universe.

Arthur sighed.

"Well," he said, "either I'm dead, or the nursing home finally upgraded their entertainment."

Iris smiled.

"Welcome back, Arthur."

"Good to see you too," Arthur said. "Although technically, I didn't come here voluntarily. I was trying to nap."

"You did nap."

"Apparently with benefits."

She placed a glass in front of him. Steam rose from it in soft spirals of gold and pale blue.

Arthur eyed it.

"What is it this time?"

"Memory steeped in time," Iris said.

Arthur squinted at the drink.

"Smells like burnt coffee and shame."

"Those are common ingredients."

Arthur lifted the cup and took a sip.

He winced.

"Yep. That's shame, all right."

Behind Iris, the massive viewport stretched across the wall like a cosmic television screen.

Arthur noticed something turning slowly in the dark.

A planet.

Blue and green and white. A respectable planet. The sort of planet that probably had traffic jams and taxes and people arguing about soup recipes.

Arthur pointed at it with the hand holding his drink.

"What's that one?"

Iris followed his gaze.

"A populated world."

"They all are."

"This one is particularly interesting."

Arthur leaned forward on the bar.

"What's the gimmick?"

"There's no gimmick," Iris said. "They simply talk."

Arthur blinked.

"They talk," he said. "That's it?"

"Yes."

"That's the feature?"

"They talk constantly."

Arthur stared out the viewport.

The planet rotated slowly below them. Cities glimmered faintly in the darkness. Lightning flickered in distant storms.

"So they're like humans," Arthur said.

"Very similar."

"God help them."

Arthur took another sip.

"What do they talk about?"

"Work. Weather. Plans. Entertainment. Small grievances."

Arthur nodded.

"Classic conversation material."

"They communicate across vast networks," Iris continued. "They send messages instantly across their entire world."

Arthur whistled softly.

"Impressive."

"They never stop talking."

Arthur gestured toward the planet.

"And yet you're telling me this is interesting."

"It is."

Arthur leaned back on the stool.

"Alright," he said. "What's the catch?"

Iris rested her seven fingers lightly on the counter.

"They hesitate."

Arthur frowned.

"About what?"

"Certain things."

Arthur snorted.

"Let me guess. Taxes."

"No."

"Politics?"

"No."

Arthur scratched his chin.

"Parking?"

Iris shook her head.

"They hesitate to say certain truths."

Arthur stared at her.

"What kind of truths?"

Iris spoke calmly.

"Some hesitate to say I forgive you."

Arthur nodded slowly.

"That tracks."

"Some hesitate to say I was wrong."

Arthur laughed.

"Now that one's universal."

Iris continued.

"Many hesitate to say I'm afraid."

Arthur took another drink.

"Yeah," he said quietly. "That one too."

Iris looked back at the planet.

"And the most fragile phrase of all."

Arthur waited.

"I love you."

Arthur was quiet for a moment.

Then he laughed.

"Seriously?"

"Yes."

"That's the big problem?"

"They believe there will always be time later to say it."

Arthur stared out the viewport again.

The planet turned peacefully below them.

Millions of people were probably having conversations at that very moment. Talking about grocery lists. Talking about the weather. Talking about television shows, sports, and neighbors who mowed their lawns incorrectly.

Arthur rubbed his forehead.

"So they talk all the time," he said, "but skip the one sentence that matters."

"Yes."

Arthur pointed at the planet again.

"That's ridiculous."

"Yes."

Arthur shook his head.

"Whole civilization built on emotional procrastination."

Iris tilted her head.

"That's an accurate description."

Arthur leaned forward, resting his elbows on the counter.

"You know," he said, "I was just looking at photographs before I got here."

"I know."

"My father."

"Yes."

Arthur exhaled slowly.

"Never told him I loved him."

Iris said nothing.

Arthur tapped the side of the cup.

"And Margaret."

"Yes."

Arthur stared into the drink.

"Didn't tell her either."

Iris rested one cool hand on the bar.

"Many people believe silence protects them."

"Protects them from what?"

"Embarrassment. Rejection. Vulnerability."

Arthur snorted.

"Terrifying stuff."

"Yes."

Arthur looked back out at the planet.

Somewhere down there, two people were probably sitting across from each other at a kitchen table. Maybe one of them was about to say something important.

Maybe they wouldn't.

Arthur sighed.

"You'd think a species that invented language would get better at using it."

"Language isn't the problem," Iris said.

Arthur looked at her.

"What is?"

"Courage."

Arthur nodded slowly.

"Yeah," he said.

He lifted the drink again.

"Funny thing," he said. "The hardest conversations in the universe are also the shortest."

Iris smiled.

Arthur watched the planet rotate below them.

Millions of voices.

Billions of conversations.

And somewhere down there, someone was probably about to say the words that mattered.

Or not say them.

Arthur finished his drink.

"Sad planet," he said.

"Yes."

Arthur shrugged.

"Good view though."

Iris poured him another cup.

Arthur looked at it.

"You trying to keep me here?"

"No."

"Good."

He took the cup anyway.

Arthur Trent sat at the bar of The Great Beyond, watching a world full of people talking.

Talking.

Talking.

Talking.

And saving the important sentences for later.

Arthur closed his eyes.

When he opened them again, the chrome barstool was gone.

Fluorescent light hummed overhead.

His walker's googly eyes stared at him with permanent astonishment.

For a moment, he could not tell whether he had lost something or been given something.

He flexed his fingers.

The warmth lingered.

Chapter 11

David sat on the edge of his couch the way a man might sit on the edge of a dock—unsure whether he intended to dive in or simply dangle his feet above something deep and uncooperative.

He had just come home from the office, the one day a week he was required to make a personal appearance. He had loosened his tie but hadn't taken it off. He was keeping his options open, just in case civilization decided to stage a sudden comeback and invited him to a cocktail party.

The apartment was dark, except for a corner lamp that gave off a yellow light so weary and pathetic it seemed to be apologizing for the invention of electricity.

The apartment had become quiet in a new way.

It wasn't the ordinary quiet of a Tuesday evening. It wasn't the peaceful quiet advertised in brochures for modern living. It was the kind of quiet that settles in after something has been permanently removed. The kind that doesn't expect interruption.

He picked up his phone.

He didn't hesitate for long. His thumb moved with the familiar certainty of habit. Gallery. Camera Roll. Years condensed into a scrollable column.

At the top were recent photos. A coffee mug. A receipt he had photographed for reimbursement. A crooked sunset taken through a dirty windshield.

He scrolled down.

And there she was.

His mother.

Margaret in a kitchen full of morning light. Flour on her hands. A smudge of it on her cheek she hadn't yet noticed. The counters behind her cluttered with bowls and measuring cups, as though cooking were a contact sport and she meant to win.

"Hold still," he said that day.

"I am holding still," she replied, while moving.

Click.

He scrolled.

Another photo. A birthday cake leaning slightly to the left like a tired soldier. Candles burning enthusiastically. Margaret mid-laugh, mouth open, eyes bright, the room around her overexposed by happiness.

He scrolled slower.

Margaret sitting on the back porch with a blanket around her shoulders, sunlight threading through her hair. She'd been thinner by then, though it wasn't yet a topic anyone addressed directly. The body had begun its quiet negotiations.

He swallowed.

The glow of the phone made everything feel underwater. His face reflected faintly in the glass, superimposed over hers. It looked as though they were sharing the same expression.

He scrolled further.

Hospital.

The lighting changed abruptly in the timeline. Fluorescent, unforgiving. Margaret in a pale gown, a plastic wristband hugging her arm with bureaucratic precision. The camera angle careful. The smile measured.

"You don't have to take that," she said.

"I want to," he replied.

"Make sure you get my good side."

"You have two good sides."

She rolled her eyes. "Flattery won't save you."

Click.

He paused on one where she was propped up against white pillows, a tray of gelatin beside her, the television remote resting like a scepter near her hand. Her smile was present but disciplined, as if it had been told to behave.

He zoomed in.

The image expanded obediently. Pores. Fine lines. The faint blue of veins beneath thinning skin.

He zoomed out again.

Scroll.

Then he found it.

The filtered one.

He remembered that afternoon with painful clarity. She had insisted on seeing the picture before he sent it to anyone.

"Let me see," she said.

"It's fine," he told her.

"David."

He handed over the phone.

She tapped something. A sparkle icon. A wand. He couldn't remember exactly. The screen shifted. Her wrinkles softened. The shadows under her eyes lightened. Her skin became a uniform brightness that belonged to no actual human being.

"There," she said. "That's better."

"That doesn't look like you."

"It looks like me on a good day."

He didn't argue.

Now, in the quiet apartment, he tapped between versions. Filtered. Unfiltered. Filtered. Unfiltered.

In the filtered one, her eyes were brighter but flatter. Her cheeks smoother but less expressive. The light in the room seemed artificial, like stage lighting attempting sincerity.

In the unfiltered version, the lines around her mouth were deeper. They folded into themselves like parentheses holding in a lifetime of private jokes. Her eyes were tired but alert, as though aware of a punchline no one else had yet grasped.

He tapped the filtered one again.

The smoothing algorithm had blurred the small scar near her chin from when she'd fallen off a bicycle at twelve. It had softened the crease between her brows—the crease that appeared whenever she read fine print or considered whether someone was lying.

He zoomed out.

He toggled back.

The filtered image felt distant. It felt like a polite stranger who knew her biography but not her habits.

He exhaled slowly.

"You hated the hospital lighting," he said aloud to the empty room.

The room didn't respond. It simply absorbed the statement.

He scrolled faster.

Birthday. Porch. Kitchen. Hospital. Porch again. A Christmas tree tilted precariously. Margaret wearing reindeer antlers with an expression of theatrical dignity.

He slowed down.

A photo appeared of her laughing mid-sentence. Not posing. Not correcting her posture. Laughing because someone—probably him—had said something stupid and she had chosen to reward him with amusement.

There was no filter on this one.

Her head was tilted back slightly. The lines around her mouth deep and unapologetic. Her eyes half-closed in motion. Her teeth visible, imperfect, and alive.

He felt the air in the room shift.

The lamp's glow seemed to hesitate. The refrigerator in the kitchen hummed and then fell silent, as if also listening.

He zoomed in.

The image pixelated slightly but held.

He could almost hear the laugh. The intake of breath before it. The way she'd touch his forearm mid-laugh, as though steadying herself against joy.

"You hated that one," he whispered to no one.

She had hated it because her eyes were nearly closed. Because her chin looked "odd from that angle." Because she wasn't composed.

"That one makes me look old," she had said.

"You are old," he replied, smiling.

She smacked his arm lightly. "Delete it."

He didn't.

Now his thumb hovered over the screen.

Delete.

The word was small but definitive. A red trash can icon waiting for an answer.

He didn't press it.

Instead, he stared.

The lines around her mouth weren't flaws. They were cartography. Evidence of laughter repeated enough times to leave marks. The faint asymmetry in her smile suggested a preference for irony over politeness.

He tapped the heart icon.

The photo became a favorite.

A tiny red symbol appeared in the corner, a badge of distinction. As though the phone understood something about reverence.

He set the phone down on the coffee table.

The screen dimmed but didn't go dark. Her frozen laugh remained faintly visible through the fading light.

The apartment exhaled.

He leaned back against the couch cushions and closed his eyes. For a moment, he imagined the photo suspended in the air in front of him, unmediated by glass or circuitry.

You can't edit a life, he thought, though he wasn't sure where the thought originated. It arrived fully formed.

He picked up the phone again.

Scroll.

Another filtered image. Another softened face. Another attempt at correction.

He toggled.

Filtered.

Unfiltered.

Filtered.

Unfiltered.

The filtered one looked like it belonged in a brochure for resilience. The unfiltered one looked like it belonged in a memory.

He whispered, “I’m sorry.”

He wasn’t sure what he was apologizing for. For the filters? For the hospital? For every time he’d suggested she rest when she wanted to argue?

The room held its breath again.

He scrolled slower, as though each image were fragile glassware.

Kitchen sunlight. Porch wind. Hospital white. Porch again.

He noticed how the later photos grew more careful. The smiles measured. The posture upright even when exhaustion was evident. The way she’d lift her chin slightly, as though refusing to concede visual ground.

He zoomed in on another unfiltered image. Her eyes tired but bright with something stubborn and unmistakable.

“That’s you,” he said softly.

He imagined her response.

“Well, of course it’s me. Who else would it be?”

He smiled faintly. The first flicker of something like humor, though it didn’t fully form.

The phone slipped slightly in his grip. He adjusted it.

Scroll.

He stopped on the earliest photo in the album. Margaret holding him as a child. The image grainy, colors slightly off. Her face young and unlined. His expression confused and damp.

He compared it to the last unfiltered one.

Two different faces. Same woman.

There was no filter that could reconcile them. No slider that could adjust for time.

He set the phone down again.

This time, he let the screen go dark.

The apartment returned to its full, unapologetic quiet.

He stared at the blank screen, which now reflected only his own face. The lines there were faint but beginning. Evidence of laughter. Evidence of worry.

He reached for the phone once more.

Scrolled back to the laughing, unfiltered photo.

Looked for the heart.

The red symbol remained.

He placed the phone face down on the table.

The lamp continued to glow.

The quiet didn't feel quite as sharp.

And in the dimness, the unedited memory held.

Sunny Meadows dining hall had the atmosphere of a train station that had misplaced all its trains.

It was midday, which meant the residents had been wheeled, guided, or stubbornly self-propelled into rows of small laminate tables under lights that hummed like indecisive bees. Outside the windows, the sun shone with bureaucratic indifference. Inside, trays were arriving.

Lunch in institutions doesn't arrive casually. It arrives with purpose. It arrives with wheels. It arrives as though it's been approved by a committee and signed in triplicate.

David stepped through the double doors carrying nothing but his phone and a sense of mild dread. He'd promised himself he'd come more often. He'd promised this several times since he became friends with Arthur (if 'friends' was the correct term), meaning it was an official promise in the same way New Year's resolutions are official.

Arthur was already seated at their usual table, which was near a ficus that had outlived three administrators. He was staring at the room as if auditing it.

"You're late," Arthur said.

"It's twelve-oh-three."

"Exactly."

David sat down. "You've been waiting a whole three minutes."

Arthur nodded. "Longest three minutes of my life. And I've had a few contenders."

A cart squeaked past them, distributing trays like subpoenas. The smell was neutral, which was impressive in its own way.

David brightened artificially. "I brought something to show you."

Arthur narrowed his eyes. "Last time you said that, it was an article about fiber."

"This is better."

"Low bar."

David pulled out his phone and swiped to the photo. "I want to show you something."

He turned the screen toward Arthur.

Arthur leaned forward and squinted. His cataracts made every object look like it was negotiating a fog bank. He tilted the phone left, then right, then up toward the ceiling as though it might confess under interrogation lighting.

"Is that your mom?" he asked. "What'd you do to her face?"

"Nothing bad," David said quickly. "I just—adjusted it."

Arthur leaned back. "Adjusted."

"Yeah. You know. A filter."

Arthur said nothing. He just stared at him in the way a judge might stare at someone who'd used the phrase "creative accounting."

David swiped again. "Look. Here's the original."

Margaret stood in the garden at Sunny Meadows, sunlight caught in her silver hair. Her smile was slightly crooked. The lines around her eyes radiated like tributaries.

Then David swiped back to the edited version.

The lines were softened. The shadows lifted. Her skin was smoother. Her eyes brighter. The photo looked like it belonged in a brochure for affordable serenity.

Arthur's nose wrinkled.

"She looks like she's running for office," he said.

"It's just a filter," David insisted. "It smooths things. Enhances contrast. Corrects lighting."

"Corrects," Arthur repeated. "From what?"

"From—" David hesitated. "Imperfections."

Arthur snorted. It was a dry, efficient sound.

"She looks better in wrinkles than in filters."

He leaned forward again and tapped the unfiltered photo with a knuckle that'd once known factory work and a firm handshake.

"That's a life," he said. "That other one's a campaign ad."

David half-smiled despite himself. "You're being dramatic."

"I'm being accurate," Arthur said. "Technology is trying to launder experience."

"That's not what it's doing."

"Of course it is. It takes an image and makes it look nicer."

Another cart rolled past. A tray was placed in front of Arthur with the solemnity of a court summons. On the tray, a bowl with a lid. The lid rattled slightly. There was no steam.

Arthur lifted the lid an inch and peered inside.

"Ah," he said. "Today's soup is invisible."

David glanced over. The surface of the soup was flat and reflective. It gave no sign of ever having been hot.

Arthur pointed at his own face. "These lines? Earned. Every one of 'em."

He traced a deep crease beside his mouth.

"This one's from my father," he said. "He once tried to assemble a grill without instructions. Nearly killed us both."

David laughed.

Arthur tapped his forehead. "These are from worrying about things I couldn't fix. Taxes. Engines. Life."

"Me?"

"You're like all humans. Very breakable."

Arthur leaned closer to the phone again, studying the filtered Margaret. He tilted the device once more, suspicious.

"You smoothed out her eyes," he said. "That's where she kept the stories."

"It's subtle," David protested. "Most people wouldn't even notice."

Arthur looked around the dining hall.

Half the residents were hunched over trays, moving slowly, deliberately. One man was staring at a roll as if it might reveal its secrets first.

"They would notice," Arthur said quietly. "They'd just be polite about it."

David shifted in his seat. "It's just what people do now. Everyone uses filters."

Arthur's eyebrows climbed.

"Everyone jumps off bridges, too," he said. "That doesn't make it landscaping."

David laughed again, though it came out thinner.

Arthur's gaze sharpened.

"You edit your own photos?" he asked.

David felt something in his chest tighten.

"Sometimes," he admitted.

Arthur didn't blink.

"Thought so."

"It's not a big deal."

"It is if you're erasing yourself."

"I'm not erasing myself."

"You're sanding," Arthur said. "You're sanding the evidence of life."

The tray in front of David arrived. It landed with a soft thud. A plastic cup of juice trembled.

David lifted the lid on his soup. It was identical to Arthur's: a lukewarm, beige uncertainty.

"No steam," Arthur observed. "Even the soup has raised the white flag."

David stirred it experimentally. The spoon made a sound like mild disappointment.

Arthur nodded toward the phone again.

"Why?" he asked.

David hesitated longer this time.

"I don't know," he said finally. "It just looks better."

"Better to whom?"

"To—" David stopped. "To everyone."

Arthur shook his head.

"There's no everyone," he said. "There's just a bunch of nervous individuals pretending they aren't nervous."

He picked up his spoon and dipped it into the soup. It parted obediently.

"You think your mother wanted to look younger?" he asked.

David considered.

"She never said."

"She didn't have to," Arthur said. "She wore every year like it was a medal."

He gestured at the unfiltered photo again.

"That one line around her mouth? That's from laughing at my jokes. Which, I'll admit, was generous of her."

David smiled.

Arthur continued, softer now.

"The ones around her eyes? That's from squinting at sunsets. And at you when you lied."

"I didn't lie."

"You absolutely lied. Everyone does."

They both smiled.

Arthur took a sip of soup and made a face.

"This isn't soup," he declared. "This is an apology."

"For what?"

"For having expectations."

David shook his head.

Arthur looked back at the filtered photo one more time.

"She doesn't look like herself," he said.

"She looks good," David insisted weakly.

"She looks edited."

"That's the point."

Arthur leaned back in his chair.

"Your generation thinks the point is presentation," he said. "Ours thought it was endurance."

"That's not fair."

"Of course it's not fair," Arthur replied. "Nothing is. That's why we get wrinkles."

A woman at the next table dropped her fork. It clattered loudly. No one seemed surprised.

Arthur tapped the phone again.

"You know what those filters really do?" he asked.

"What?"

"They make everyone look like they haven't lived yet."

David stared at the screen.

Margaret's filtered face looked bright, smooth, almost expectant. The unfiltered one looked grounded. Present. Finished in the best sense of the word.

Arthur nudged the phone back toward him.

"Keep that one," he said, pointing to the original.

David nodded slowly.

Arthur squinted at him.

"And stop sanding your own face."

"I don't sand it that much."

Arthur gave him a look.

"You hesitated."

David sighed.

"It's just—there's pressure."

"From who?"

"Everyone."

Arthur leaned forward again.

"Again, there's no everyone," he repeated. "There's just you deciding whether you're allowed to look like your own life."

David stirred his soup again, though it hadn't improved.

Arthur lifted his spoon in a mock toast.

"To topographical proof," he said. "May we remain geographically accurate."

David clinked his spoon against Arthur's.

"To wrinkles."

"To evidence of love," Arthur corrected.

They both tasted the soup at the same time and winced.

Arthur nodded solemnly.

"Cold," he said. "As foretold."

David laughed.

Arthur looked around the dining hall—the bowed heads, the trembling hands, the patient chewing.

"This place," he said, "is full of original prints."

David followed his gaze.

Arthur continued.

"No filters. No corrections. Just the long version."

He looked back at Margaret's unfiltered photo, still glowing faintly on the screen.

"That's the one," he said.

David deleted the edited version.

Arthur saw the movement and raised an eyebrow.

"Good," he said. "Let the record show she was real."

The trays sat between them like small, edible verdicts.

Outside, the sun continued shining without enhancement.

Inside, under fluorescent lights that seemed to smooth out no one, they ate their cold soup.

The soup sat between them like a small, gray lake that had given up.

Arthur pushed his spoon through it with ceremonial slowness. The surface parted reluctantly, closing behind the metal like a failed ambition—visible for a moment, then swallowed whole.

"What do you think this is?" Arthur said, peering into the wake he'd made.

David looked at the bowl. "That's soup."

"That," Arthur corrected, "is evidence of something. Just don't know what."

He pushed again. Another thin trench. Another disappearance.

The dining hall of Sunny Meadows was having one of its quieter afternoons. The fluorescent lights hummed like insects who had forgotten the point of being insects. The other residents leaned over their meals with the seriousness of jurors. No one was acquitted.

Arthur set the spoon down, leaned forward, and pointed at David with a finger that had known machinery, grief, and at least three kinds of arthritis.

"Wrinkles mean you lived," he said. "Don't ever erase them."

David blinked. "I wasn't planning to."

"Good," Arthur said. "Because the erasers are winning."

David glanced instinctively at his phone resting near his elbow. Its dark screen reflected the ceiling in sterile, obedient lines.

Arthur noticed the glance. Arthur noticed everything he pretended not to.

"Those filters . . . are just wrong," Arthur continued. "Swipe your face left, suddenly you're twenty again. Skin like a peeled grape."

David smirked. "You'd look good as a peeled grape."

"I'd look like produce," Arthur replied. "Discount produce."

He stirred the soup again. The spoon made a faint clink against the bowl. The sound carried farther than it should have.

David hesitated, then asked, "Did you think my mom minded aging?"

Arthur stopped stirring. The spoon remained half-submerged, like it was considering escape.

He shook his head. "She minded pretending."

He leaned back slightly, remembering without permission. "But as you know, she was a strong woman. She never let the aches and pains bother her."

David smiled at that. "Yeah. I know."

His eyes sharpened a little, as if polishing an internal lens. He pulled up a photo on his phone and showed it to Arthur.

"I had a cousin's wedding," he said. "It was a circus. They had a chocolate fountain the size of a small waterfall. Even a woman who was a makeup artist."

"A makeup artist?"

"Yup," David added darkly. "It was like she was prepping soldiers for war."

"And your mom?"

David's laughter softened. "Mom at first refused. Sat right there in that little hotel chair and said, 'I earned my face.' But then she relented."

David could see it clearly now. His mother in front of the mirror. The makeup artist hovering like a confused hummingbird.

"No heavy foundation, or contouring," David said. "She said the only contour she needed was gravity."

David felt something tighten gently behind his ribs.

"She looked beautiful," he said quietly.

Arthur nodded once. "Because she wasn't hiding."

They both looked down at the photo on the phone. Margaret smiling into sunlight. No smoothing. No blurring. Just light and time working together.

David studied it again.

He noticed details he hadn't before—creases near her eyes that deepened when she smiled. Lines at the corners of her mouth that looked less like wear and more like parentheses. As if her joy required punctuation.

"She never complained about those," David murmured.

"Why would she?" Arthur said. "Those are receipts."

"For what?"

"For showing up."

Arthur picked up the spoon again and held it over the soup like a conductor about to lead a reluctant orchestra.

"You start editing the surface," he said, "you forget what's underneath."

He glanced around the dining hall. Mrs. Davenport chewing with dignified suspicion. Mr. Kline asleep upright, spoon suspended midair like a surrender flag.

"Place like this?" Arthur said. "We're all unfiltered."

David looked around, too. There were liver spots and tremors and scars and oxygen tubes. There were stories leaking out of everyone, whether they approved or not.

He picked up his phone and, without quite knowing why, slipped it into his pocket.

Arthur noticed that too. He didn't smile. He simply nodded, as if a minor but necessary treaty had been signed.

David wasn't fully convinced. He still liked the idea of adjusting brightness, cropping out clutter, and selecting the best angle of a life. But he felt something move inside him—like furniture being rearranged quietly in the dark.

Arthur lifted the spoon and tasted the soup.

He paused.

His face went through several administrative stages of disappointment.

"Yup," he said. "Still cold."

David tasted his own.

Confirmed.

Arthur squinted at the bowl as if it'd betrayed him personally.

"You think," he began slowly, "they could filter the soup, too."

David grinned. "Oh no."

"Warmth adjustment," Arthur continued, waving his hand over the bowl as though applying an invisible setting. "Texture smoothing. Reality enhancement."

He leaned closer to the soup. "Hashtag Rustic Chill."

David laughed. "You know that hashtag stuff."

"Saw it on the TV," Arthur insisted. "Hashtag Rustic Chill. They can call it artisanal."

"Farm-to-table disappointment," David added.

Arthur nodded gravely. "Locally sourced indifference."

The humor landed, but softer than usual. It hovered rather than bounced.

Arthur stared into the soup again. The surface trembled faintly—not from heat, but from the faint vibration of the building's old ventilation system.

"Can't fix temperature with illusion," he muttered.

David felt the parallel slide into place like a key.

He didn't say it aloud. Neither did Arthur.

But it was there.

You can't warm a life by adjusting the contrast.

Arthur dipped the spoon again and, with the stubbornness of a man who once repaired machines no one else would touch, began to eat.

The spoon clinked against porcelain.

Clink.

Pause.

Clink.

The sound stretched slightly, as if the room had inhaled and forgotten to exhale.

The fluorescent hum above them thinned. The edges of the dining hall softened, like a photograph left too long in the developing fluid.

Arthur's eyes grew heavy. Not dramatically. Just gradually, like curtains being drawn by someone careful not to wake the house.

David noticed. "You okay?"

Arthur blinked slowly. "Just considering whether the afterlife has microwaves."

"That's your big theological question?"

Arthur's mouth twitched. "Efficiency matters."

The spoon slipped from his fingers and struck the bowl.

The sound lingered longer than physics would normally allow.

The walls of the dining hall seemed to pull back, dissolving into pale abstraction. The other residents blurred into silhouettes, then into suggestion.

Arthur's voice, softer now, floated between them.

"You can't digitally improve lived reality," he said. "It either warms you or it doesn't."

The soup's surface became mirrorlike. For a moment, David thought he saw something else reflected there—not the ceiling lights, but something vast and dim, glowing red at the edges.

Then the hum stopped altogether.

Silence moved in like a careful tenant.

Arthur's head tilted forward slightly. Not asleep. Not gone. Just elsewhere.

David reached out instinctively, steadying the old man's shoulder.

The bowl of soup sat untouched again, its surface smooth and unaltered.

No filter.

No enhancement.

Just exactly what it was.

Arthur arrived standing up. This was a real bother, mostly because he couldn't remember the part where he stopped being at Sunny Meadows.

One moment, he was sitting at a table with some cold soup. There was a spoon involved, and some fluorescent lights overhead that were doing a very poor impersonation of hope. They were humming just for the sake of humming.

Oh, and there was David.

And then, suddenly—no more soup. No more humming lights. No more David. Instead, he'd been provided with a great deal of sky and a very solid floor.

He stood on the surface of a planet so reflective it seemed less like ground and more like an agreement. The sky—wide, pale, faintly red at the edges like an embarrassed sunburn—stretched beneath his shoes as perfectly as it did above his head. Arthur looked down and saw himself looking up at himself.

"Well," he muttered, "that's unnecessary."

Around him, rising from the curved horizon, stood mirrors.

Thousands of them.

No—millions.

They followed the curve of the planet, if you could even call it a planet. It was more of a giant, spherical joke made of glass and existential commentary. Everything was a reflection of a reflection, which is a very crowded way to exist.

Each mirror stood upright and tilted slightly inward. They looked like polite, silver-plated mourners. They seemed to be listening for a sound that never came.

Arthur turned slowly.

Every mirror contained him.

Not the same him.

Just him.

One mirror showed a young Arthur in a factory uniform. Shoulders straight. Jaw set. Grease on his hands and the kind of certainty that comes from believing your back will never hurt.

Another showed a middle-aged Arthur at a kitchen table, leaning forward mid-argument. His hands were animated, his face flushed, his certainty now sharpened into defensiveness.

Another showed an elderly Arthur seated beside Margaret, laughing. Not politely. Fully laughing. Head tilted back. Eyes half-closed.

Arthur took a careful breath. It sounded very loud in a world made of silence.

He stepped closer to the nearest mirror.

The young factory Arthur didn't notice him. He was busy tightening something invisible with heroic confidence.

Arthur studied him. "You thought you were indestructible," he said.

The reflection kept working.

Arthur moved on.

In another mirror, he was alone. Sitting at a table. The chair across from him empty. The light too bright.

In another, he was weeping. Not dramatically. Just leaking.

In another, he was already gone. The mirror showed a hospital bed. Sheets folded. No body. Just absence arranged neatly.

"That's rude," Arthur said.

The reflections shifted continuously. The young Arthur grew older in a blink. The older Arthur became a boy again. The weeping Arthur dried his face and began laughing. The laughing Arthur faded into shadow.

None of them held still long enough to be selected.

Arthur frowned.

"This is poorly organized," he informed the horizon.

The horizon didn't respond.

He walked further. The planet curved gently under him, but the mirrors kept their posture. Each one contained a possibility he had already exhausted.

Then he saw her.

Margaret stood in a mirror slightly to his left.

Not young. Not retouched. Not glowing like a perfume advertisement.

Her face was lined. Fully lined. Beautifully lined.

The creases near her eyes deepened when she smiled. The corners of her mouth carried parentheses of memory. Her hair was threaded with silver like intentional decoration.

She stood beside him in the reflection—an older him. They were close but not touching.

Arthur felt the instinct rise in him. The same one from before. The reaching. The grabbing. The desperate need to confirm substance.

He didn't reach.

He simply looked.

"Well," he said softly, "there you are."

Margaret in the mirror didn't wave. She didn't perform. She simply existed. Entire. Unfiltered.

Arthur swallowed. "You look exactly like you should."

The reflection shifted. She aged slightly more. Then slightly less. Then she laughed at something he could not hear.

Arthur exhaled slowly.

He moved on.

Another mirror caught his eye.

This one showed him younger again. Not factory-young. Post-factory. Pre-regret. He looked leaner. Sharper. Certain in the way only the not-yet-humbled can be.

Arthur stepped closer.

"That one," he said. "That one I could work with."

He lifted his hand and pressed his palm against the glass.

The surface was cool.

The reflection changed instantly.

The younger Arthur aged beneath his hand like fruit left too long in the sun. Lines formed. Hair thinned. Shoulders curved. The certainty dissolved into something gentler and less negotiable.

Arthur jerked his hand back.

"No," he snapped. "Hold still."

The mirror refused.

He turned to another.

In this one, he sat in the dining hall at Sunny Meadows, talking. He could see the whole room. Margaret sat across from him, quiet, smiling.

The image fractured suddenly into three versions.

In one, he apologized.

In another, he argued, grabbed his walker and left.

In the third, he said nothing at all, and the silence calcified.

Arthur felt irritation crawl up his spine.

"Pick one," he demanded. "Just pick one."

The reflections multiplied. Three became six. Six became twelve.

He spun around. Everywhere he looked, versions of himself flickered, shifted, dissolved. Young, old, angry, kind, alive, dead.

"I want one," Arthur barked. "Just one I prefer."

The mirrors didn't obey.

The young factory Arthur's back began to ache. The laughing elderly Arthur began coughing. The weeping Arthur began laughing. The dead Arthur sat up and looked confused.

Arthur's breathing grew shallow.

"This isn't how reflection works," he insisted. "You're supposed to show me what I am."

The nearest mirror flickered. It showed him exactly as he stood—wrinkled, slightly hunched, frustrated.

Then it shifted to show him as a boy.

Then a corpse.

Then nothing at all.

Arthur's temper, which had survived management and cold soup, finally snapped.

He stepped forward and punched the glass.

The mirror shattered outward in absolute silence.

No crash. No clatter. Just a bloom of fragmentation.

Shards hung suspended in the air like frozen rain.

And in each shard—

Arthur.

Infinite Arthurs.

Tiny ones. Distorted ones. Sideways ones.

In one shard, he was smiling. In another, he was mid-argument. In another, he was sitting beside Margaret. In another, he was alone.

Even broken, the truth multiplied.

Arthur staggered back, breathing hard.

"Fine," he said to no one. "Multiply."

The shards slowly drifted downward. As they touched the reflective ground, they dissolved—not into nothing, but into surface. The mirror reformed. Not perfectly. A faint seam remained. But whole.

Arthur stared at it.

"You repair yourself?"

The planet offered no explanation.

He turned slowly, taking in the endless curvature of upright glass. The sky burned faintly red at the edges. The ground reflected everything without commentary.

He looked down at his own reflection beneath his feet.

It didn't change.

It simply mirrored him as he was. Breathing hard. Eyes damp.

He felt something inside him loosen. Not break. Just loosen.

"You don't get to pick," he murmured.

The words felt less like defeat and more like instruction.

The horizon shimmered.

The mirrors thinned into brightness. The reflective ground softened into something less exacting.

And then Arthur was seated on a barstool, as though he'd always been there.

The Great Beyond throbbed gently around him. The bar curved in impossible geometry. The stars outside the panoramic window rotated like patient thoughts.

Iris stood behind the counter, polishing a glass that seemed to contain dawn. Her plum-colored skin glowed softly. Her many eyes regarded him with professional curiosity.

"How was the excursion?" she asked lightly. "The Planet of Mirrors?"

Arthur stared at his hands. They were intact. Slightly trembling.

"Crowded," he said.

Iris poured him a drink that emitted a faint golden steam.

Arthur accepted it. "I broke one."

"Yes," Iris said pleasantly.

He squinted at her. "You saw that?"

"I see many things," she smiled. "It's all these eyes I have."

Arthur chuckled and took a sip. It tasted like something honest.

"I wanted to pick the version of me I liked," he admitted. "Thought maybe I could settle on one. Streamline the inventory."

Iris tilted her head. "And?"

"They wouldn't hold still," Arthur said. "Even broken, they multiplied."

Iris nodded. "You can't edit truth."

Arthur snorted softly. "I figured that out."

"Down there," Iris continued, gesturing vaguely toward wherever down was, "broken glass reforms. Repairs itself. Not perfectly. But whole."

Arthur considered that. "So, the cracks stay."

"Yes."

He looked into his drink. His reflection shimmered in it. Older. Present.

"I saw Margaret," he said.

Iris's eyes softened. "Yes."

"She wasn't smoothed," Arthur said. "No enhancements. Full lines."

"As she was."

Arthur nodded slowly. "She once told her son she earned her face."

"And she did."

He looked at Iris. "Reflection isn't revision."

"No."

"Wrinkles are proof."

"Yes."

He exhaled. "Cold soup is still soup."

Iris smiled faintly. "And truth doesn't take edits."

Arthur lifted his glass slightly. "You're very calm about this."

"I've had practice."

He took another sip. The warmth traveled outward from his chest like a rumor of sunrise.

"So that's it?" he asked. "No filter?"

"No filter," Iris confirmed.

Arthur nodded.

"Fine," he said. "Don't have a choice. I'll keep the whole set, then."

Outside the window, the stars turned without distortion.

Chapter 12

The television in the common room had achieved a kind of minor divinity.

It glowed blue and constant, like a cheap god that accepted no offerings except attention. The residents of Sunny Meadows sat arranged before it in vinyl chairs that sighed when occupied. The light washed over their faces in patient waves, bleaching them into a congregation of blinking parishioners.

On the screen, four politicians shouted at once. The network had arranged them into tidy split-screen boxes, as though civility could be achieved through geometry.

It hadn't been achieved.

David paused at the doorway. Today, he could tell where Arthur was by the density of irritation in the air.

There he was. Slumped in his usual vinyl throne, his walker nearby standing guard. The googly eyes attached to it stared at the television with permanent astonishment.

Onscreen, a man in a navy suit jabbed a finger toward the camera. In the adjacent box, a woman in red did the same thing, though perhaps more elegantly. Beneath them crawled a red banner announcing BREAKING NEWS in letters that seemed permanently broken.

Arthur didn't blink.

"Morning," David said, taking the chair beside him.

Arthur nodded toward the screen. "I see the circus arrived early."

David glanced at the split-screen shouting match. "You're watching it."

"I also watch hurricanes," Arthur replied. "Doesn't mean I support them."

The volume was slightly too loud. It'd been set by someone who believed hearing loss could be defeated through sheer amplification. The panelists' voices overlapped in competitive indignation.

David leaned closer. "What are they even arguing about?"

Arthur squinted. "Hard to say. They're all winning simultaneously."

Onscreen, a moderator attempted to regain control, speaking in a tone normally reserved for kindergarten teachers and hostage negotiators.

Arthur sniffed. "Used to be simpler."

David raised an eyebrow. "Politics?"

"Circuses," Arthur clarified.

David smiled faintly. "You don't think it was always like this?"

Arthur considered the question with suspicious seriousness. "Oh, we had our villains," he said. "Big ones. Some of them had impressive mustaches. But at least they believed in something. Now . . . all this . . . it's performance art."

On the screen, the image cut to archival footage of a rally. Then to a graph. Then, to a man standing before a digital map glowing red and blue like a malfunctioning Christmas tree.

"It's fragmented," Arthur continued. "Nobody's driving the car. They're all honking."

David watched the scrolling headlines beneath the chaos. Each sentence was engineered to spark a minor heart attack.

"You don't think the stakes are higher now?" David asked.

Arthur tilted his head. "The stakes are always high. That's the trick. You keep people convinced the sky is permanently falling. They'll never notice who's holding the ladder."

David folded his arms. "You sound cynical."

Arthur shook his head. "No. Cynicism implies I expect better."

Onscreen, a commentator declared the nation to be "on the brink." The word brink appeared in bold type, as though the network had personally measured it.

Arthur leaned back in his chair. The vinyl groaned in sympathy.

"You know what this is?" he said.

"What?"

"An outrage economy."

David blinked. "That's a phrase."

"The outrage economy manufactures nothing and sells everything," Arthur said. "You see, outrage is renewable. Self-sustaining. Doesn't require facts. Just volume."

The split screen multiplied briefly into six smaller windows. All six faces appeared indignant, as though outrage were a competitive sport with strict training regimens.

Arthur gestured vaguely at the television. "They don't want agreement. Agreement doesn't trend."

"Trend?" David echoed. "You know about that?"

Arthur glanced sideways at him. "I read things."

David laughed. "I thought you didn't like the internet."

"I don't like the soup either," Arthur said. "Doesn't mean I don't know what temperature it's supposed to be."

A younger resident—Robert, who wore athletic sneakers as though preparing for a sprint that would never be announced—leaned forward from the couch behind them.

"Did you see what Senator Wilkes tweeted this morning?" Robert said eagerly. "It's blowing up."

Arthur didn't turn around. "Explosions are rarely productive."

Robert persisted. "No, seriously. It's exposing everything. People are furious."

Arthur exhaled slowly. "People are always furious. That's the point."

Robert frowned. "But this is different."

Arthur turned then, fixing Robert with a look that'd once quieted machinery.

"The good Senator's angry tweet won't save the republic," he said evenly. "Actions are always required for such things."

Robert blinked.

David coughed to disguise a smile. "You're going to get banned from the common room."

Arthur shrugged. "They need me. I'm the balance."

Onscreen, the moderator declared a commercial break. The panelists froze mid-expression, caught between fury and dental advertisement.

The commercials arrived in cheerful formation—insurance that wasn't needed, medication with names you couldn't pronounce, and a luxury cruise to a tropical paradise that no one in Sunny Meadows had heard of.

David leaned back. "So what was it like when you were younger?"

Arthur considered. "Quieter."

"That's it?"

"Quieter arguments," Arthur clarified. "Fewer microphones. If someone wanted to yell at you, they had to come to your house. Or you read it in the newspaper."

David nodded. "And now?"

Arthur gestured at the screen, which had returned to its shouting quartet. "Now they rent space in your pocket." He pointed a shaky finger at David's chest.

David looked down. There was his smartphone, nestled in his shirt pocket like a polite accomplice. It was a little black box full of lightning and opinions, waiting for the right moment to tell him the world was ending.

"Politics," Arthur muttered, leaning closer, lowering his voice as if revealing a sacred truth. "Is just traffic with fancier cars."

David laughed. "What?"

"Think about it," Arthur said. "Everyone insists they're in the right lane. Everyone believes the other drivers are idiots. Nobody wants to slow down. And there's always some guy merging without signaling."

Onscreen, the debate intensified. A graphic labeled CRISIS NOW flashed repeatedly.

David shook his head. "So what's the solution? Stop watching?"

Arthur eyed the television. "You can't stop watching completely. You just have to remember it's a show."

The blue light flickered slightly as the signal adjusted. It cast the residents in cool tones, making them look like statues of thoughtful disappointment.

Arthur leaned forward.

"They figured out something important," he said. "Fear keeps you seated. Outrage keeps you clicking. And division keeps you predictable."

David glanced at the other residents. Mrs. Davenport nodded along as if personally consulted. Mr. Kline snored softly, immune to brinksmanship.

"And you?" David asked. "What keeps you watching?"

Arthur considered that longer than expected.

"Habit," he said finally. "And curiosity. I like to see which direction the wind claims to be blowing."

The moderator on television demanded order again. The panelists ignored her in perfect unison.

Arthur sighed. "Look at them. None of them are listening. They're just waiting for their turn to shout."

David studied the screen. It was hard to tell who was speaking at any given moment. The captions attempted heroism.

"Do you think it's worse now?" David asked quietly.

Arthur stared at the shouting faces.

"No," he said after a moment. "It's just louder."

The room fell briefly silent during another commercial break. The blue light softened.

Arthur shifted in his chair. "You want to know the real danger?"

David nodded.

"When you start believing the performance is the substance," Arthur said. "When you forget that politics is supposed to be boring. Roads. Budgets. Soup temperatures."

David smiled faintly. "Soup again."

"It's always soup," Arthur said. "Sooner or later."

Onscreen, the debate resumed. The chyron now read FINAL SHOWDOWN.

Arthur watched for another minute, then reached forward and muted the television.

The screen continued its frantic pantomime, but no sound accompanied it.

The room felt larger immediately.

Arthur leaned back, satisfied. "See?"

David looked at the silent shouting faces. They appeared almost ridiculous without volume.

Arthur folded his hands again. "Much better."

The blue light still washed over them. But without noise, it felt less like a tide and more like decoration.

The lunch carts arrived at precisely eleven forty-five, which was the official time for surrender.

They rolled into the common area with the solemnity of parade floats and the enthusiasm of tax auditors. Stainless steel compartments rattled softly, releasing faint aromas that had once been vegetables.

Arthur watched them approach with the expression of a man who had seen civilizations invent the wheel, perfect the wheel, argue about the wheel, and finally decide walking was simpler after all.

"Brace yourself," he muttered.

David adjusted in his chair. "It's just soup."

Arthur turned his head slowly. "That," he said, "is how civilizations fall."

The cart stopped beside their table. A young aide with determined cheerfulness set down two trays, each with a bowl of split pea soup.

Steam didn't rise.

Steam had apparently filed for retirement.

Arthur stared into the bowl. He didn't immediately touch it. He studied it the way archaeologists study ruins.

"It's reflective," he said.

David leaned in. "Different color, at least. It's green."

"It's cold," Arthur corrected.

He dipped his spoon cautiously, as if checking for structural integrity. He lifted it halfway. A sluggish ribbon of soup dripped back into the bowl with a soft plop.

Arthur froze.

He closed his eyes briefly, as if centering himself before delivering difficult news.

Then, with ceremony, he raised the spoon high above his head.

The movement drew mild attention from neighboring tables. Mrs. Davenport paused mid-chew. Mr. Kline blinked twice, which for him qualified as civic engagement.

Arthur held the spoon aloft like a protest sign. Split pea trailed downward in slow, resigned threads.

"Ladies and gentlemen," he began, voice steady but resonant, "I stand before you today in the shadow of a great injustice."

David groaned softly. "Oh no."

"Oh, yes," Arthur continued, ignoring him. "We gather once again beneath fluorescent tyranny to confront the failure of Thermal Responsibility."

A few residents turned their heads. The room had little else to offer.

Arthur pointed the spoon at his bowl. "Observe. A liquid allegedly intended for nourishment. Yet lacking the fundamental quality of warmth."

He leaned toward David. "Feel it."

David placed a fingertip against the rim. He recoiled. "Okay. Yeah. That's chilly."

Arthur nodded gravely. "Stone-cold," he announced. "Colder than a campaign promise in February."

He lowered the spoon slightly, then lifted it again for emphasis.

"If I were a politician," Arthur declared, "I would run on a platform of Thermal Integrity."

David folded his arms. "You're running now?"

"I've always been running," Arthur said. "Just usually from responsibility."

He turned slightly in his chair, addressing the room more broadly.

"Ask yourselves," he continued, "how can a leader who cannot keep split pea soup at a respectable temperature possibly manage a national budget?"

A murmur drifted across the dining hall. It might've been agreement. It might've been dentures adjusting.

Arthur pressed on.

"You start with cold soup," he said, "and next thing you know, you've got lukewarm infrastructure."

David rubbed his temples. "That's not how infrastructure works."

"It's exactly how it works," Arthur insisted. "It begins with temperature neglect."

He gestured toward the kitchen doors. "Today it's split pea. Tomorrow it's fiscal policy."

Mrs. Davenport gave a faint clap, perhaps out of habit.

Arthur acknowledged her with a dignified nod.

"My administration," he said, "would guarantee a minimum thermal standard. No bowl below regulation warmth. No spoon left shivering."

David laughed despite himself. "And how would you fund this revolutionary heating agenda?"

Arthur paused, considering. "Common sense," he replied. "And possibly a microwave."

The aide who'd delivered the soup pretended not to hear any of this. She rearranged napkins with exaggerated focus.

Arthur lowered the spoon just enough to inspect the soup again. The surface quivered faintly from his earlier theatrics.

He sighed.

"Do you know what this is?" he asked David.

"Soup."

"No. It is symbolic negligence."

David picked up his own spoon and stirred experimentally. The liquid moved with reluctant cooperation.

"Maybe it's meant to be this way," David offered.

Arthur narrowed his eyes. "No sir. Warmth implies intention."

He leaned closer to the bowl as though interrogating it. "Were you ever warm?" he demanded softly.

The soup declined to answer.

Arthur leaned back again and resumed his speech posture.

"My fellow diners," he announced, "we deserve better."

Mr. Kline's spoon slipped from his hand and clattered onto his tray. Arthur pointed at the fallen utensil.

"See? Despair."

David shook his head, smiling. "You're impossible."

"I'm principled," Arthur corrected.

He lowered the spoon and finally tasted the soup.

He paused.

His face underwent several quiet recalibrations.

"Still cold," he confirmed.

David tasted his own. The verdict matched.

Arthur placed the spoon carefully on the table, aligning it parallel to the bowl as though preserving evidence.

"You know," he said more quietly now, "temperature matters."

David studied him. "It's soup."

"It's expectation," Arthur said. "You're told it will warm you. You believe it. You open yourself up to that possibility."

He tapped the side of the bowl. "And then—this."

David didn't respond immediately.

Arthur's tone shifted again, losing some of its campaign energy.

"When something is meant to comfort," he said, "it should at least try."

The fluorescent lights hummed overhead, impartial as ever.

David glanced around the room—the bent shoulders, the careful chewing, the long pauses between bites.

"You're saying it's not all about the soup."

Arthur gave him a sideways look. "I'm saying," he replied, "if you can't get the small things right, people stop believing in the big ones."

David looked down at his bowl. The surface was smooth again, reflecting pale ceiling light.

Arthur picked up his spoon once more, though not as high this time. He regarded it thoughtfully.

"You think they'll ever heat it properly?" David asked.

Arthur considered this with theatrical seriousness.

"Not without oversight," he said.

"And you're volunteering?"

Arthur gave a faint smile. "I'm retired from pretty much everything," he said. "But not from standards."

He dipped the spoon back into the soup.

For a moment, he held it there, feeling the cold against the metal.

Then he ate another spoonful.

It wasn't better.

He chewed slowly, swallowed, and nodded once as if confirming a long-held suspicion.

"Campaign begins tomorrow," he said.

David laughed. "I'll design the posters."

Arthur looked satisfied. Not because the soup had improved. It hadn't. But because he'd named the problem.

And sometimes naming a thing was the closest you could get to warming it.

The television was shouting again.

It always was.

Two commentators with symmetrical haircuts were arguing about the fate of civilization as if civilization were a casserole someone had left in too long. Their voices rose and collided, sharp and indignant. A red banner crawled across the bottom of the screen announcing CATASTROPHE in bold, patriotic font.

Arthur stabbed his spoon into the soup. It sort of gurgled.

Plastic trays clattered around him. Someone coughed in the corner. A nurse laughed too brightly at something that wasn't funny. Shoes shuffled against linoleum with the determination of people who'd nowhere urgent to go.

Arthur glared at the television.

"You see this?" he muttered to David. "They're yelling about the end of the world between pharmaceutical commercials."

David played with the two peas in his soup, moving them around in a circle. "It keeps people informed."

"Informed of what?" Arthur snapped. "That everyone's furious?"

On screen, one anchor leaned forward and declared something "unacceptable." The other nodded gravely, as if unacceptable things were their specialty.

Arthur lifted a finger toward the screen. "There. That one. He looks like he irons his jeans."

David snorted. "That's your issue?"

"It starts there," Arthur insisted.

He tried to hold onto his indignation. It'd always served him well. Indignation was structure. It was scaffolding. If you were mad enough at the world, you didn't have to admit the world might simply continue without consulting you.

But the shouting kept going.

The words began to blur into rhythm rather than meaning. Urgent phrases repeated.

Crisis.

Outrage.

Historic.

Unprecedented.

The anchors' voices braided together until they sounded less like debate and more like chanting.

Arthur felt something inside him sag.

"Does anyone ever fix anything?" he asked.

David shrugged. "Sometimes."

"When?"

David considered this. "After they finish yelling?"

Arthur leaned back in his chair and let his head rest against the wall. The cool surface pressed against his skull.

The television's neon glow shifted from angry red to a strange violet as his vision softened. The scrolling text at the bottom of the screen smeared into a single luminous ribbon.

Plastic trays clacked. Forks scraped. The anchors kept talking.

Arthur closed one eye. Then the other.

The noise didn't stop. It simply rearranged itself.

The shouting became less pointed, more musical. The repetition of phrases formed a rhythm, almost gentle. Almost hypnotic.

He'd spent decades being a critic. He had opinions about soup, about politics, about the proper temperature of coffee, and the improper temperature of civilization. He'd even believed, with admirable stubbornness, that commentary mattered.

But the world on the screen didn't pause for his corrections. It didn't request edits. It didn't lower its voice.

His spoon slipped from his fingers.

It struck the tray with a soft metallic clink that sounded disproportionately small compared to the volume of the apocalypse on television.

David looked over. "You okay?"

Arthur didn't answer immediately.

His chin had begun its slow descent toward his chest.

The violet haze thickened. The anchors' voices melted into a steady drone, like distant machinery operating without oversight.

Arthur exhaled through his nose.

"For once," he murmured faintly, "I'm clocking out."

His head settled forward.

The television continued shouting.

Arthur, at last, did not.

Arthur opened his eyes, expecting fluorescent lighting and the faint medicinal perfume of disinfectant. He was prepared for the aroma of chilled split pea soup—the institutional bouquet of overcooked vegetables and lowered expectations.

Instead, he inhaled something expensive.

Ozone, faintly metallic and clean, braided with the smoky sweetness of aged bourbon. It was the kind of smell that suggested someone had dusted the universe and polished it afterward.

Arthur was sitting on a barstool that knew how much it cost. Before him stretched a polished counter so flawless it reflected him with unnerving honesty.

"Well," he muttered, inspecting the reflection. "Either I'm dead, or the soup improved."

Behind the bar stood Iris.

She was as poised as a cathedral that'd never known scaffolding. Her plum-colored skin carried the subtle luminescence of something older than fashion. Her many eyes regarded him not with surprise, but with the professional patience of someone who had seen civilizations argue themselves hoarse.

Outside the massive panoramic windows of the star cruiseship The Great Beyond, a violet nebula coiled lazily, as if stirring itself for dramatic effect. Within that glowing cloud hung a planet—round, theatrical, and brimming with activity. The Arena Planet.

Arthur squinted. "What's the circus this time?"

Iris slid a glass toward him. The liquid inside was amber and perfectly chilled, though it emitted a warmth that defied refrigeration.

"Back so soon, Arthur?" she asked lightly, wiping an invisible speck from the counter with a cloth that appeared to be woven from starlight. "You look like you've just come from a riot."

Arthur picked up the glass. The rim caught the nebula's glow and fractured it into delicate prisms. He watched, through localized projection fields embedded in the windows, as figures on the Arena Planet below swung glowing staves at one another.

"Are they arguing over soup?" he asked, gesturing vaguely toward the galaxy.

On the planet's surface, a man in ceremonial armor—labeled Sector Senator in floating holographic text—leapt forward dramatically. His staff collided with another leader's in a cascade of sparks that appeared calibrated for visual impact rather than injury.

Camera drones hovered like obedient dragonflies.

Iris leaned slightly, observing the spectacle with detached interest. "It's the annual Nutritional Crisis," she explained.

Arthur took a slow sip. The warmth traveled down his throat and into his ribs, settling there like an old friend who knew when to speak and when not to.

"They look serious," he said.

"They're rehearsed," Iris corrected.

Below, one of the Leaders—an athletic woman with a cape that rippled at precisely photogenic intervals—shouted something about equity and seasoning. The drones zoomed in. Her opponent countered with a manifesto about tradition and proper broth viscosity.

Despite the sparks and acrobatics, no blood appeared. No wounds. Just spectacle.

Arthur leaned forward. "You telling me none of them actually get hurt?"

"Not in ways that interrupt funding," Iris replied.

A Senator took a theatrical dive, clutching his side as though pierced by ideological shrapnel. The drones swarmed him sympathetically. A medic hurried in—not to treat, but to reposition him for a better angle.

Arthur snorted. "Looks familiar."

"Sunny Meadows?" Iris asked.

"Everywhere," Arthur said. "Everybody swinging sticks at each other about soup temperature. Nobody tasting it."

He glanced at his glass. The amber liquid shimmered as if it understood the comparison.

On the Arena Planet, a giant holographic banner unfurled above the battlefield: For the Future of Flavor. The crowd—projected, amplified, algorithmically intensified—roared on cue.

Arthur shook his head. "When I argued at the kitchen table, at least there was a kitchen."

Iris raised one brow—she had many, and could spare one for punctuation. "You believe the stakes were higher?"

"I believe the soup was real."

Another leader twirled her staff and delivered a speech about authenticity. Her voice echoed dramatically across the nebula, edited for resonance.

Arthur watched as her image flickered, subtly smoothed by invisible filters. Lines softened. Jaw sharpened. Light corrected.

"They've filtered them," he said.

"Yes," Iris answered.

"Why?"

"To make conviction more symmetrical."

Arthur huffed. "Conviction isn't symmetrical."

Below, the so-called wounded Senator sprang up miraculously revitalized. The crowd roared again.

Arthur took another sip. "They ever solve anything?"

"Define solve."

"Soup gets warmer. People eat. Nobody swings glowing sticks."

Iris considered. "They recalibrate the recipe annually."

Arthur stared. "You're joking."

"I don't joke," Iris said calmly. "I only describe."

He leaned back on the stool. It adjusted itself to his spine like a respectful chiropractor.

"So, what's the point?" he asked.

"Attention," Iris said. "Attention is the currency. Conflict is the advertisement."

Arthur watched the Arena Planet more closely now. The Leaders' movements were precise. Choreographed. Sparks erupted at predictable intervals. The manifestos rhymed suspiciously well.

One shouted, "For the purity of broth!"

Another countered, "For the freedom of spice!"

Arthur blinked. "They sound like children arguing over crayons."

"They are," Iris said gently. "The crayons are expensive."

Arthur's gaze drifted beyond the Arena Planet to the violet nebula swirling around it. The gas clouds shimmered with indifferent beauty. No banners. No manifestos. Just physics.

"Do they know?" he asked.

"Know what?"

"That it's theater."

Iris polished the counter again, though it needed nothing. "Some do. They call it necessary."

"Necessary for what?"

"Continuity."

Arthur grunted. "Continuity of what?"

"Belief."

On the planet below, the Leaders paused mid-skirmish to deliver synchronized closing statements. The drones hovered closer. The lighting intensified.

Arthur shook his head slowly. "All that energy over soup."

"Soup is never just soup," Iris said.

He narrowed his eyes at her. "You're going philosophical on me."

"It's an occupational hazard."

Arthur stared at the Senator who'd taken the dramatic dive earlier. The man now stood victorious, raising his staff as if he'd personally served justice.

"No blood," Arthur murmured.

"Not today."

"And tomorrow?"

"Tomorrow is another broadcast."

Arthur let that settle. The counter reflected his face—lined, unfiltered, exactly as it was. He studied the wrinkles near his eyes. They didn't shimmer. They didn't smooth themselves.

"Down there," he said, gesturing toward the Arena Planet, "they could warm the soup. But they don't. Instead, they fight about it."

Iris nodded faintly. "Warmth is quieter than conflict."

He looked back at the battlefield. The Leaders were bowing now. Applause cascaded like artificial rain. The banner dissolved into sponsor logos.

Arthur tapped the rim of his glass thoughtfully. "You ever think maybe they're scared?"

"Of?"

"Tasting it."

Iris tilted her head. "Go on."

"If they taste it and it's still cold," Arthur continued, "then all the arguing was for nothing."

Iris's eyes reflected the nebula in miniature. "You suspect the temperature is irrelevant?"

"I suspect," Arthur said, "that nobody wants to admit they're hungry."

The nebula pulsed faintly, as if amused.

Arthur took the last sip of his drink. Warmth bloomed in his chest. "Back at the home," he said, "we complain about cold soup. But we eat it anyway."

"Yes."

"We don't stage duels."

"No."

"We just grumble."

"That's your species' quieter art form."

Arthur watched the Arena Planet dim as the broadcast concluded. The Leaders exited through concealed hatches. The drones powered down. The planet's surface lights shifted to standby mode.

Without the projection filters, the surface looked smaller. Less heroic.

"Looks tired," Arthur observed.

"It is."

He set the empty glass on the counter. It made a soft, satisfying sound. Real. Unamplified.

"You ever serve them drinks?" he asked.

"Occasionally."

"They tip?"

"Generously," Iris replied. "With promises."

Arthur chuckled. "Figures."

Silence settled, but it wasn't the sterile silence of a hospital corridor. It was the spacious kind—the kind that allowed thoughts to stretch without bumping into fluorescent lights.

Arthur leaned his elbows on the counter. "So, what's the lesson?"

Iris regarded him. "Must there be one?"

"There's always one," Arthur said. "Otherwise, why bother."

Iris considered this. "Perhaps the lesson," she said slowly, "is that spectacle is easier than sincerity."

Arthur nodded. "And cold soup is easier than admitting you don't know how to cook."

"That too."

Outside, the violet nebula continued its patient swirl. No manifestos. No camera drones. Just light bending around gravity like it always had.

Arthur slid the empty glass forward slightly.

"You think they'll ever stop fighting over soup?" he asked.

Iris refilled the glass halfway. The amber liquid caught the starlight and held it without distortion.

"When they decide to taste it together," she said.

Arthur considered that. He lifted the glass but didn't drink yet.

"And if they don't?"

Iris's smile was gentle, eternal, and not particularly optimistic.

"Then they'll keep swinging glowing sticks," she replied.

Arthur finally took another sip.

Warmth returned to his bones again.

Chapter 13

Arthur sat alone on a worn wooden bench in the garden at Sunny Meadows, though "alone" was relative. A water fountain burbled somewhere nearby, like it had secrets it would never tell. The birds flitted between the bushes and the rose trellises as if rehearsing some very minor catastrophe. The sunlight fell in dappled patches on the flagstones, but Arthur didn't notice the flowers. He stared at his hands.

They were gnarled, a lattice of veins and knuckles like twisted roots dug out of dry soil. He flexed them. The skin creaked. It didn't sound like skin. It sounded like wood—a branch being coaxed into shape, reluctantly, with the wrong tools.

David appeared quietly at the garden gate. He paused for a moment, taking in the little courtyard with its carefully pruned hedges, its iron benches, and a fountain that dribbled in what might've been poetic rhythm—or just neglected plumbing.

"Well, this is a first," David said.

Arthur didn't look up.

"I mean, why have we never visited it together?" David asked.

Arthur's mouth quirked, but only slightly. Not a smile. Not a frown. Something between recognition and resignation.

"This is my special place," he said. "Used to be. Now . . . it isn't. Not anymore."

David sat on the bench next to him. "Used to be?"

Arthur's eyes still didn't leave his hands. "Margaret used to bring me here," he said. "She had a way of making the air smell like it had secrets. The roses, the lavender, even the old bench under the elm—it all seemed to breathe with intention. But I was a child then. I didn't notice much, except that I liked being here . . . with her."

David nodded, cautiously. "Is . . . something wrong?"

Arthur finally looked up. It took a while, like the signal had to travel a long distance through bad wiring. His voice came out slow and scraped, the way an old record sounds when it insists on being played anyway. It had weight in it—not drama, not theatrics, just the dull, honest gravity of a man discovering that time doesn't steal things so much as it misplaces them and refuses to help you look.

"It's the ticking," he rasped. "Not the clocks. Not the ones on the walls, the ones in my hands that go round and round. It's the ticking in the marrow. My knees click when I stand. My pulse thumps in my ears like a drum in a basement. It goes on and on. Constant. Relentless. A rhythmic reminder that the machinery, my body, is grinding down. My mind wants to sprint, but the biological chassis is stuck in low gear, dragging itself through mud."

David shifted, uncomfortable with the sound of it—though the sound was internal, not audible. He waited for Arthur to continue.

"My grandfather," Arthur said, voice catching, "once told me, 'Never grow old.'"

David blinked.

"I laughed at him," Arthur admitted. "A child's laugh, sharp and dismissive. I thought him ridiculous. Foolish. A man afraid of shadows."

He looked down again at his hands, and his fingers twitched, as if they were considering escaping from the bones that held them.

"Now I get it," he said. "Every tick is a little stab, every heartbeat a memo from the universe saying, 'Sorry, pal, time never belonged to you. It never will. And it'll keep marching, with you, over you, and right past you.'"

David watched him, unsure if he should speak. There was nothing to say. The air felt too thin for platitudes.

"You ever get the feeling," Arthur said, "that time is a lousy jailer? Life hands you a row of doors, one after the other, and each one just dumps you into another hallway. You walk, you stumble, you think you're moving forward— but really, you're just practicing the motions. The walls sneak up behind you while you're busy picking the next lousy door."

David swallowed. "I think . . . maybe. Sometimes."

Arthur's gaze returned to his hands.

"Sometimes?" he said. "Time isn't polite. It doesn't wait for hesitation. It doesn't allow reconsideration. You miss a second, and it becomes a minute. You miss a minute, and it becomes an hour. Hours collect into days. Days into years. And then—one day—you realize the doors are fewer, the corridors longer, the walls higher. And the ticking is louder. Much louder."

David reached out and placed a hand lightly on Arthur's shoulder. "You're . . . not going to stop ticking," he said. "You shouldn't feel trapped by it."

Arthur looked up then, eyes polished black in the shadow of his lashes.

"You think you get it," he said, voice soft, like a man explaining gravity to a goldfish. "You don't. You can't. You're too young to have watched yourself rust from the inside out, muscles waving goodbye, joints sneaking off to their own schedule, mind remembering too much while the body forgets. You think time is kind. It's not kind at all. It's cruel. Time's a pendulum swinging with no regard for mercy or apology."

David blinked. "But maybe . . . maybe some of it's our fault," he said, careful. "The way we waste the time we get?"

Arthur let out a harsh laugh, dry as twigs. "Fault?" he said. "Do you think the sand waits to be blamed? Fault is a human illusion. Time doesn't punish. It merely continues. You're punished only by noticing, by existing long enough to recognize the decay, the shrinking of the horizon, the exhaustion of options."

David swallowed again, the words heavy in his throat. "So, what can we do?"

Arthur's hands, now resting in his lap, trembled slightly. He flexed the fingers. The wooden knuckles creaked. "Nothing. We can't stop the clock. Nothing that changes the marrow's beat. All we can do is notice. Hang on. Make something out of it while it passes. And we don't curse it. Not yet. Not until it arrives."

David frowned. "Hang on? That's it?"

"That's it," Arthur said. "Hang on. Observation. Silence. If you're lucky, you'll notice something beautiful in the cracks. If you're not . . . you'll miss it."

The garden was quiet again. The fountain dribbled. A small beetle struggled up a rose stem. A butterfly hesitated in the air, then fluttered onto a petal.

Arthur's voice softened, almost imperceptibly. "This garden . . . used to hold my childhood in its hands. I thought the petals could protect me from the tick, from the ache, from knowing that time wouldn't be still. Now . . . now it only reminds me. Reminds me that all the doors have already been opened, all the corridors walked, all the choices made. And yet . . ."

He lifted his gnarled hands slightly. "And yet the ticking goes on. No pleading can stop it. No wishing can still it. The pulse is relentless. It won't be silenced. And I . . . I'm not younger. Never younger. Only older. Step by step. Echo by echo."

David swallowed again. "Do you . . . regret?"

Arthur's laugh was like dry leaves. "Regret?" he said. "Perhaps. But regret is also a door, one of those I spoke of. You can knock on it, peer inside, and see . . . nothing. No remedy. Only what was. Only what will be. Time is patient, David. Patient and indifferent."

David reached out again. His hand hovered over Arthur's trembling fingers. "Then why tell me?"

Arthur finally looked at him. Eyes polished black, deep enough to drown in. "Because," he said, "to tell another is a rebellion of sorts. It doesn't change the tick. It doesn't alter the rhythm. But it acknowledges it. And acknowledgment . . . is a small victory. A quiet one, yes, but one nonetheless. You'll learn that later. That's what my grandfather was doing when he told me not to grow old. Winning a little battle against time."

David nodded. "I . . . think I understand."

Arthur leaned back slightly, the weight of years pressing into the stone bench beneath him. "Maybe you get it. Maybe you never will. Maybe it isn't about getting it at all. Maybe it's merely about noticing."

A shadow moved across the garden. The light shifted. The petals shivered in the breeze.

Arthur flexed his knuckles once more. They groaned like old timber. The ticking continued.

"You should come back here again," he said finally, almost gently. "Sit. Watch. Hang on. Notice. And maybe—just maybe—you'll get it—how time can be patient but in a most cruel way."

David didn't speak. He didn't move. He simply sat and observed.

And the ticking went on.

And Arthur's hands—gnarled, wooden, mercilessly honest—remained in his lap.

David had sometimes thought about the "golden years," about time mellowing the mind and softening the edges of life. But Arthur's words stopped him cold. There was no softening, no mellowing. There was only the raw, jagged edge of impatience and dread pressing against the skin.

David looked down at his own hands, smooth, unscarred, unremarkable. He flexed his fingers slowly, noting the absence of creaks, the absence of the tiny betrayals that Arthur's joints so audibly proclaimed. He looked back at Arthur's hands. They were twisted, a topography of age and experience. Each knuckle a hill, each vein a riverbed. David felt something sharp in his chest—a sudden pang, a taste of future grief, the knowledge that he too would one day inhabit those hands.

"I get it," David said finally. His voice was cautious, uncertain, but sincere. "Sometimes . . . I feel it too. Not the clicking, not the grinding machinery, but the rush. Like I'm standing in a river, and the water is moving too fast for me to grab anything. I try to listen to someone talk. But my brain is already three seconds behind, mourning the second that just passed."

Arthur's eyes found David's. Surprise tried to dance across his face, but he shooed it away like a stray cat. His shoulders loosened an inch, maybe two, not enough to matter, except that it did.

He leaned back, the bench groaning in sympathy—or complaint. Hard to tell which.

"That's the secret, kid," he said, voice low, rough, like gravel pressed into fabric. "You have to acknowledge the rust. If you pretend the clock isn't ticking, you'll go mad trying to keep time. Mad and polite. The worst combination imaginable."

He tapped a gnarled knuckle to his temple, a deliberate, almost ritualistic motion. "The lesson is simple: say the soup is cold. Say the world is spinning too fast. That your knees are yelling at you. That your pulse is drumming a war march in your ears. Name the demon before it names you. If you don't, it'll gnaw on you from the inside out."

David nodded, the metaphor landing with a weight heavier than expected. "But . . . sometimes it feels selfish, doesn't it? Complaining? Saying out loud what hurts?"

Arthur's eyes flicked to him. A glint of humor, thin and fleeting, passed across the shadowed expanse of his face. "Selfish? Maybe. Human? Definitely. And that's the point. Say it before the demon moves in and lodges itself between your ribs. But don't be a martyr. Nobody likes a martyr. Not even the moon, which has seen worse and still won't clap."

David chuckled softly. "So . . . just say it? Out loud?"

Arthur let out a bark of laughter that was equal parts amusement and exasperation. "Out loud. In your head. To the cat. To the neighbor's dog. Doesn't matter. Just don't swallow it until it solidifies into a bone. Speak your truth. Let it echo somewhere. Anywhere."

David leaned back, letting the sunlight touch the back of his neck. He imagined the ticking in his own body, soft at first, almost polite, then gathering volume, a steady metronome of his eventual decay. The sensation was oddly comforting, less a terror than a reminder of life, of presence.

"I think I get it," David said slowly, "Everyone's walking around with their own ticking. And they all pretend they're fine. But they're not. Everyone's just . . . drowning in invisible rivers."

Arthur nodded. "Exactly. And if you don't acknowledge it, you start judging everyone else for splashing. For gasping. For failing to keep up. Then you become one of those people who's angry all the time for no reason. Angry at the wind. Angry at the clock that refuses to pause. Angry at the soup. You become a complaint waiting to happen."

David tilted his head. "So, the soup is cold, the knees ache, the pulse drums . . . and we're allowed to say it. Without guilt?"

Arthur's expression softened, a rare thing. "Without guilt. Without shame. But with precision. You can't just scream into the void and call it a lesson. You have to name what's wrong, but also . . . how it makes you feel. Otherwise, the demon thinks you're negotiating, and you'll lose before you begin."

He flexed his wooden knuckles again, slow and deliberate.

"See this?" He held them up. "These aren't just hands. They're journals. Each crease, each ridge, each tremor—it's a story. You can't polish them away without erasing the narrative. And the narrative . . . that's all you really have in the end."

David's stomach knotted. He understood. Not fully, not yet, but the shape of it, the silhouette of the lesson, was beginning to form. The soup was cold, yes, but there was also a story in that coldness. There was meaning, even if bitter, even if unappetizing.

"I think . . . I understand," he said. "It's not about stopping the ticking. Because you can't. It's about . . . acknowledging it. Naming it. Letting it live with you."

Arthur smiled faintly. A twitch of the lips, more weary than amused. "Kid, that's exactly it. It's the difference between letting life pass you by like a freight train and actually riding in the caboose long enough to notice the sparks off the rails. And let me tell you . . . those sparks are glorious if you look."

David laughed softly, but it was hesitant, uncertain, like someone testing ice before stepping onto it. "Even cold soup has its place in the story."

Arthur's eyes sparkled for the briefest instant. "Exactly. Cold soup. Aching knees. Pulse drumming like a basement drumline. Life isn't polite. It doesn't check in or ask permission. It slaps you in the face, and you either call it out or it calls you out first."

David nodded again. His gaze drifted to the garden, to the shadows between the hedges, to the way the sun caught the petals of a rose just so. He realized, suddenly, that noticing was a form of defiance. A quiet rebellion against the ticking, against the slow grind of the marrow, against the inevitable rust.

"So . . . that's why you sit here," David said.

Arthur let out a sound somewhere between a chuckle and a groan. "Whenever I need to remind myself that I'm still in the story. That the ticking hasn't won yet. That the soup is still soup, and I'm still me, however gnarled and creaking."

David nodded. "I think . . . I think I want to learn that. To notice."

Arthur gave a slow, approving smile. "Good. That's the first step. The next steps . . . well, kid, they're yours to figure out. Nobody can hand them to you. You walk. You stumble. You acknowledge. You speak. And sometimes, if you're lucky, you laugh at the absurdity before it swallows you whole."

The garden remained quiet. The fountain dribbled. A small bird hopped across the stone path. A butterfly flitted past, unaware of any ticking, any rust, any cold soup.

David exhaled, long and deliberate. "I think… I'm ready to start noticing."

Arthur's knuckles creaked once more, a punctuation mark. "Noticing," he said, "is all we have. Until the clock stops, until the marrow obeys, until the soup is just soup, and nothing more."

They sat in silence after that. Side by side. Two observers of the relentless rhythm.

And the ticking went on.

And the garden, like life, continued without apology.

Arthur felt the warmth of the sun pressing through his shoulders, a gentle, golden weight that should've been comforting, but it only made the ticking in his knees more apparent. He'd closed his eyes for a moment, just a breath, just a blink, and when he opened them, the garden of Sunny Meadows had dissolved into something impossible. David was gone. The soil, the hedges, the roses—they were gone. In their place stretched a crystalline plateau, smooth and transparent, reflecting violet and gold light that pulsed in rhythm with a heartbeat he didn't recognize as his own.

He was sitting on a barstool that looked like it had been designed by someone who distrusted both chairs and human spines. The air was clean in a suspicious way, like it had never known dust and didn't intend to. The lighting came from nowhere obvious, which meant it came from everywhere, which meant someone had spent a great deal of money avoiding lamps.

Before him stretched a window. Not a window, really. Windows have edges. This thing had ambition. It curved, very large, a great transparent idea separating him from the universe.

And the universe was showing off.

A planet hung there, enormous and patient. Blue, green, and streaked with white, like it had been painted by someone with steady hands and no deadlines. Storms spiraled lazily. Continents drifted in silence. It looked alive in the way that made humans uncomfortable—because it didn't need them.

Arthur blinked once.

"Ah," he said. "There it is."

Behind the bar stood Iris.

She polished a glass that didn't need polishing. This was a theme. Iris always had something to do, even when there was nothing to be done. It was either a personality trait or a cosmic joke. Arthur had stopped trying to determine which.

"You're late," she said.

"Didn't know I had a schedule," he said.

She smiled. "Everyone has a schedule."

Arthur looked down at his hands.

They were not gnarled.

They were not young either. They were . . . cooperative. A middle ground. A diplomatic agreement between decay and denial.

He flexed them. No creak.

"That's suspicious," he muttered.

"Everything here is," Iris replied. "Drink?"

Arthur considered the question as if it had moral weight.

"Do I have a choice?"

"No," she said. "But you get to pretend you do."

"Good," Arthur said. "I've always enjoyed pretending."

She poured something amber into a glass that probably cost more than his first car, assuming his first car had been a mistake, which it had.

He took it. Sipped.

It tasted like memory and poor decisions.

"Ah," he said again. "Nostalgia. It's your specialty. Do I detect a hint of regret."

"House special," Iris said. "And yes . . . a bit of regret."

Arthur turned back to the window.

The planet rotated, slowly, like it had nowhere else to be. No urgency. No ticking. No knees clicking in protest. No pulse hammering out reminders of expiration dates.

Just motion. Endless, indifferent motion.

Arthur leaned forward slightly.

"Looks peaceful," he said.

"It isn't," Iris replied.

"Of course it isn't."

"Zoom," Iris said.

The window obeyed.

It wasn't a zoom in the technical sense. There was no sense of movement, no rush forward. The universe simply decided Arthur should see more, and so he did.

Clouds parted.

Storms revealed themselves—not poetic storms, not the kind painters enjoy, but the messy, violent kind that rearrange coastlines and cancel plans.

Lightning stitched the sky together in brief, violent threads. Waves rose and collapsed with the enthusiasm of things that do not understand moderation.

On a continent below, something moved. Cities, maybe. Or the idea of cities. Lights flickered in patterns that suggested intelligence or at least electricity.

Arthur watched.

"Busy place," he said.

"Very," Iris said.

"Ticking?"

"Oh yes."

Arthur nodded. "Of course."

He took another sip.

"You know," he said, "I was just explaining to a kid that time is a lousy jailer."

Iris raised an eyebrow. "And?"

"And now I'm here, watching a planet that doesn't seem particularly imprisoned."

Iris set the glass down. "You're making a common mistake."

Arthur sighed. "I specialize in those."

"You're confusing scale with mercy."

Arthur paused.

That was inconvenient, he thought.

He looked again.

The planet turned. Storms came and went. Somewhere down there, someone was being born. Somewhere else, someone was ending. Somewhere, someone was probably complaining about soup.

"Cold?" Arthur asked.

"Very," Iris said.

"Of course it is."

Arthur leaned back on the stool, which continued to distrust him.

"So, what's the lesson?" he asked. "There's always a lesson. This place runs on them."

Iris smiled, which was dangerous.

"The lesson," she said, "is that the ticking never stops."

Arthur gestured to the planet. "Tell me about it."

She moved beside him, looking out at the same impossible view.

"Every storm down there," she said, "thinks it's the whole story."

Arthur nodded slowly.

"And every calm moment thinks it earned the silence," she continued. "It didn't. It just arrived."

Arthur snorted. "Uninvited, I assume."

"Always."

Arthur tapped his glass lightly.

"So, all that business about acknowledging the ticking—naming the demon—"

"Still applies," Iris said. "Especially down there."

Arthur frowned. "But the planet doesn't care."

"No," Iris said. "But the people on it do."

Arthur watched a storm unravel itself over an ocean.

It didn't ask permission. It didn't apologize. It didn't check a calendar. It simply existed, did its work, and moved on.

Time, he thought.

Not cruel. Not kind. Just… thorough.

He looked at his hands again.

Still cooperative.

"My hands," he said. "Everything about my body. It will eventually fall apart.

"Yes," Iris agreed.

"Good," Arthur said.

She blinked. "Good?"

"If it lasted," Arthur said, "I'd start to think I'd won something."

"And you haven't?"

Arthur laughed. A real one this time. Short, sharp, honest.

"No," he said. "But I noticed."

He turned back to the window.

"That's the trick, isn't it?" he said. "Just . . . noticing."

Iris nodded.

"And saying it out loud," Arthur added. "Before it turns into something unpleasant and internal."

"Like a creaking bone," Iris said.

"Exactly like a creaking bone."

They stood there for a while.

The planet spun.

Storms came and went.

Somewhere, a sunrise happened. Somewhere else, something ended quietly, without witnesses.

Arthur watched it all with the expression of a man who had finally realized the joke was not at his expense.

It was just a joke.

"You going back?" Iris asked.

Arthur considered that.

He thought of the bench. The fountain. David, sitting there, trying very hard to understand something that couldn't be handed over like a pamphlet.

He thought of his hands. The real ones. The honest ones. The ones that told the story whether he liked it or not.

"Yes," Arthur said.

"Why? You know you can stay here if you'd like."

Arthur finished his drink.

"Because the soup is still there," he said. "And it's probably cold."

Iris smiled. "It is."

Arthur slid off the stool.

The ship hummed around him, full of quiet luxury and expensive indifference.

He took one last look at the planet.

"Hey," he said.

Iris tilted her head. "Yes?"

Arthur gestured toward the window.

"Nobody down there knows they're part of something this . . . big."

"No," Iris said. "They don't."

Arthur nodded.

"Good," he said. "They'd ruin it."

And then—

Without announcement. Without ceremony. Without permission. Arthur was gone. Back on the bench. Hands gnarled again. Honest again. The fountain still burbled its useless secrets.

David sat beside him, mid-thought, mid-breath, as if nothing had happened. Which, in a way, was true.

Arthur flexed his fingers. They creaked. The sound made him smile.

"Kid," he said.

David looked up. "Yeah?"

Arthur stared at the garden—the roses, the beetle, the butterfly that didn't care about any of this.

"Say it out loud," Arthur said. "Whatever it is. Even the cold soup. The universe won't file a complaint. Doesn't matter."

David blinked. "I will."

Arthur leaned back, like a man negotiating with gravity and losing politely.

"Do it before the ticking gets the better of you," he said. "And you can't hear anything else."

David looked at him then—not at the advice, not at the cleverness of it, but at Arthur himself. The hands. The posture. The way he occupied the bench like a well-read book no one was ready to close.

And it hit him, sudden and unfair.

The ticking wasn't personal. It was everywhere. In the roses. In the stones. In him. In Arthur. Only Arthur's was louder now, like a clock that had stopped pretending it would run forever.

A lump rose in David's throat, thick and immovable, like something that had decided to stay. He swallowed once, hard, as if that might push it back where it came from. It didn't. His eyes burned anyway.

He turned slightly, pretending to study the roses, because that's what people do when they're about to cry and would prefer not to advertise it. And all he could think, stupidly, helplessly, was that there wasn't enough time. Not for this. Not for him. Not for any of it.

The garden continued. The ticking continued. The story, stubborn and unimpressed, continued.

And Arthur—who had seen the whole ridiculous thing from a barstool in the stars—sat there and noticed.

Chapter 14

Arthur had begun to disappear in small, bureaucratic ways.

Not all at once. Not with trumpets. Not with a memo posted on the bulletin board beside the daily menu ("Tuesday: Cream of Something"). He simply began removing himself from the equation of daily life. It was subtraction, pure and simple.

"He hasn't been feeling well." That was how Nurse Kelly put it, in the same tone one might use for describing a late delivery of paper towels.

She made it sound as though wellness were a physical garment—a nice, warm overcoat, perhaps—that Arthur had simply misplaced somewhere between the garden bench and the dining hall.

David noticed it first in the spoon.

Arthur's hand, once capable of scooping up a pea from his soup with the precision of a duelist, now shook as if it had forgotten what a duel even was. The spoon rattled against the ceramic bowl like an impatient insect. It seemed offended by the journey.

"Don't know if I want to eat it," Arthur muttered one afternoon, eyeing the soup, "or propose to it."

His voice, which had once snapped like a dry twig underfoot, now sounded like paper rubbed between fingers. Papery. Thin. As if the air itself had to work harder to carry it.

David smiled the way people smile when they're trying not to panic. He looked down at his bowl of soup.

"I think it's staring back at me," David said.

Arthur blinked slowly. "That's your reflection. You look terrible."

There it was—the joke. The old blade. But it landed softly, like a butter knife.

Over the next several visits, the subtraction continued. Arthur grew weaker. Thinner. His cheeks hollowed as if someone had scooped a little bit of him out each night with a careful spoon. His collarbones rose into prominence beneath his shirt, sharp parentheses framing a sentence that was running out of words.

He slept more.

The nurses noticed it first because nurses notice everything. They noticed he no longer narrated the weather like a disgruntled anchorman. He no longer criticized the wallpaper. He stared less out the window. He spoke only when spoken to, and even then, as if speaking were a bill he'd to decide whether to pay.

Nurse Kelly wrote things down on a clipboard. Clipboards are where mystery goes to pretend it's paperwork.

"He's just tired," she told David one morning.

"Tired of what?" David asked.

She offered a small, diplomatic shrug.

"Living," she said. "It's exhausting."

Arthur would've approved of that line. He'd always maintained that existence was an endurance sport with no medals.

David tried not to catalog the changes. He tried not to notice how Arthur's hand rested longer on the arm of the chair before pushing himself up. How his breathing seemed to count the stairs even when he was sitting still. How sometimes his eyes drifted somewhere inward, as if reviewing footage from a previous life.

Once, in the garden, Arthur sat without commentary for a full five minutes.

Five minutes.

The roses trembled in a light breeze. A bee committed petty theft. Somewhere beyond the confines of Sunny Meadows, a lawn mower grumbled about its purpose. And Arthur said nothing.

David glanced sideways. "You're unusually quiet."

Arthur didn't look at him. "I'm conserving."

"For what?"

Arthur considered this. "For the end of the argument."

"What argument?"

Arthur closed his eyes. "The big one."

David laughed. He was supposed to laugh. That was the rule. Arthur said something ominous; David reframed it as wit. It was their little trade agreement.

But Arthur's eyelids fluttered as if even sarcasm had grown heavy.

Then one afternoon, it happened, David arrived at Sunny Meadows with the kind of optimism that borders on superstition. He had a cup of coffee, black, a rebellion against the institutional goo of the dining hall.

He checked the garden first.

Arthur wasn't on the bench. It looked strangely unoccupied, as if it'd misplaced its most dedicated critic. The sunlight spilled over the slats without being evaluated. No one squinted at it. No one accused it of being theatrical.

David waited a moment, half-expecting Arthur to materialize from behind the roses, muttering, "You're late. Time is a scam."

Nothing.

He moved inside.

One common area contained three residents and a television program about competitive baking. No Arthur.

The hallways—no Arthur.

David's optimism thinned.

He checked the dining hall even though it wasn't mealtime. The chairs were stacked in military formation. A cart waited in the corner like an obedient dog.

Arthur was nowhere.

It's remarkable how quickly the body understands before the mind agrees. David felt it first in his stomach, a small inward drop. Not panic. Not yet. Just more—subtraction.

He found Nurse Kelly at the station, reviewing a chart. The fluorescent lights hummed overhead with bureaucratic indifference.

"Hey," David said, aiming for casual and landing somewhere near brittle. "Have you seen Arthur?"

Nurse Kelly looked up.

There are pauses, and then there are pauses that contain information.

She didn't answer immediately. Her eyes softened in a way that made David wish they wouldn't.

She looked down. A small movement. Almost imperceptible.

Then she gently shook her head.

"He's in his room," she said softly. "In bed."

The words landed heavier than they should've. In bed. As if Arthur were simply indulging in laziness. As if beds were temporary.

"In bed?" David repeated, as though translation might improve it.

"He was tired today," she said. "Wanted to stay in his room."

David nodded, because nodding is what one does when the alternative is to demand a different script.

"Thanks," he said.

The hallway to Arthur's room had never seemed long before. It now stretched with theatrical cruelty. The hum of fluorescent lights grew louder, or perhaps David had simply lost the ability to filter it out. The carpet absorbed his footsteps with funereal politeness.

He passed Room 214, where a man argued gently with a crossword puzzle. He passed Room 218, where someone laughed at a television laugh track. Life continued its low-budget production.

David walked more slowly than usual.

He told himself it was respect.

He told himself it was nothing.

When he reached Arthur's door, it was slightly ajar.

He knocked anyway.

"Arthur?" he called, too brightly.

No answer.

He pushed the door open.

Arthur lay beneath a thin blanket, as if someone had tucked him into a story that was nearly finished. His eyes were half-closed. His breathing was shallow but steady, a quiet tide moving in and out.

The room seemed smaller.

Arthur's face, once animated by commentary and complaint, was still. The sharp angles remained, but they no longer looked defiant. They looked exposed.

"Arthur?" David said again, stepping inside.

Arthur's eyelids flickered. It took effort. That was visible now—the effort behind small things.

"You're . . . loud," he murmured. "And you look terrible."

The voice was papery. Fragile. It had to travel farther to reach the air.

"Can I get you anything?" David said automatically. "Soup?"

Arthur blinked.

"Hot or cold?" he sort of laughed.

David smiled, faintly. "Cold, of course."

Arthur considered the offer. "Good," he said. "I'd hate to go into the Great Unknown with a burnt tongue. Might spoil the conversation."

There it was again—the old rhythm—but faint, like music from another room.

David pulled a chair closer to the bed and sat.

Up close, frailty was undeniable. Arthur's hands rested atop the blanket, veins raised like faint blue rivers on a thinning map. His wrists looked narrow, the bones too close to the surface.

"You look terrible," Arthur whispered.

David smiled. "You already used that one."

Arthur's mouth twitched, almost a smile. "Oh, did I?"

They sat in a quiet that felt different from the garden quiet. The garden had been full of sound—bees, wind, the fountain, distant traffic. This quiet was padded, insulated. Clinical.

"How you feeling?" David asked.

Arthur took his time answering, as if evaluating the market value of honesty.

"Like a library book," he said finally.

David frowned. "A library book?"

"Overdue."

The line hung in the air between them.

David let out a breath that wasn't quite a laugh. He was going to respond—

"Don't," Arthur said gently.

"Don't what?"

"Turn everything into a joke. You'll miss it."

"Miss what?"

Arthur's eyes shifted toward him fully for the first time since he'd entered.

"This."

David swallowed.

For the first time, he saw not stubbornness—but something else. He saw someone who was finished. Done with everything.

No big, dramatic performance of defiance Arthur used to carry around like a heavy sword. This was something much smaller, more honest, something simpler. A man whose body was performing its final edits.

"You're just tired," David said, as if repetition could stabilize reality. "That's all."

Arthur didn't argue.

"Maybe," he said.

His breathing remained steady, shallow, deliberate. Each inhale seemed negotiated.

David looked at the thin blanket rising and falling. He noticed how small the movement was.

He'd always thought of Arthur as immovable. Annoying, yes. Sharp, certainly. But fixed. Permanent in the way that grumpy old men in stories are permanent.

Now he saw it clearly—the end nearing.

Arthur shifted slightly, wincing at the effort.

"Sit," he murmured.

"I am sitting."

"No. Sit."

David stilled. No adjusting. No checking his phone. No rehearsing conversation. He simply occupied the chair.

Arthur closed his eyes again.

For a long moment, there was nothing but the quiet hum of the building and the soft exchange of breath.

David realized he'd been holding onto the idea of Arthur as invincible through sheer personality. As if sarcasm were structural support.

It wasn't.

Arthur's hand twitched slightly on the blanket. David hesitated, then placed his own hand gently over it.

Arthur's skin was warm.

Arthur's eyes opened again, just a fraction.

"You're late," he whispered.

"I checked the garden."

Arthur exhaled something that might've been a laugh.

"Always chasing," he murmured.

David didn't argue.

He looked at the man in the bed—the sharp critic of soup, the reluctant philosopher, the stubborn resident of Sunny Meadows—and saw, for the first time, how thin the boundary was between presence and absence.

Arthur had begun to fade.

Not dramatically. Not cruelly.

Just quietly.

Like a sound carried a little too far.

Arthur lay in the narrow bed. He looked smaller than David remembered, as if someone had quietly let a little air out of him overnight. His face had taken on that pale, almost translucent quality of paper that'd been folded too many times. The light from the window rested on his cheekbones like something trying to decide whether to stay.

David was carrying a lot of sadness, which is awkward because sadness is heavy and the universe doesn't offer pockets or handles. He decided he'd try to break the sadness into smaller, more manageable pieces by using words.

"Well," he started. He was making noises with his mouth to fill up the silence, which is what people do when the silence starts to feel like a giant, invisible foot about to step on them. "Beautiful day out there. The sun's finally doing its job. The garden's looking good. They trimmed the roses."

Arthur didn't move.

"And the roses are bright," David continued. "They're red. Very red. Aggressively red. Like they're trying to win something."

Arthur's eyelids fluttered open. He looked at David the way a cat looks at a vacuum cleaner: with resignation and mild irritation.

David pressed on. "And the soup at lunch—well. You'll be thrilled to know that I believe it will be worse than usual. I think they've found new ways to remove flavor. It's almost scientific."

Arthur's fingers twitched against the blanket. His hand, thin and veined like a map of a country no one visits anymore, lifted a few inches off the mattress. It hovered there, wobbling like a question mark in a bad novel, then—because gravity had bills to pay—came down.

"Stop it," Arthur whispered.

It wasn't loud. It didn't need to be. The word landed between them like a gavel.

David blinked. "I was just—"

"You're still chasing," Arthur said.

His voice was dry and fragile, like leaves rubbed together. Each syllable seemed to cost him something.

David fell quiet.

He'd always hated silence. Silence meant there was nothing to fix, nothing to manage, nothing to polish into something presentable. Silence meant you had to sit with what was there. David preferred improvement projects. He preferred narratives with upward trajectories.

Arthur shifted slightly in the bed. The movement drew a small wince across his face. He waited for the pain to pass, then gathered what looked like the last of his strength as though he were assembling a speech from spare parts.

"Just sit still," he said.

David leaned forward. "Do you need water? I can get Nurse Kelly. Or I could adjust the pillow. It looks—"

Arthur's eyes sharpened, just for a second.

"Sit," he repeated.

David sat.

Arthur's breathing rasped in and out, like someone slowly dragging sandpaper across wood. He stared at the ceiling for a moment, collecting himself.

"Stop chasing," he said.

He paused, breathed.

"Stop fixing."

Another breath.

"Stop proving."

The words came in fragments, like they'd been rationed.

David opened his mouth to argue, but the words got lost somewhere between his brain and his tongue. He'd built his life on chasing, fixing, proving. Chasing promotions. Fixing problems where he could. Proving that he was competent, intelligent, and indispensable. It'd seemed like a noble life.

"Watch the world shuffle by," Arthur said.

His hand lifted again, this time only a few inches, and tilted faintly toward the window.

David turned.

Outside, clouds drifted across the sky with no visible ambition. They weren't striving. They weren't networking. They weren't optimizing. They simply moved because that's what clouds do.

"It's the only peace you'll ever find," Arthur whispered.

There it was. The thesis statement. The last lecture from a man who'd spent a lifetime disguising advice as criticism.

David swallowed.

He didn't argue.

This was new.

Normally, he'd have countered that stillness was laziness with good marketing.

Instead, he looked at the clouds.

They were unimpressed by him.

A clock on the nightstand ticked. It had a second hand that jerked forward in small, decisive motions, like it was impatient with the rest of existence.

Tick. Tick. Tick.

A cart rolled distantly down the hallway, its wheels squeaking in uneven protest. Someone coughed. A door clicked shut.

Life, shuffling by.

Arthur closed his eyes, not in dismissal but in something like surrender.

David shifted in his chair, feeling the old urge to perform. The urge to entertain, to reassure, to solve. He wanted to say something wise. Something quotable. Something that'd prove he'd understood.

Instead, he said nothing.

Silence settled over them, not heavy but dense. Like fog.

David studied Arthur's face. The sharpness had gone from it. What remained was something simpler, almost boyish. Without the constant motion of complaint and commentary, Arthur looked less like a man fighting the world and more like someone who'd finally stepped off the battlefield.

"You know," David said softly, before he could stop himself, "I just . . . I don't want you to feel alone."

Arthur's eyes opened again.

A corner of his mouth twitched.

"Idiot," he murmured.

It wasn't cruel. It was affectionate, in the way Arthur did affection—by pretending it was something else.

"You think sitting there quietly makes me alone?"

David hesitated. "I just thought—"

"You think your noise keeps death away?" Arthur asked, almost amused.

There it was.

There was the word.

David closed his eyes. He had no answer.

Arthur's gaze drifted back to the window. "Noise is for the living who are scared," he said. "Silence is for the living who are not."

The clock ticked.

Tick. Tick. Tick.

David considered this. He'd been very noisy his entire life. He'd filled rooms with plans, with strategies, with updated spreadsheets and analyses. He'd turned conversations into action items.

He looked down at his hands. They were clenched.

He forced them open.

Outside, a bird landed briefly on the windowsill, cocked its head, and flew away again. No announcement. No applause.

Arthur's breathing steadied. It was still shallow, still fragile, but less strained.

David realized something unsettling: his presence, stripped of chatter and performance, seemed to be enough.

He didn't have to improve the moment.

He didn't have to frame it.

He only had to occupy it.

"You're quiet," Arthur muttered, eyes still closed.

"I'm sitting," David replied. "I'm sitting still."

"Good," Arthur said.

Another pause.

"Harder than it looks, isn't it?"

"Yes," David admitted.

Arthur let out something that might've been a laugh. It was small and dry, but it was there.

"Told you," he said.

A cart squeaked again in the hallway. A nurse's voice murmured something unintelligible. The building continued its quiet industry of endings and continuations.

David felt an unfamiliar sensation creeping up on him. It wasn't panic. It wasn't urgency.

It was grief, but not the dramatic kind. Not the kind with speeches and clenched fists. It was the simple awareness that this—this small room, this ticking clock, this man breathing beside him—wouldn't repeat itself indefinitely.

He didn't try to fix it.

He didn't reach for his phone.

He didn't narrate the moment into something inspirational.

He let it be—ordinary.

Arthur's hand slid weakly toward the edge of the bed. David noticed and, without ceremony, placed his own hand beneath it.

Arthur's fingers were cool and light. They rested there without gripping.

"See?" Arthur murmured. "You're learning."

"Learning what?" David asked.

"To stop auditioning," Arthur said.

David smiled despite himself. "I didn't know I was auditioning."

"You always are," Arthur replied. "For someone. For something. For approval. For immortality."

"And sitting here changes that?"

Arthur's eyelids fluttered. "No," he said. "But it's a start."

The clock ticked.

David found himself counting the seconds, then deliberately stopped. Counting was chasing by another name.

They sat.

Minutes passed. Or maybe only seconds. Time, deprived of commentary, became elastic.

Arthur's breathing, which'd been ragged earlier, smoothed out into something almost peaceful. Not strong. Not vigorous. Just steady.

David felt the urge to say something meaningful one last time. To capture the lesson in a neat phrase. To secure it like a diploma.

Instead, he watched a cloud stretch thin and dissolve into the blue.

He felt his own breath, in and out.

In and out.

He realized that doing nothing in this room wasn't laziness. It was participation. It was staying.

Arthur shifted slightly and sighed.

His eyes were open, but they'd gone translucent somehow, like old photographs left in the sun.

"You still here?" Arthur asked, his voice a dry hinge.

"I'm still here," David said.

"Good. Someone ought to witness this nonsense."

David smiled faintly. "Didn't you tell mom the world needed a stenographer? Or something like that."

"It needs better copy editors," Arthur muttered. Then he winced. Even muttering cost him now.

They sat with that.

David felt Arthur's hand twitch.

After a while, Arthur spoke again.

"You think there's anything?"

David leaned closer. "Anything?"

"After." Arthur's eyes moved toward the ceiling, as if the tiles might provide schematics. "You think I'll see . . . them?"

Them.

The word hung in the air like a coat with no hook.

"Who?" David asked gently.

Arthur swallowed. "My father. My mother." He paused. His jaw tightened. "Your mom . . . Margaret."

"You're thinking about them?" David asked.

"Of course I'm thinking about them," Arthur said. "What else is there to do? I can't exactly start a new hobby."

David let out a small breath that might've been a laugh.

Arthur continued, his voice softer now. "My father rarely finished a sentence in his life. Always trailed off. Like he was afraid of being wrong." He closed his eyes briefly. "I used to think I'd outtalk him forever. Now I wonder if he's waiting somewhere, finally finishing his sentences."

"You hope so?"

Arthur hesitated. "I don't know. I'm not sure hope is the right word. Curiosity, maybe. Suspicion."

"And your mother?"

Arthur's lips shifted into something almost like a smile. "She believed in heaven the way other people believe in bus schedules. Certain it would arrive. Certain it would run on time."

"Do you?" David asked.

Arthur turned his head slightly. The movement looked monumental. "I believe in . . . possibilities."

"That's vague."

"In my condition, I'm allowed to be vague."

They both sat with that.

"And my mom?" David asked quietly.

Arthur gave him a look that was almost sharp, almost familiar. "Your mother once told me that if there was an afterlife, she hoped it didn't involve harp music. 'If I have to listen to amateur harpists for eternity,' she said, 'I'm going to have to file a complaint with the big man upstairs.'"

David smiled. "Sounds more like you."

"She believed we'd see each other again," Arthur said. "Not because of religion. Because of stubbornness. 'You don't get rid of me that easily,' she told me once."

The room seemed to shrink around the bed.

"Do you think you'll see them all again?" David asked.

Arthur stared at the ceiling. The tiles offered no revisions.

"I don't know," he said finally. "I've spent my life complaining about the present. It would be just like the universe to give me more of it."

David leaned back slightly. He felt the urge to offer reassurance wrapped in confident words. You'll see them. Of course you will. Love doesn't disappear.

But Arthur had trained him better than that.

"What do you want most?" David asked instead.

Arthur considered this as though it were a complex riddle. "I don't want . . ." He stopped to breathe. "I don't want Margaret to be alone."

The simplicity of it cracked something open in David's chest.

"You think she is?"

Arthur's eyes flicked toward him. "I don't know how it works. That's the point. Maybe she's nowhere. Maybe she's everywhere. Maybe she's reorganizing eternity."

"That sounds like her."

Arthur's mouth twitched. "If she's somewhere, I hope she's annoyed I took so long."

"You think she'd wait?"

Arthur exhaled slowly. "I surely hope so. I think she can manage eternity."

They both chuckled then, softly, carefully, as if laughter itself might bruise the air.

Arthur's face grew serious again. "But what if there's nothing?"

David swallowed. "Nothing?"

"No reunion. No pearly gates. No celestial complaint department. Just . . . lights out. Darkness."

A fluorescent light above punctuated the thought with a flicker.

David chose his words with care. "Then you won't know the difference."

Arthur looked at him. "That's your comfort?"

"It's not comfort," David admitted.

Arthur stared up at the ceiling for a long moment. "At least," he said. "You didn't say something stupid like . . . it's math . . . or whatever miserable thing people say when they're out of ideas."

"I'm learning. At the feet of the master."

Arthur shifted again, the effort visible. David held onto his hand. It wasn't choreography. It was instinct.

Arthur's hand was beginning to feel lighter to David. As if parts of him had already begun to leave.

"You think they'll recognize me?" Arthur asked suddenly.

David blinked. "Recognize you?"

"My father and mother. I'm not exactly the man I was. Thinner. Meaner. Better dressed."

"You're still you."

Arthur snorted faintly. "My father always said I talked too much. My mother said I didn't talk enough about the right things." He paused. "You think they'll recognize this version?"

David squeezed his hand gently. "If there's a place where recognition matters, I think it's built into the architecture."

"That's almost . . . poetic," Arthur murmured.

"Don't get used to it."

Arthur's eyes drifted closed for a moment. David thought he'd fallen asleep, but then he spoke again, barely audible.

"I'd like to see my father finish a sentence."

"You might," David said.

"And my mother," Arthur continued, "she'll probably check her watch."

David smiled. "She'll tell you you're late."

"I am late," Arthur said. "Took me long enough to figure things out."

"You figured them out," David said.

Arthur opened his eyes again, fixing him with a fragile intensity. "Did I?"

"Yes."

"If I see your mom," he whispered, "I'll tell her you finally learned to sit still."

"Please don't," David said. "I've a reputation."

Arthur's fingers tightened once more around David's hand. Then loosened.

"You'll stay?" Arthur asked, though the question seemed more reflex than doubt.

"I'll stay."

Arthur nodded almost imperceptibly. "If there's nothing," he murmured, "it won't be so bad. I've had enough of whatever this was."

David swallowed hard. "Okay."

"And if there's something," Arthur continued, his voice thinning, "I hope there's no harp music."

"Mom will file a complaint on your behalf."

"Good."

Arthur exhaled slowly. The sound was softer now, softer than the hallway, softer than the world.

David felt his own breath, in and out.

In and out.

He didn't rush the silence. He didn't fill it.

Arthur's chest rose once more.

David stayed.

He didn't look for signs in the ceiling tiles. He didn't search the air for Margaret's stubborn silhouette or a father finishing a sentence mid-cloud.

He simply held Arthur's hand a little longer.

Participating.

David breathed in.

Breathed out.

"Whatever you do," Arthur muttered. "Promise me you won't turn this into a story.""

David blinked. "What?"

"In your head," Arthur said. "Don't make it heroic. Or tragic. Or poetic."

David almost laughed. "What should I make it?"

"Nothing," Arthur said. "Just . . . this."

Just this.

The words were there, uncomplicated.

The clock ticked.

A cart rolled.

Clouds drifted.

Arthur's breathing steadied further, as if it had found a rhythm it trusted.

David sat still.

For the first time in his life, he didn't try to outrun the moment. He didn't try to add to it or subtract from it. He let it shuffle by, ordinary and enormous at the same time.

He understood then—quietly, without fireworks—that sitting there, doing nothing, wasn't surrender.

It was love.

Not the loud kind. Not the kind that announces itself with declarations and grand gestures.

The kind that stays.

The kind that watches the world move and doesn't demand that it move faster.

Arthur's fingers shifted faintly in his hand.

"You're doing good," Arthur whispered.

And they sat there together, in the small room that smelled of disinfectant and carrots and something like peace, while the world shuffled by outside the window.

That night, after visiting hours had ended, Arthur's room at Sunny Meadows was dim and still, like a theater after the audience had left and the stagehands had swept away the popcorn. The overhead light was off. Only the small lamp by the bed glowed, yellow and patient.

The hallway, which by day hosted the parade of carts and conversations and rubber-soled urgency, had quieted to a distant murmur. The building sighed the way old buildings do. Pipes ticked. An elevator groaned somewhere far away, reconsidering its life choices.

Arthur lay in bed, propped slightly on one pillow that'd known better decades. His hands were folded loosely on his chest, not in prayer exactly, but in a posture of administrative resignation. He'd spent a lifetime filing complaints with the universe. Tonight, he'd apparently closed the office.

Just a bit past 10 p.m., Nurse Kelly eased open the door. She'd perfected the art of entering a room without disturbing whatever fragile treaty existed inside it. She stepped in, sneakers whispering against linoleum.

She looked at Arthur, gently taking his hand and checking his pulse.

"Well," she said softly, not expecting an answer. "Still with us, Arthur."

Arthur didn't reply. He was asleep, or something very much like it. His mouth was slightly open. His breathing came shallow and thin, as if each inhale had to travel a great distance to find him. And there was a gurgle to it now.

Nurse Kelly adjusted the blanket by an inch. This was a skill nurses learned in school: how to move fabric without moving hope.

"I'll see you in the morning," she told Arthur. "Sweet dreams, dear friend."

Friend.

Arthur didn't hear it. Or maybe he did. And if he did, he didn't have the energy to argue with the universe about it.

He lay still.

She slipped out, closing the door with a click so small it could have been imagined.

Inside the room, nothing dramatic occurred. No thunderclap. No sudden confession. Arthur didn't sit bolt upright and declare a final, perfectly worded lesson about soup or sorrow or the uselessness of ambition.

His breathing simply slowed.

Inhale.

Exhale.

A pause.

Inhale.

Exhale.

The pauses grew longer, like ellipses in a sentence that'd decided to trail off rather than end with a period. One breath stretched longer than the others, wandering off the map. It didn't seem especially significant at first. After all, Arthur had always taken his time with things he didn't particularly enjoy.

Then the next breath didn't come.

The room didn't react. The lamp didn't flicker. The building's systems didn't gasp. The clock didn't stop ticking. The universe, which had endured far louder exits, continued minding its business.

Arthur's face settled into something almost peaceful. The lines that'd tightened around his mouth for years loosened their grip. His brow, accustomed to skepticism, smoothed. He looked less like a man bracing for disappointment and more like someone who'd finally put down a heavy suitcase.

As if he'd stopped chasing, too.

In the early morning, Nurse Kelly returned with the weary grace of someone who realized that the sun is just another lightbulb that occasionally needs a rest. She opened the door, already sensing the difference. Rooms, like people, have moods.

She stepped closer. She knew something was off.

"Oh," she said gently.

There was no panic in her voice, only recognition. She touched his wrist, feeling for a pulse, then gave his shoulder a jiggle, as if confirming that he'd, in fact, gone somewhere without leaving a forwarding address.

"Well, Arthur," she murmured, "you finally got some rest."

A single tear performed a brief, lonely dance on her cheek before she wiped it away with a sniffle.

The room felt different—emptier, yes, but lighter too. As though something dense and stubborn had been lifted. The lamp continued to glow. The hallway continued to hum.

And Arthur, who'd spent so many years narrating the world's imperfections, had at last fallen silent.

Chapter 15

The phone rang at 6:12 a.m., which is the hour when the world pretends it's innocent. The light outside David's apartment window was gray and undecided. The kind of light that hasn't committed to being morning yet.

He stared at the screen before answering. He knew the number. He knew what numbers like that meant at 6:12 a.m. Sunny Meadows wasn't calling to congratulate him on winning the cosmic lottery—certainly not at 6:12 a.m.

"Hello?" he said. He sounded like a man stepping onto a frozen pond, waiting for the first crack.

It was Nurse Kelly. Her voice was professional but padded with something softer, like she'd wrapped the words in gauze.

"I'm so sorry, David. Arthur passed peacefully during the night."

Passed peacefully. As if he'd taken a nap on the couch and never got up. As if he'd slipped out the door and the universe hadn't noticed.

David closed his eyes. He'd known when the phone rang. He'd known the day before, when Arthur looked like newsprint left out in the sun too long—pale, thin, the kind of fragile that makes you worry you'll blink and tear it.

"The big nap," David whispered.

"I'm sorry, what was that?" Nurse Kelly asked.

"Oh, nothing. Thank you," David said. Because that's what one says to a messenger of inevitability.

He hung up gently. The room felt too small for grief, so he left it.

Sunny Meadows smelled the same as always: lemon disinfectant and overcooked vegetables. The receptionist looked up when he walked in, her mouth already shaping sympathy. David nodded before she could speak and kept walking.

He said nothing. He didn't trust his voice.

He passed through the many hallways. He passed a common area where a television muttered to itself. He pushed through the doors to the small garden courtyard.

The bench waited for him. It creaked when he lowered himself onto it. The exact same sound the bench made when he and Arthur sat there together.

He turned to his side. He saw Arthur sitting next to him, clear as a bell.

David knew perfectly well that it couldn't be Arthur. Arthur was someplace else. But in the theater of his mind, Arthur was there anyway, occupying the wood and the air and the afternoon.

"This bench," Arthur said. "It's going to collapse one day. Probably under someone more important than us."

David stared up at the sky. The same patch Arthur once criticized for being "too dramatic."

"Look at that," Arthur grumbled at him. "Clouds acting like they're auditioning for a postcard. Nobody asked for theatrics."

Today, the sky was doing its best impression of endlessness. Blue stretched wide and indifferent. Clouds drifted lazily, as if they'd nowhere better to be. Which David supposed, they didn't.

Memories came, not the cinematic kind with orchestras swelling, but the ordinary ones. The kind that scratch instead of shimmer. Arthur grumbling about hobbies becoming assignments. How he despised the modern obsession with likes, followers, and phone apps. And of course, every cold bowl of soup he'd ever cursed, which, in the grand scheme of things, might have been the most honest complaint of all.

"You know, I can hear your thoughts," Arthur told him. "Let me remind you, soup shouldn't have a skin. If it has a skin, it's a crime."

"It's fine," David said aloud to no one.

"Fine is what people say when they've given up."

David let out a small breath that might've been a laugh. Or a leak. Hard to tell.

Then came the insults disguised as wisdom.

"You work too much," Arthur said.

"I told you, I have responsibilities."

"You have distractions."

And then the uncomfortable truths that stung more than they soothed.

"You don't listen," Arthur said.

"I'm listening right now."

"No. You're waiting to respond. That's different."

David realized, sitting there on the bench that might or might not collapse under someone more important, that beneath the sarcasm had been something relentless. Arthur had insisted on awareness, the way some men insist on punctuality. He refused to let moments slide by unnoticed. Even bad ones. Especially bad ones.

Arthur leaned toward David, the wooden bench wheezing under the shift. He gestured with a gnarled finger, his voice dropping into that familiar, sandpaper grit.

"Remember to complain properly," Arthur said. "If you're going to suffer, at least articulate it."

David felt Arthur's presence tighten. He knew Arthur wasn't about to let him drift. Wasn't about to let him romanticize about the past.

"Don't try to polish a memory into something gold and glowing," Arthur told him, using a metaphorical sheet of coarse-grit sandpaper to strip the finish. "Remember, it wasn't better back then. You were just younger and dumber."

Arthur took a deep breath. "And above all, remember to stop chasing."

David smiled and nodded. He looked at his hands now, resting uselessly in his lap. He didn't reach for his phone. Didn't check the time. Didn't check his messages or emails. Didn't doom scroll through news headlines.

He simply sat.

It was astonishing how difficult that was.

There came a sound. Nurse Kelly appeared, pushing a small cart just outside the door to the small garden. She paused when she saw him alone on the bench.

"Oh, David," she said. Her voice carried the kind of sympathy that doesn't try to rearrange the universe. "I'm so sorry. We all are. Arthur . . . he kept things . . . interesting."

"Interesting," David said. "That's one way to put it."

She smiled, relieved at the hint of humor. "He certainly had . . . opinions."

David just nodded. Smiled. Because sometimes nodding and smiling is the only honest response the universe allows.

She hesitated, then lifted a tray from the cart. A bowl of soup trembled slightly in its bowl.

"We have extra from lunch prep," she said. "Would you like some?"

David looked at it. It was pale and unassuming. Steam wasn't visible.

He shrugged, which is what humans do when they're willing to be reasonable.

"Sure," he said. "I'll take it."

She handed it to him carefully, as if it were ceremonial.

"If you need anything—" she began.

"I know," he said gently. "Thank you, Kelly."

She nodded and wheeled the cart away, the small rattling sound fading into the hallway.

David stared at the soup.

"Temperature unacceptable," Arthur said. "Texture suspicious. Flavor absent without leave."

David dipped the spoon in. The surface resisted slightly, forming that thin skin Arthur had despised. He broke it.

He tasted it slowly. Deliberately.

Of course, it was cold.

He almost laughed. Exactly the kind of thing Arthur would've held up as evidence that the universe had absolutely no sense of humor—or perhaps too much.

He took another spoonful. It tasted awful, but he kept eating.

Not because it was good. Not because he was hungry. But because it was there. Because it was offered. Because it existed in this moment, imperfect and bland and undeniably real.

The sky stretched wide above him.

Clouds drifted lazily, unbothered by grief. They didn't pause. They didn't dim. They didn't rearrange themselves into condolence cards.

David watched without trying to interpret them.

He didn't search for faces in the vapor. Didn't assign meaning to their shapes. Didn't construct metaphors about journeys or gates or staircases to heaven.

He simply watched.

Arthur was still there, approving in that quiet, passive way old men have when they know the universe is messy and they don't care.

"Sometimes a cloud is just unemployed water," he said.

David let the spoon rest in the empty bowl. He folded his hands again and breathed in. Breathed out. The air smelled faintly of mulch and distant laundry detergent.

For a moment—brief and almost imperceptible—he thought he saw something shimmer among the clouds.

Not a shape exactly. More like a distortion. A folding of light.

He squinted.

There—just at the edge of vision—a faint outline of something elongated. Sleek. Improbable. Glistening.

A starship of some kind folding into brightness, as if slipping between pages of the sky.

His heart gave a small, involuntary leap.

"Well," he murmured to Arthur. "That's new."

Arthur smiled, the way people do when they already know the punchline to the universe.

"Looks like this is my stop," he told David. "Well, be sure to keep all the stupid wisdom I gave you. It's all I've got to leave to humanity."

David looked at him and grinned. "I'll do my worst."

The shimmer of light flickered once more and vanished.

Arthur went with it.

The clouds drifted again—unemployed, unbothered, and entirely innocent.

David didn't stand.

He didn't call out.

He didn't chase the vision with an explanation. No cosmic metaphors. No grand conclusions about The Great Beyond or interstellar bartenders or planets made of sound.

If it'd been real, it didn't need him to validate it.

If it hadn't been real, it didn't need him to dismantle it.

He simply sat there, breathing in, breathing out.

The bench creaked softly under his weight, as if reminding him that wood ages, too.

Somewhere inside Sunny Meadows, a door closed. A phone rang. A television audience laughed on cue. Life continued its shuffling procession.

"The world keeps going," David said to no one. "It just spins and spins. It doesn't ask your permission."

He nodded slightly. "And I'm not chasing it."

The world shuffled by. Clouds moved. Nurses changed shifts. Soup cooled.

David stayed.

He let the sky be dramatic if it wanted to be. He let the bench creak. He let the absence sit beside him without trying to fill it.

He breathed in.

He breathed out.

And wouldn't you know it, he suddenly got it: life wasn't about the money, the shiny objects, or the stories we tell to keep from screaming. It was about sitting up straight and paying damn attention, refusing to drift through one's own life unnoticed.

Arthur had left him that little cosmic joke.

So, David sat on the worn wooden bench in the small courtyard garden of Sunny Meadows and did the hardest thing imaginable.

He did nothing.

The world shuffled by.

And he let it.

ABOUT THE AUTHOR

Philip Mazza is a novelist with a boundless imagination, captivating readers with the epic fantasy series *The Harrow Saga* and the sci-fi thriller *The Neon Hive*. Born in New York in 1959, he earned a degree in Business from LeMoyne College and an MBA, later holding leadership roles in human resources and operations. Now a professor at the Madden School of Business and Economics, Philip dedicates his time to his students and writing. *Conversations Over Cold Soup* is his twentieth literary work. He and his wife enjoy travel and continue to live in Key West and upstate New York.

www.ingramcontent.com/pod-product-compliance
Lightning Source LLC
LaVergne TN
LVHW090549110826
845146LV00001B/81